A Bandit's Request

by

Micki Miller

Request Series, Book 2

A Bandit's Request

Cover Art by *Rae Monet, Inc. Design*

The Wild Rose Press, Inc.
PO Box 708
Adams Basin, NY 14410-0708
Visit us at www.thewildrosepress.com

Publishing History
First Tea Rose Edition, 2019
Print ISBN 978-1-5092-2729-7
Digital ISBN 978-1-5092-2730-3

Request Series, Book 2
Published in the United States of America

"You're very petite, for an ogre." His smile grew full then and devastating to her woman's good sense. "I think I should like to see your face."

He was close enough to grab her. The beast maintained the grin of his obvious advantage. Panic set in and gripped her. This man she had just saved from certain death held the power to ruin her in every way. He knew it. The smug rake was enjoying himself. She should have let Lord Beaumont shoot him.

"Come now, don't be shy. You saved my life. I shall keep your secret. You have my word as a gentleman."

Dove didn't worry about her snort giving her away, as it was very unladylike. Some fine gentleman he was, having a liaison with another man's wife, and under the lord's own roof, no less! The insult of her snort did not affect him.

"You've stirred my curiosity into quite the frenzy. Grant me just a peek at you."

Dove darted around him but stumbled on the outstretched arm of Lord Beaumont.

The rake caught her before she hit the ground. He wrapped his arms around her, gentle, but firm. His strong hold was akin to a binding caress. One hand climbed up between her shoulder blades. The other encircled her waist. Lord Worthington held her not as a criminal detained, but as a woman desired.

Dedication

To Kathy Myers,
keeper of the only other key to the vault,
and with whom I share so many great memories

Chapter 1

London, 1814

"He was a brute of a man, troll-like in his bearing, with huge hands, legs like tree trunks, and forearms as big as my thighs!"

The retelling of her terrifying encounter with the Creeping Bandit had Lady Ashbury retrieving her vinaigrette from her orange-beaded reticule. Three concerned ladies, in varicolored ball gowns, stood near her chair waving their painted fans in her face to help fend off a swoon. One of the gentlemen in her captivated audience fetched and set before her an upholstered footstool, which she put to immediate use.

The dramatic crimson gown worn by Lady Ashbury, a full-set woman, did a poor job of containing her mass. Her plump arms bulged like rising dough from her short, gathered sleeves, and the bodice must have required extra stitching to contain the woman's voluminous bosom. Blonde sausage curls stacked around her orb-like face in so many layers she could use her hair as a pillow.

Her theatrical recitation gave all in attendance the belief she was on the verge of losing consciousness. This, however, was belied by her vibrant coloring, robust hand gestures, and strong tone of voice as she told the story for at least the fourth time since entering the ball.

She glanced at the circle of a dozen or so ladies and gentlemen surrounding her. Their attention rapt; their sympathy overflowing. Another quick sniff of her vinaigrette, followed by tipping her head back for a full minute to take in the fan breeze, and she was ready to continue her accounting.

The musicians at the Beaumont's lavish ball were taking their quarter hour respite, facilitating the flow of unencumbered conversation. Chatter of the latest events dominated all other entertainments. It bloomed in large and small patches about the vases of early white azaleas and white and pink hyacinth.

Many of the hundred or so guests fed each other the latest gossip at the buffet tables. Other groups and pairs stepped outside to take in the fresh air while discussing the most recent break-in.

Viscount Andrew Worthington's tall form drifted in and out of the circles of conversation until he found whom he sought. Lady Beatrix Beaumont, along with the others gathered around Lady Ashbury, listened wide-eyed to the recounting of her close call with death at the hands of the Creeping Bandit.

The night the Bandit broke into the Ashburys' was the only time anyone had seen the miscreant. She and Lord Ashbury were to be at the theater that night with Lord Ashbury's brother, but she'd not been feeling well, and her husband had their driver take her home. She'd walked in and caught the brazen man searching her private chambers.

"He was dressed all in black with a black hood over his head," Lady Ashbury continued. "Larger than any man I'd ever seen. He tried to grab me, but somehow I managed to escape the fiend and ran screaming from the room before he could get his hands on me."

She opened her silver vinaigrette box for yet another sniff. Two of the ladies continued to fan her while the third touched her shoulder and gifted her with a sympathetic mewl.

"Strange thing, that Bandit," said Lord Linden as he adjusted his over-starched cravat. "For the life of me, I can't understand why he goes to all the trouble and risk of breaking in, yet he never steals a thing. He just moves small items about the room, making certain his presence there would be known. It makes no sense a-tall."

Others in the small gathering nodded. Someone mumbled a comment about the oddness. One of the men declared the Bandit's lack of sound mind made him more dangerous. Nods of agreement tipped all around, mixed in with at least one "Indeed."

Andrew, Drew to those who knew him, half heard, as he was in the depths of a furtive eye conversation with the fair and buxom Lady Beatrix Beaumont. He feigned attention to the talk as a means of discretion. Not that discretion ever earned his concern. His reputation as a rake wasn't a secret even amongst the less social, and he cared not a whit.

However, the lady presently holding his focus would be put off if anyone should discover their trysts. Most especially, her ill-tempered husband.

Beatrix excused herself from the small gathering. Drew followed. When she slipped into the washroom at the end of the hall, he found an empty salon she would have to pass on her way back. Moments later, his hands darted out to the corridor, and he snatched her into the privacy of the salon. Her anxious lips met his before words had a chance to pass. Within seconds, Drew had her against the wall, lifting the batiste skirts of her empire style gown as his mouth feasted on her luscious neck, exposed to suit both their pleasures.

"Not here," Beatrix said, drawing air to catch her stolen breath. "Someone might walk in."

"I want you, Beatrix." He nipped at her earlobe and suckled her throat.

Her head lolled back. Her words rushed out on her heated breath. "Drew, you are insatiable."

He ran a hand down her back until he cupped her backside, drawing her into the rough intimacy she always appreciated. Beatrix gasped as she moved with him, sliding her hand inside his waistcoat. "As are you, my dear."

Her eyes fluttered closed before popping open again. She used the palms of her hands to shove him back. "Meet me in my chambers in fifteen minutes." She spun toward the door before glancing back over her shoulder. "You remember where it is, don't you?"

He hadn't a clue. Going by her implication, he must have been there before, but who kept track of such things? The perplexing situation gave him pause. If he asked for directions, Beatrix would know the placement of her bedchamber held little space in his realm of importance. Yet, if he did not get directions, he could spend the rest of the evening poking his head into empty rooms.

Lady Beaumont laughed. "If you had my heart, Lord Worthington, I'm afraid I might be quite hurt."

Drew gave her a wry and grateful smile. How he

loved women! He loved the adventure of deciphering their contrary natures, their scents, their softness, even their occasional rough edges. He loved them in all sizes, heights, and colorings. Some, such as Beatrix, had aggressive sensualities stocked with unexpected pleasures. When there was expressed interest sans aggression, Drew thoroughly enjoyed playing the seducer.

The only thing he couldn't suffer was their tears. Those warm, salty drops leaking from female eyes melted his every resistance. To his detriment, his younger sister, Olivia, discovered this weakness at an early age. The wise little chit wielded her weapon on many occasions.

Beatrix didn't cry, though. Her heart was as uninvolved as his, for which he was ever thankful. Instead, she raised her wheat-colored brows, and through a smile as wry as his own, said, "Up the stairs, first right, third door on the right."

Beatrix spun on her dainty slipper and was gone. Fifteen minutes later, in the flickering of the branch of candles in her bedchambers, she shoved Drew backward so he sat on the edge of her bed. Lips locked, hands devouring his shoulders and chest, she climbed atop his lap to straddle him.

"Drew, you are the most masculine, most fine-looking man I've ever felt. I mean, known, um...I mean—not that I've known..."

Drew saved her from her own words by taking her lips. He clasped her hips. "You drive me mad," he told her. "If I can't have you now, I'll surely awake in Bedlam."

It was his signature line, and he'd been considering

a change. But the words, when infused with just the right amount of passion, did seem to please the women. He didn't believe all of them had heard it yet. Had Beatrix?

If she had, Lady Beaumont did not appear to care. She wrestled with the front of his trousers while he worked to yank up the layers of her skirts. Once he found her ankle, he took a slow finger-crawl up her gossamer stocking.

Drew caressed the lovely female roundness of her knee, before gliding up to clasp her thigh. Ah, skin! Beatrix sucked in a breath as his hand neared the apex of his upward journey.

It was as far as they would get.

The door burst open. Lord Beaumont, his stout figure taut with rage, lunged into the room. "Unhand my wife!"

Beatrix screamed, and in her startled twist, tumbled off Drew's lap. Drew stood and offered a hand she didn't see. Her panicked expression stayed on her husband. The way she was composing her features, fear molding into exaggerated relief, did not bode well for Drew.

"Benjamin!" Beatrix shouted to her husband, a man more than twenty years her senior. A fair amount of gray dulled the man's blond hair. Years of leisure had softened his strong frame. "Thank God you've arrived! This man must have followed me to my chambers. He tried to ravish me!"

Drew stared down at the rumple of mussed hair and tangled skirts with an incredulous take, which he then shifted to the lady's furious husband. Had neither Lady nor Lord Beaumont comprehended *she* was the one atop *him*?

"Are you hurt, my love?" Lord Beaumont asked his wife after she threw herself into his arms.

"You've arrived just in time, Benjamin, thank God! Another minute and…I can't even think about what he may have done to me."

In another minute, Drew would have followed through with her lead and done exactly as she'd wished him to do.

"Thank God you arrived, darling," Beatrix repeated, her breath still heavy from the shocking interruption to their brief encounter with pleasure. Beatrix accentuated her drama by slapping the back of her hand against her forehead. "I'm near to a faint with terror over what might have happened."

"Oh, for all that is holy," mumbled Drew.

In the span of less than a minute, the lying adulteress thrice gave thanks to the lord. Drew nearly laughed aloud at the hypocrisy. Then Lord Beaumont withdrew a pocket pistol from inside his jacket, executing Drew's mirth with frightening efficiency.

"Benjamin, no!" Beatrix shouted.

"Go downstairs, love," Lord Beaumont said to his wife. "I shall handle this situation in short order."

"Benjamin, you can't kill him."

Drew raised a brow. *Well, at least she draws the line at my murder.*

Lord Beaumont cast a critical eye toward his wife. "You sound as if you bear affection for this villain."

"No, of course not. I simply…um…" Beatrix flapped her hand in front of her face. "I'm afraid I'm quite overwrought."

"Of course you are, my dear. Leave us now. Go

into my chambers and lie down for a while. This is no situation for a lady with delicate sensibilities."

Drew gave an airy chuckle, earning him a scowl from both Beaumonts. He couldn't help it. Had her husband been delayed another minute or so, he would have caught his wife and her delicate sensibilities riding her occasional lover into oblivion.

Beatrix extricated herself from her husband's protective arm and scurried behind him. At the door, she glanced back at Drew. Her lovely face formed a sympathetic expression and she mouthed to him, *I'm sorry.*

With her husband standing before him, angry and armed, Drew was not feeling the least bit open to forgiveness. His expression must have told her so. Beatrix turned up her nose, spun on her traitorous little feet, and was gone, closing the door behind her.

Drew said, "Now, if you will allow me but a moment to explain."

Lord Beaumont responded with a chilling glower. The truth would get Drew killed, and any lie he told this cuckolded husband had better be a good one.

"What you witnessed was a simple matter of mistaken identity. If you'll notice, there are hardly enough candles burning," Drew said, even though an entire branch of candles was lit and gave sufficient light to the room. "I believed I was trysting with a different woman. I've done no harm, as you entered this chamber but a moment after we did. So, you see, shooting me would be a grave mistake on your part, tantamount to murder."

"Do not take me for a fool," Lord Beaumont sneered. "I shall end your libertine life this night and be named a hero, for I will have slain the Creeping Bandit."

"The Bandit! You can't be serious. I am not the Bandit."

"I am quite serious. You snuck into my wife's private rooms. She happened upon you before you could play your little game and rearrange her belongings. We fought." Lord Beaumont used his pistol to tip over a vibrantly painted vase of yellow roses on Beatrix's dressing table. The vase rolled off, fell to the floor, and shattered. "I was forced to shoot you."

Lord Beaumont was truthful about only one thing. The man was serious about killing him.

"Wait," said Drew. He raised placating hands, palms out to his assailant. Panic tinged his calm tone and tightened his skin. "You're acting in a manner of regrettable haste."

Lord Beaumont raised his arm.

"Good God, man, think this through."

"Prepare to meet your maker."

As Drew wished desperately for said maker to intervene, it struck him how undeserving he was of any divine assistance. Perhaps this was his comeuppance. But others would suffer in this wake.

Since his father died when he was but a lad of fifteen, leaving him fortune and title, he'd done nothing but seek his pleasures. Women, gaming, spirits, one, or all called to him daily.

Even his tolerant mother was beginning to worry. Of late, her mantra consisted of all the many reasons it was time for him to mature. He'd returned her concern with little more than polite, indulgent smiles, and compliments meant to deflect. Now his mother would grieve, as would Olivia, his young sister.

Not a single good argument arose in his mind for him to put forth in plea for his life. How could that be? How could he have lived twenty-eight years and not have accomplished anything worthy? And how, until this very minute, had he not cared?

But such was the way of it. The sad truth was he would leave a legacy of naught but debauchery. His mother and sister would have nothing by way of remembrance but a few vague recollections of him passing by them on his way out, or in, and shame. They would have an abundance of shame and scandal were he to be named the Bandit.

Lord Beaumont took aim.

Then, a heartbeat before Drew's heart would stop beating, the wardrobe doors flew open. And out leapt the Creeping Bandit.

A Bandit's Request

Chapter 2

Dove Barrow cursed her reckless conscience. She cursed her blasted luck. She cursed both Lord and Lady Beaumont. Most of all, she cursed the lying, disreputable rake whose worthless life she was about to save.

Lord Beaumont spun around. Dove was ready. She held the toes of her hard-soled half boots in each of her hands. With all the strength she could muster, she clapped the heels on either side of Lord Beaumont's head. He stood frozen for a moment. Then, as his shocked expression slackened, the man dropped to the floor with a heavy thud.

The rakehell standing on the other side of the fallen lump expelled an audible breath.

Dove had prepared what she would say to him when he pleaded for his life, for the second time tonight. He would, of course, believe he was in mortal danger, as all of London's elite feared the Creeping Bandit. Dove couldn't help but smile beneath her hood.

Yes, she'd caused quite a stir. The gossips only helped her cause with their theories and exaggerations. It was her second goal, to make them fear the Bandit, to fear what he might do to them. And they did.

Rumors did what rumors do, especially when mixed in with a fair amount of facts. She'd been breaking into their homes for months. She'd never

11

taken a thing, but Dove made sure they knew she'd been there. The whole of London's aristocracy was on edge. Facing the dreaded Creeping Bandit, this man must be terrified.

To her great dismay, when the shock of seeing the Bandit passed, the man did not give the impression of being the least bit frightened. If she didn't believe it impossible, she might think the rogue recognized she was not a man beneath her disguise.

Perhaps men such as this scoundrel had heightened sensitivities about women. But that was absurd, her imagination taking her on a merry ride. She'd been very careful in choosing her disguise for the Bandit.

His analytical gaze floated down her length, and the honey gold of his eyes took their time on the return climb. Dove stood still as he took in her black-stockinged feet, her legs clad in black trousers, a plain, black shirt and cropped riding coat a size too large. The coat encumbered her movements. Should anyone catch sight of her, however, the shapeless garment served to mask her woman's curves, as well as give her a larger appearance.

She'd pinned up her mass of dark hair and capped it with the black hood, which was long enough to cover her face and neck. She'd cut holes in the hood for eyes, and a strip for her mouth. Black gloves covered her woman's hands. Much thought had gone into her disguise. No, he couldn't tell she was a woman. No one could.

"My deepest gratitude," the man said. He gave a slight bow. "Viscount Andrew Worthington, at your service."

Dove held her silence. She didn't believe she could

alter her voice well enough to fool him. It had been her hope in his panicked relief he would run for help, and she could slip out the window and shinny down the massive oak, the way she'd entered. Renny awaited her in the carriage not far off around the corner. She would change back into her gown and reappear at the Beaumont's ball posthaste, before anyone realized she had gone. Even grandfather, her dear chaperone, would remain oblivious to her activities.

In accordance with the disastrous way this evening was playing out, however, the big oaf didn't have sense enough to be intimidated when facing the scourge of London. In fact, Dove could almost swear she detected a hint of amusement on his dashing countenance.

The man took a single step toward her. "I would have thought someone of such an ominous reputation would be in possession of far deadlier weapons than footwear."

Dove narrowed her eyes. He was toying with her, the rogue. Where was the terror? Where was the desperate need to escape the clutches of the dreaded Creeping Bandit? This fool showed no fear whatsoever. In fact, the knave took another step in her direction.

Dove held her tongue. Except for Lady Ashbury, and now a brief glimpse by Lord Beaumont, none of London's upper classes had ever seen her as the Bandit. Lady Ashbury's skewed description helped her by enhancing her reputation. If this ne'er-do-well did not flee in fear, he could ruin everything.

"Who *are* you, beneath that hood?" he asked.

The viscount's deep voice rolled on a seductive curve. Did the man have no sense at all? She was the Creeping Bandit!

Dove gave him no answer. The man took another slow step in her direction. She straightened her spine, attempting to appear taller, more intimidating. Perhaps she should start padding the shoulders of her coat. Though she doubted it would have mattered tonight. A bit above average height for a woman, she was still a head shorter than this fool.

"Rather bold, breaking in with half of London's nobility below stairs." He rounded Lord Beaumont's still form and took another smooth step toward her, and then another, until he was but a foot or two away.

She could see how a woman might be enticed to engage in an affair with him. The man was beyond handsome. He was taller than most, and broad across the shoulders. His features were strong, might have even been harsh if not for the softness of his amber eyes and the playful lift at the corner of his lips. Faint streaks of red shone in the candlelight against the sandy waves of his hair, one lock of which hung across the edge of his forehead in a careless fashion.

"You're very petite, for an ogre." His smile grew full then and devastating to her woman's good sense. "I think I should like to see your face."

He was close enough to grab her. The beast maintained the grin of his obvious advantage. Panic set in and gripped her. This man she had just saved from certain death held the power to ruin her in every way. He knew it. The smug rake was enjoying himself. She should have let Lord Beaumont shoot him.

"Come now, don't be shy. You saved my life. I shall keep your secret. You have my word as a gentleman."

Dove didn't worry about her snort giving her away,

as it was very unladylike. Some fine gentleman he was, having a liaison with another man's wife, and under the lord's own roof, no less! The insult of her snort did not affect him.

"You've stirred my curiosity into quite the frenzy. Grant me just a peek at you."

Dove darted around him but stumbled on the outstretched arm of Lord Beaumont.

The rake caught her before she hit the ground. He wrapped his arms around, her, gentle, but firm. His strong hold was akin to a binding caress. One hand climbed up between her shoulder blades. The other encircled her waist. Lord Worthington held her not as a criminal detained, but as a woman desired.

"Let me go," she ordered.

He grinned wider, for her voice confirmed her gender. She tipped her head up. The way he gazed down into her eyes made her feel as if he not only saw through her hood, but through the rest of her disguise, as well. He trailed a finger along her cloth-covered jaw, just a single finger. It amazed Dove, the power of so simple a touch. The tingle shot like a velvet lightning bolt all the way to her toes.

He dragged his fingers down her throat, lingering to tease the bottom edge of the hood. One finger slipped beneath. Dove gasped and leaned back. "No!"

Lord Worthington sighed and dropped his hold. "Very well, then. If you wish to keep your identity a secret, I'll not push the matter. In fact, when Lord Beaumont regains consciousness and claims to have witnessed the Bandit in his upstairs rooms, I'll deny I was even here. He must have fallen and bumped his head." The viscount tipped his head toward the broken vase on the floor.

Dove nodded. For a moment, he held her with naught but his fascinated gaze. Then Lord Worthington's hand drifted up again. Through the fabric covering her entire head, he traced the rim of her ear. Somewhere in her mind, Dove had a vague notion Lord Worthington was going to lie for her benefit. It was hard to say for sure, as his touch was scrambling her thoughts.

The viscount stroked the underside of her lip, his finger just barely breaching the edge of the cutout. Dove wondered if one could swoon from such a sensation.

He bent down, with an ever so slight brush of his nose, and nuzzled her ear before whispering, "Might I thank you, with a kiss?"

"Yes."

The word slipped from her lips without her permission. Never had Dove allowed a man such a liberty. Maybe it was simple curiosity. Perhaps it was the disguise, masking her proper demeanor as well as her identity. Whatever the reason, she didn't put up so much as a smidgeon of protest when he brushed a kiss across her hooded face all the way to her lips. In fact, she welcomed him.

His strong arm wrapped around her again and drew her closer to his body. With the brush of bare touches, his kiss teased, and then he delivered. His slow sensuality diluted her wits. Dove's fingers let go and her boots landed on the rug with two light thuds.

She ran her hands up the surface of his hard chest to grip the rounded strength of his shoulders. At the audacious touch of his tongue, extraordinary sensations fluttered through her, and with less than a thought at what she was doing, Dove opened to what he gave.

She met his bold kiss with an uncertain one of her own, learning what to do from his every shift and nuance and following his bold escalations. He welcomed her initiative by leading her further.

Dove adapted to his lessons of tease and reward by returning them to him, tentative at first, then emboldened with a command she'd not known she possessed. Her fingers dug into his shoulders and her body leaned into his as her kiss flourished on instinct. The viscount sucked in a breath. She affected him. Dove savored her dominion. The empowerment was unequalled. She wanted more.

Before she could explore the possibilities, Viscount Worthington retreated. In a gradual change, smugness replaced his stunned expression. Her cooling passions summoned the return of her senses and Dove was grateful for the cover of her hood, as her heated blush would only embarrass her further.

"My dear Bandit, you are a fast learner. Tell me; was that your first kiss?"

She stared at his white cravat, askew from the evening's events. It *was* her first kiss, but she certainly wasn't going to admit such a thing to this rogue.

Dove took a step back. Lord Worthington stepped toward her.

"Come now, Bandit. Our fun has just begun. Do you not hunger for another kiss?"

Yes. "I do not."

"Do you not understand the power you hold?"

He'd reacted to their kiss. His breath had grown heavy, his body taut beneath her fingers. Even now, heat burned in the deep amber of his eyes. It was because of her. The experience was new, and heady.

"Your mystery is an aphrodisiac." Wonder grew in his hooded eyes as his focus on her deepened. "You've cast a spell on me, Bandit."

She drifted to him, under the same spell. Was it true, unique, this attraction toward one another? It was to her. Before she left this place, Dove wanted another kiss. She would know this power a moment more.

His hands slid around her waist, fingers gripping to draw her close. He nuzzled her neck, and on a heavy breath, whispered into her ear. "You drive me mad. If I can't have you now, I'll surely awake in Bedlam."

Dove stiffened, and then stepped back. He returned her harsh glare with a sincere expression of surprise. *The only thing sincere about him.*

Dove's black-gloved hands balled into fists. She spat her words through the slit in her hood. "You bastard."

He blinked. "I beg your pardon."

"Those are the exact same words you spoke to Lady Beaumont." She narrowed her eyes. "I'd be willing to bet you've plied many other women with your dire declaration."

At least he had the good graces to feign embarrassment. And it *was* a fraud. The man wouldn't know true authenticity if it socked him in the jaw, which is just what she was tempted to do.

"Oh, so they are. I beg your forgiveness, my Lady Bandit. I'm but a simple man with a simple vocabulary with which to express my feelings."

Dove set her fiercest glare to meet his fallen gaze of chagrin. "You are a rogue, Lord Worthington, too lazy and too shallow to devote even a single moment to the care of a woman's feelings."

His eyes widened, his head jerked back, and his mouth worked a moment before he found his words. "That's not…It isn't as though you did not enjoy yourself."

Dove gasped. "How dare you speak of such out loud!"

"How dare you act as if I gave you no pleasure." His brows met in consternation. "And you're hardly one to give a lecture on morality, *Bandit*."

Dove jammed her fists against her hips. His valid point did not dampen her anger. "You…"

"Yes?"

She huffed out a breath. "I'm leaving now."

Dove kicked her feet back into her half boots and strode to the window. She had one leg already out when the viscount grabbed hold of her arm. Alarm fused through her. The way this night was going, she should have known this escape would not be easy.

"We're high on the second floor," he said. "You cannot leap from this window!"

"Just because I tolerated your bumbling kiss, do not think me a fool."

His jaw tightened, and he crossed his arms. "Do forgive my error, Bandit."

"Ease your nerves, rake. I am not jumping. An elm grows along the house. It's how I gained my entrance into these chambers."

Lord Worthington's arms dropped to his sides. "You *climbed* all the way up here?"

"I could hardly have the butler announce my arrival as I pranced through the front door looking like this."

"Well, I suppose not." He rubbed his chin with his thumb and forefinger. "I just assumed you snuck in at the ground floor and took the servant's stairs."

"Most often, I do. Tonight was an exception." *Many times over.*

"Still, it is quite a distance down. I would hardly be a gentleman if I allowed you to undertake this dangerous feat."

"I am the Creeping Bandit! It is not up to you to allow or forbid anything. And," Dove added, unable to stop. "From what I witnessed in the slight opening between the wardrobe doors, you are hardly a gentleman."

"This from the spying Bandit."

"I was not spying! You left me no choice but to hide in the wardrobe. I certainly had no desire to witness your shameful indiscretion."

"Only to partake."

Dove sucked in a breath and concluded Lord Worthington was the lowest of the low. "It is your good fortune I had less desire to witness your murder, you, you, cad."

"Miscreant."

"Libertine."

"Peeping Tom."

"Peeping...This is absurd and pointless. I'm going now. Do try to stay out of a woman's skirts long enough to form a plausible tale for Lord Beaumont. Both our necks are on the chopping block. If someone catches me, I'm sure to take most of the blame for this debacle."

He scowled at her. "And you take care making

your escape down the tree. It will spoil my lie beyond repair if the Creeping Bandit is found dead on the ground."

Following a brief pause, Dove laughed. She couldn't help it. The night had spun in a most bizarre downward spiral. "I give you my word I shall do my best not to die. I have but one request."

He crossed his arms, a sneer tugging on his face. "Do tell."

"Tame your sarcasm. You owe me."

Lord Worthington sighed. "Very well. What do you want?"

He sounded so put upon, Dove almost laughed again. "I want you to curb your curiosity and leave me be. Do not search for me, tonight, or ever."

This time, Lord Worthington laughed. "I will have everlasting joy should our paths never cross again."

She glared at him, refusing to acknowledge the reason for her chafe. *His kisses could transport a woman to a world full of wonder.*

"I feel quite the same." With those parting words, Dove slipped from the window.

Once on the ground, she tipped her head back. He stood at the window, watching. Viscount Worthington gave her an exaggerated salute. Dove spun on her heel and fled.

****

Drew stared out the window long after she disappeared into the darkness. A tad bit taller than the average woman, trim build, vibrant sapphire eyes, and a hint of honeysuckle at her throat. He hadn't meant to kiss her. His intent had only been for a bit of fun teasing, letting her know she hadn't fooled him for a second with her masculine disguise. Before he knew what he was about, he had his hands on her, her soft lips beneath his.

The woman had more passion than experience. Her innocent lust nearly dropped him to his knees. For the first time, his pat words of fearing for his sanity proved true. *He'd nearly taken a virgin.* That was something he simply did not do, ever.

It had taken a great force of will for him to put a stop to their carnal progression. He may be a rake, but he did not seduce innocents, even if they were the infamous Creeping Bandit. Drew chuckled at his latest near conquest, the blasted Bandit, of all things!

How he wished he'd had more time with her. The myriad of mysteries pranced through his mind. Why did she go to all the trouble and risk of sneaking into homes, and then not take anything? Why did she rearrange items? Most of all, who in the blazes was she? That question plagued him the most. He should have held on to her, just a bit longer. But the woman had saved his life. On his honor, he had to let her go.

Drew chuckled again, though his humor soon fell into a strange fade. Had his relationship with honor grown so distant? He didn't have to delve far into his past for the answer, or the twinges of fear still pinching his insides. Tonight, the distance between his actions and his honor almost cost him his life.

He glanced at Lord Beaumont. The man lay in a lump on the floor, breathing, but still unconscious. The pistol was but a foot or two from the man's hand. He hadn't even thought to kick it away. As usual, his mind had focused on a woman. If not for a miraculous coincidence, he might well have died this night. Along with the gooseflesh, those pre-death images returned, as if he needed a reminder.

His last thoughts, before the Creeping Bandit leapt to his rescue, had been of his mother and sister. Drew now considered the deficiency he would have left behind. In truth, though, had it not been for the Creeping Bandit, his legacy would have been far worse than a mere deficit of substance.

Drew slumped against the window frame. Yes, far worse than nothing for which his mother and sister could be proud. He would have left an irreparable scandal for them to bear.

Even upon, say, an accidental death or one due to illness, his mother would have to fabricate tales of his honor and good standing if she were to retain any dignity at all. His exploits were no secret amongst the *ton*. However, she would never be able to recover from the scandal of her son shot dead in the bedchambers of a married woman. Worse still, Lord Beaumont was prepared to declare him the Creeping Bandit.

Furthermore, the rampage of dishonor he left behind would not stop with his mother. The scandal would annihilate his little sister's chance of a good match. Even with money and title, Olivia would be lucky to wed an impoverished baron three times her age.

Until now, Drew hadn't given a ghost of a thought as to how his lifestyle might one day affect them. He'd thought only of his own pleasures. How could he have been so selfish? He was the family patriarch. He had been since the age of fifteen, though a pitiful one, he now conceded. Never, in all truth, had he considered himself amongst London's cluster of self-seeking cads.

This night shone a harsh but accurate light on all he was, and all he was not.

Tonight, he'd pushed his debauchery to its limit. How long had it been since he'd acknowledged a boundary? He used to have them. In fact, they'd been quite stringent. At what point had they softened, and then dissolved? When had it become acceptable to take up liaisons with married women? There was a time when he would not have considered such a thing.

Perhaps his lifestyle had grown beyond his control. The very idea he'd lost command of his life was alarming. He had, though. Whatever moral restraints he'd once had were lost in ruffles of skirts, coins stacked on gaming tables, and bottomless pits of brandy-filled glasses.

He'd just barely escaped a pistol ball to the chest, yet in the aftermath, all he'd thought about was seduction. He dipped his head at his own shameless decadence. To lose his own life was bad enough, but to ruin his mother and sister was inexcusable. Drew straightened and gazed out the window through purposeful eyes.

Well, no more. If the fates saw to it to give him another chance, he would not squander it.

A groan drew his attention. Lord Beaumont stirred on the floor before falling still again. Drew stepped over and knelt, lifting the man, no small feat, onto his wife's bed. Perhaps Lord Beaumont would awaken believing he had too much drink, stumbled in here, bumped his head, and had a nightmare. Beatrix could help convince her husband of such. The lovely minx owed Drew at least that much.

Already heading for the door, he stopped. The

window beckoned his return, where he stared into the darkness. There was no sign of the Bandit. He hadn't expected one. Of course, she was long gone. He searched anyway.

Just as his lifestyle had caught up with him this night, sooner or later, the Bandit's would catch up with her. So, Drew arrived at a decisive conclusion. He would prove he was a man of honor and return the saving of his life by saving hers. It was a good start to a moral life.

His old self had one last vow to break. The Bandit requested he leave her be and not seek her. It was a request he would not honor.

Chapter 3

Dove swung open the door and spoke into the darkness outside the carriage. "All right, Renny. You can turn around now."

Renny, her coachman in full black and silver livery, her lifelong friend, and the closest thing she'd had to a father since her own father's death, took her hand and helped her step out of the carriage. She turned around and Renny got to work on the long row of buttons down her back. His nimble fingers took more time than usual, and she was quite sure it had nothing to do with the lack of light.

"What dreadful thing happened?" he asked, the fret in his voice softening the bluntness.

Dove glanced back over her shoulder. Even in the sliver of moonlight, she could see worry deepening the creases fifty-four years on this earth had set in his face. Was his hair grayer than it was yesterday? If there was more age to him, it was her fault. Renny was the only one who knew of her secret identity as the Bandit. All the worrying about her fell on his shoulders.

"What makes you think something dreadful happened?"

"Dove," he said, using her given name as he always did when they were alone. "You were gone considerably longer than usual."

Dove swung her head forward and faced the

carriage. As much as she wanted to lie to Renny to protect his tender heart, as well as save herself a lecture, she could not deceive this man.

"Things got…complicated."

Renny finished the buttons, took her by the shoulders for a gentle spin until she faced him. Since he was only a bit taller than she was, they were practically eye-to-eye. "Tell me."

So, she told him everything, leaving out the kiss. She couldn't even tell Renny about her first kiss. It was too embarrassing, especially considering the circumstances. Besides, she was still trying to sort it all out. A few minutes later, she was glad she'd held back that part of the story. As it was, by the time Dove finished her tale, Renny sat on the carriage step holding his palm to his brow.

Dove sat down beside him and patted his back. "There, there, Renny. Calm yourself before your heart begins to flutter again. Everything turned out well. I escaped unscathed."

"You were *seen*."

"We always knew it was a possibility, hence the disguise. Besides, it's not as if I haven't been seen before."

"By a woolly-headed woman whose telling of you is so exaggerated no one would ever guess your identity, much less your gender. In fact, after Lady Ashbury's description of the Bandit, not a person with any eyesight whatsoever could look upon you with suspicion. This man, this Lord…"

"Worthington."

"Worthington. He heard your voice. He knows you're a woman."

Dove's fingers floated upward until her fingertips brushed her lips. Yes, Lord Worthington had no doubt she was a woman. Her hand curled into a ball and dropped into her lap. She hated anyone, especially *him*, knowing she was not a man.

"He still hasn't a clue as to who I am."

"Suppose he should seek out the woman behind the mask? You know these types. They get bored. They're always searching for some new amusement."

Dove shook her head. "We parted on great and equal amounts of dislike. Neither of us ever wants to see the other again."

Renny laid his hand upon hers and squeezed. "Quit, Dove. As the town grows more fearful, so grows your risk."

"I can't quit now."

Renny sighed and drew back his hand. She worried he would argue his point, again. They'd had repeated debates, and with his present pallor, she did not want to cause him any more upsets. But he must have accepted her decision. With the history of his previous failed efforts to persuade her to quit this mission, he let the matter drop.

"I take it you didn't find the brooch."

The brooch! She'd forgotten all about it. She hadn't a chance to search the entire chambers before Lady Beaumont slipped into the room. Dove jumped into the wardrobe without even blowing out the branch of candles she'd lit. It gave her a clear view of the proceedings through the opening, as she couldn't risk the click of closing the doors all the way. Dove shook her head. She hadn't even left her signature, rearranging small items enough so the owner would know the

Bandit had been there.

"No, I didn't find the brooch. I'll go back another time."

"Dove, my sweet, you know I love you as if you were my own daughter."

Ah, so he hadn't surrendered his attempts to convince her to quit. She couldn't be angry with Renny, though. His efforts were all because he cared.

"Growing news of your escapades has made the *ton* more alert. They're specifically looking for you. With each of the Bandit's ventures, it becomes more dangerous. I've heard some of them have taken to hiring guards to patrol their grounds."

"I too have heard such," she said. "I can't quit, not until I've searched for the brooch in the private chambers of every member of the upper classes."

"I've made this point before, but I wish you'd give it more thought. It is possible the murders were indeed no more than a tragic matter of highwaymen, and not a grand scheme set upon your parents. As horrible as it is, these things do happen, you know."

"I know, Renny. But I can't stop thinking there is more to their murder than a simple robbery gone awry. You know many of them looked down their noses at my mother because of her Shawnee heritage, and my father for marrying her. Perhaps far more so than we know about."

"Yes, little bird, but murder..."

Dove glanced away for a moment before twisting back to face her dearest friend. "Please be patient with me, Renny, for a while longer. I have to know, for my parents' sake."

"And what would your parents think of you rotting

away in Newgate Prison? Oh, now," Renny said when her eyes filled. He palmed her head, bringing it to his shoulder and used his other hand to pat her back. "Very well."

Dove sniffed and Renny handed her his handkerchief.

Blotting her eyes, she said, "Thank you. When I've crossed the last of the homes off my list, I'll accept what you say and put the Bandit behind me. I promise." She clutched the handkerchief to her chest and breathed deep. "Oh, Renny, I don't know what I'd do without you."

"Nor I you. Without these escapades of yours I'm afraid this old coachman would live a rather dull life."

Dove smiled her gratitude. She had no doubt Renny would relish a dull life.

"Well," he said. "We'd best fix your hair and return you to the ball before your grandfather begins a search for you."

Upon standing, Renny teetered a bit and Dove caught his arm to stabilize him. "Is your leg in a bad way tonight?"

"Not too bad. Just a little stiff." After a quick, hard rub on his right thigh, Renny produced a brush from a pocket in his jacket. He removed and replaced several pins in her hair, smoothing, tucking, and then scrutinizing his work. "It's hard to be sure, with so little light. Check yourself when you get back inside."

Dove smiled. "You make a fine lady's maid, Renny."

"Ah, well, another secret for us to keep between us." Renny stepped back, pointed a finger toward the ground, and spun it. She rotated for his inspection.

"You are lovely beyond compare, little bird."

Dove blushed, even though she knew it was flattery and nothing more. The half of her Shawnee heritage she carried gave her skin a diluted, ocher appearance, unlike the fashionable fair-skinned beauty of her peers. They would never step foot out of doors without their parasols to prevent their skin from darkening.

Dove loved the sun on her face, which served only to deepen her complexion further. Her hair was so dark, Elsa, her lady's maid, said in the sunlight it shone with a hint of plum. The bright blue of her eyes, though, her father's eyes, gave lightness to her appearance, and along with her grandparents' influence, gained her a good measure of acceptance.

Every time Dove looked in a mirror, she saw both of her parents in her features. It was always a bittersweet experience. It had been three years since their murder. Instead of diminishing, her pain and anger had grown until she could no longer sit idle. She had to find her mother's brooch. For through that stolen piece of jewelry, she would find whoever was responsible for their deaths.

"Are you ready?" Renny asked.

Dove nodded. "I am."

Five minutes later, Dove slipped in a side entrance of the Beaumont residence and blended into the crowd. Music floated from the ballroom and wove through the rest of the party. Laughter punctuated the light mood. As she made her way past conversations, she still caught an occasional mention of the Bandit. As the evening had gone on, though, topics had shifted to politics, fashion, and of course, gossip.

Dove kept a surreptitious eye out for both Lord

Beaumont and Lord Worthington. She saw neither man, though she spotted Lady Beaumont in close conversation with a lord she did not recognize. The lady showed no sign of the evening's events, save for an occasional sly glance toward the staircase.

Dove found her grandfather in a heated discussion with Lady Havisham over which tarts were preferable for breaking one's fast, strawberry, or blueberry. The moment he saw Dove, the man's entire face smiled.

"Dove, my dear," her grandfather said, a squint over his smile. Have you been gone a while, or not? I can't remember."

Even in his advanced years, her grandfather appeared hale and hearty. His shoulders were still strong, though his weight had diminished some over the last few years, and his legs didn't carry him as far as they once did. His hair was gray, but full. His eyes twinkled the green of spring grass every time he smiled.

After exchanging greetings with Lady Havisham, Dove answered her grandfather. "Only a moment or two. I see your punch is almost gone. Would you two like me to refill your glasses?"

"My nephew has just gone to get us some wine," Lady Havisham said. She was a trim woman, a dowager with a fine-boned face and a friendly nature who often joined them for tea.

"Very well, then." Dove smiled at her beloved grandfather.

The dear man had once been sharp as a point. Since Dove's grandmother died two years ago, his mind was slipping away in scattered patches. All the sadder since he'd always been her champion, loving her wholeheartedly right from the start regardless of her foreign heritage. It was heartbreaking to witness his mind's slow demise. However, it did make her work as the Bandit easier to accomplish. Of course, nothing about tonight had gone easy.

Normally, Dove waited until the lord and lady of the house were not in residence. She could slip away from home or an event if it was busy enough, even with her grandfather chaperoning. This was the first and only time she had she attempted to search a private chamber while a ball was underway just downstairs. Seeing as things turned out, she would not attempt such again.

It had been foolish, but the temptation was too strong, knowing the arrogance of both Lord and Lady Beaumont. They, like many of the *ton*, had spared her mother only shallow acceptance, made her feel less, and if Dove's suspicions were correct, one of London's elite had arranged the night of their murders.

"Have you danced, dear?" her grandfather asked. "Your hair is a bit mussed."

Dove patted her hair. "Um, yes. I'll go attend to my appearance right now. I'll be back to check on you later."

After fixing her one loose tuft of hair, Dove wandered through the parlors. It was too early to leave. Not for her, Dove was more than ready to put an end to this disastrous night, but for her grandfather. He so enjoyed these events and the socializing was good for his health. The man had always been so good to her, and good to her mother.

It had taken grandmother a while to adjust to a Shawnee daughter-in-law straight from the colonies, but she did. Her grandparents had enough influence to gain Dove's mother acceptance into society, well, somewhat. More than a few of the pleasantries were skimmed from the surface. But the love of her parents was solid, and their love sustained all of them. The love of her grandfather sustained her still.

Dove passed by Lady Beaumont with barely a glance exchanged. In her distraction, the wayward lady chewed on a thumbnail before catching her behavior and clasping her hands together. Lady Beaumont's smile was so forced she appeared to be in pain.

Dove walked on, also keeping an eye out for *him*. She'd not seen the man since leaving him framed within Lady Beaumont's open window. It was the only thing gone her way this night.

Perhaps Lord Worthington had enough adventure for one evening and already bid his goodnight. She hoped so. Though he couldn't possibly recognize her, Dove did not want to take the chance something about her might arouse the scoundrel's suspicions. The man had caused her enough trouble.

Dove chatted for a while with Elspeth, Lady Havisham's granddaughter. Elspeth had a rounded face with plump cheeks and walnut-colored hair that struggled to hold its curl. She was nice enough, but she had her cap set for a husband and didn't tarry long once her target strolled into view. Dove followed her line of sight.

Lord Derek Durham, a wealthy marquis, and one of the most handsome men in London, stopped to converse not twenty feet from where they stood. Other young women on the marriage market must have also spotted him, as his surroundings of fluttering eyes and twitters grew. Elspeth wasted no time extricating herself from their conversation to scurry into the fray of competition. Beneath her breath, Dove wished Elspeth luck.

For a while, Dove conversed with Lord and Lady Darington, two people for whom she bore sincere affection. They were kind, and not above getting their hands dirty for a good cause. Dove had volunteered some of her time to work with them on the Foundling Project. The reward for all their hard work was about to pay off, as the new foundling home was but a few weeks away from being ready for the children.

Rose Darington was early in the stages of her second pregnancy. At her second yawn, her husband, Burke, insisted they go home so she could rest. Rose agreed, but not until she said some goodbyes. Her husband gave her a wry smile, conveying a dubious, yet indulgent expression. Indulgent, perhaps, or bemused resignation. Everyone knew Lady Darington was a woman of her own mind. It was an oddity amongst the *ton*, how such a woman and the austere Lord Darington had found a love match with each other. But even after scandal and tribulation, they had.

Dove bid them farewell and was several feet away before she twisted a glance back over her shoulder. Burke brushed a kiss against his wife's neck. Rose gazed back at her husband. The love in her eyes equaled his, rich, full, complete. Dove spun away from them and wove back into the party.

For the next hour or so, she wandered through the crowd, exchanging cordial greetings and snippets of conversation, until a few others bid their goodnights. At that time, grandfather collected their wraps and helped Dove into hers.

At least two dozen people crowded the foyer,

making a slow stream out the door, too slow for her comfort. The closeness of all the perfumed people, the damp heat of the press, the heaviness of her cloak upon her shoulders, threatened to overwhelm her. This being stuck in a close-knit crowd left her battling a near panic. Small places did such to her. Even the few minutes she'd spent stuffed in Lady Beaumont's wardrobe had tested her fortitude.

At last, they'd gotten to the open door and the night's air sifted cool against her face. Dove breathed it in deep, releasing it as they stepped outside. A few more minutes and Renny would have them on their way home and she could call an end to this luckless night.

And then it happened.

A tingling of sorts got her attention, a tickle up her spine, a tightening of her scalp. Dove's head made a slow rotation. She didn't want to look, but like the rest of this bizarre night, the matter was not in her control. It was as if a demanding hand of fate clutched her jaw. Faces clicked by with little notice, until one didn't. Lord Worthington's rich, amber eyes locked on hers, and a jolt shot through her entire body.

Recognition gleamed in his sudden gaze, but it couldn't be. It was simply she was a woman and he was a rake in search of his next conquest. Dove spun back toward the walk, accelerating their pace as best she could through the crowd. Lord Worthington had been back several deep and still inside the doors. The blasted bounder wouldn't have seen her at all if he were not so tall.

At the end of the walk, Renny waited beside the open carriage door. Was grandfather moving at a slower pace tonight? The question no sooner ran through her mind, than when her grandfather asked, "Are we having a race, dear?"

"I'm sorry, Grandfather. I didn't mean to rush you." Dove slowed, but not much. Never had she come so close to having her identity discovered and her nerves buzzed over her skin.

"Dove dear, I know you don't much enjoy these social outings. But they are the best places for you to make a good match, and you deserve the best."

Dove didn't bother telling him she had no interest in husband hunting. His concerns were for her future, her happiness, and she loved him for it. She would have paused and kissed his cheek had she not been so rushed to escape that vexatious viscount.

Renny must have seen the worry upon her face and understood trouble was afoot, because he acted with haste installing them into the coach. Still, it took an interminable minute or so before she and her grandfather settled inside. Dove didn't peek out the window until the carriage was rolling away.

He was there, standing on the broad walk. Long legs apart, hands on hips, he held still as others flowed around him like a river around a boulder. Several carriages rolled away at the same time. When Lord Worthington's head rotated toward theirs, Dove flattened back against the squabs.

Chapter 4

He had a face, but no name. And what a face! It was not at all what he expected. He'd guessed her to be rather plain. What kind of beauty would cover herself so, and get involved in such strange criminal activity?

The audacious little chit had the gall to don her disguise and sneak about at the very party she was attending! Drew laughed out loud, catching the attention of passersby.

The only reason he'd returned to the ball was to have a serious talk with Beatrix. Her apologetic mood led her to be quite accommodating. Of course, the lie she would tell her husband about how he'd overindulged, stumbled into her room, fell, and bumped his head, was to her benefit, too. Beatrix was confident she could convince him what he'd seen had been naught but a nightmare.

Drew kept mum on the appearance of the Creeping Bandit, as Beatrix was out of the room before the Bandit made her daring appearance. The last thing that hooded rapscallion needed was more publicity. Besides, this way, when Lord Beaumont told his wife the Bandit had attacked him, Beatrix's expression of surprise would be sincere. Drew wished he could see it.

With the night's disaster tucked into his past, Drew bid his farewells. For once in his life, he was ready to call it an early night. Besides, he wanted to get a good night's sleep. For tomorrow, he would work his brain, and then commence his search for the mysterious Creeping Bandit.

Where he'd begin, he hadn't a clue. He'd figure it out tomorrow when he had a fresh and rested mind.

Before he could collect his coat and be gone, however, several acquaintances vied for his attention. Their efforts to persuade him into another round of parties failed, much to their extreme dismay. Drew, above anyone, was always up for the pursuit of indulgent pleasures. Tonight, he hadn't a drop of interest. Staring down the barrel of Lord Beaumont's pistol, seeing naught but an end to a vacuous life, had drained him of his energies.

Drew collected his coat and took a place in the back of the exiting current. He declined several more invitations to continue the night elsewhere. The assumptions following his refusals were all in the same vein.

Lord William Bradley slid a leering grin his way. "Hope she's a pretty one," said Will. The lecher raised his brows at his clear insinuation.

Lord Percy Linden elbowed Will in the ribs. "Of course she is! What else would keep our boy here from drink and game but a beautiful woman?"

Will leaned in, and in a voice mocking a conspiratorial tone said, "Two women!"

The two of them did not attempt to quell their burst of laughter as they headed back to the party. Had Will and Percy always been such obnoxious little men? Drew suffered two more similar conversations, if one considered such debasement conversation.

The only people Drew spoke with for more than a

shake was his one true friend, Lord Burke Darington, Earl of Blackwood, and his lovely wife, Rose. It was the first he'd seen of them this night, and the couple was on their way out.

"Do come by for tea this week, won't you, Drew?" Rose said. Her face was aglow with motherhood, and love for her husband.

Husband. Drew still couldn't believe Burke had gone off and gotten leg-shackled. Strange as it still was to him, his friend did appear to be quite happy in his present state of matrimony. Not so long ago, Drew would have thought such a thing impossible. Burke had sworn off marriage, until a very strange and wild set of circumstances tossed the two of them together.

"Yes," Burke said, draping his wife's warm cloak over her shoulders. "My son keeps asking when you're coming back to see him again. He quite enjoyed playing hide-and-seek with you in the gardens. He remembers you with all clarity, even though it's been several months."

Had it been months already? He'd meant to stop by and see the boy again, as he had enjoyed the afternoon. But the days had gotten away from him. Or rather, the late nights, which kept him asleep much of the day. By the time he climbed from his bed and shook off the cobwebs, it was near time to once more dive into the night's festivities.

"Of course, I'll stop by soon," Drew said, and meant it. The Darington's were his friends. He would not again be remiss keeping that in mind.

A footman handed Drew his slate gray Garrick coat with three elbow-length caplets attached to the collar. Before he could slide his arms into the sleeves, Burke leaned toward him and said in a hushed voice, "I'm sure he would like to have you all to himself before his new sibling comes along."

Drew leaned back to take in his friend's face. Burke was near to bursting with joy. It was contagious. After a handshake and a hearty clap on the back, Drew set his attention on Rose. Her eyes were bright. Her cheeks glowed the color of her namesake. She lay a hand on her belly, scarce rounded, and nodded. Drew took her in a brotherly hug and whispered his congratulations into her ear.

"We'll see you soon, then?" she asked.

"You have my word."

Burke shrugged into his coat. The Darington's were on their way out, too, anxious to get home to their son. Though young Robert was long asleep by now, Burke had told him before they were happiest when they were all within the same walls.

Drew would have accompanied them and been out the door sooner had it not been for a tug on his arm. Lord Felix Brethem, already half in his cups.

Drew nodded to Burke and his wife as they left. Just before they stepped out of the door, before several people blocked his view, Rose tipped her head up and shared a tender gaze with her husband. For a moment, an ache Drew couldn't explain tightened his heart. Then a voice with a bit of a slur drew him away from the warm loving sight, as well as the strangeness it set upon him.

"Come on, old man," Felix said to tempt him into a card game. The stakes, Felix explained, had grown enough to draw none but the most skilled of gamblers. "This game calls for a man of your expert talents."

The crowd in the foyer thickened and grew noisy with farewells. Sparks of laughter interspersed with final quips. Outside, footmen called for carriages. Drew was tired and quite ready to climb into his. He glanced down at Felix.

The man was just a few years older than Drew was. Already lined and timeworn, his body expanding with sloth and spoils, he looked at least a decade older. His lifestyle was aging him. It was Drew's lifestyle, too.

How long would it be before he tired of boxing at Gentleman Jackson's, the one source of exercise he adhered to, and his middle grew thick and soft? Perhaps his eyes already carried the same, liquid lack of clarity. Was his face also puffed and ruddy with excessive indulgences?

"Not tonight, Felix," Drew told him. He had difficulty looking at the man, fearing a glimpse into future's mirror.

Shock flashed across Felix's face before understanding replaced it.

"Ah, found yourself a lady to spend your evening with, have you?" he said, a lewd smile folding the excess skin of his face around his sottish eyes. "Well, when you've finished with her, catch up with us at White's."

Drew resisted the urge to glare at the man. Finished with her, Felix said, as if a woman was of no more importance than a game. Did he treat women so? No, he did not. He loved women, he cherished them, savored them. It's not as though he toyed with their affections. Or did he?

Women see things in a different light. Perhaps…ah, damn! He couldn't think straight in this chattering crowd. He needed to go home and sleep. On the morrow, he would sit alone for a while and let his mind work. The fastest route there was to give a nod to Felix and just leave.

That's when it happened.

From his place, crushed in the exiting crowd, a whiff of honeysuckle captured his full attention. While it was possible another woman wore the same scent, he knew better. How, he couldn't say. Perhaps the honeysuckle mixed with her personal essence to create a unique and splendid fragrance. Whatever the reason, Drew's feeling gained confirmation the instant her head rotated back, and his gaze met hers.

Her skin had a slight, exotic hue, as if she was given to taking walks without her parasol. Her hair shone like new black silk. What he recognized, though, was the radiant sapphire color of her almond shaped eyes. They were a bright blue sea sparkle of unrivaled jewels.

Her full lips parted just enough to take in a quick breath, and those fabulous eyes widened right before she spun away from him. Yes, it was her, his beautiful Creeping Bandit.

Drew shouldered his way through the crowd with the least amount of politeness spared. By the time he funneled through the door and onto the walk, however, he'd lost her. He scoured the people heading for their coaches. His search was futile. She was gone.

Several carriages rolled away at the same time. Drew couldn't tell who was in any of them. Two traveled to the right and one to the left.

It was a gamble, picking which of the three carriages to follow. Perhaps his luck in gaming would remain with him in this new eve of morality, at least for a little while.

Chapter 5

"Dove, dear, what do you think of this fabric?"

Dove shifted her eyes from the bowl of silver buttons she was sifting through, to the green swatch of fabric her grandfather held. Today he'd had a notion to take her shopping for a new gown. This was not unusual. He often did such things. Sometimes she thought it was his way of compensating for her not having a mother or grandmother. But truth be told, he did always appear to enjoy these outings.

"It matches your eyes," she said.

"Hmm, so it does." Her grandfather set the swatch down and lifted another, the color of fair blond. "Now this fabric is perfect for you."

"It's very nice," Dove said, sparing a glance. "But I don't need another gown."

"Tosh. Every woman needs another gown. Your grandmother had a new gown made for every occasion," he said.

He was so precious, giving close inspection to the fabrics, searching for what worked best for her, doing what he could to fill in the place her mother and grandmother left vacant.

He held the fabric up to her. "This will look splendid with your coloring. It's a shame we can't have it for the Frasier's soiree tomorrow night. Have you decided what to wear?"

Dove had been busy deciding which lady's bedchambers the Creeping Bandit would search. If the Beaumont's were out, she could return to their home while they were gone. She would not repeat her mistake of searching a home with guests just downstairs. Dove almost laughed at her own arrogance.

At the time, it had seemed quite logical. No one would suspect the Bandit might be sneaking about just overhead. The servants would all be busy attending to the needs of such a large event. No, her plan hadn't been arrogant. It *had* been a good idea. It would have worked, too, had it not been for the immoral behavior of Lady Beaumont and Lord Worthington.

Lord Worthington. The wastrel had nearly gotten her caught. The closeness of her demise that night haunted her. As did his kiss, damn the cad.

Did men like him have some sort of special power over women in general? Or worse, perhaps he wielded his magic over just her. It boggled her mind, that moment when she and her grandfather were leaving. How did she sense his nearness with such certainty?

Perhaps it was on her, the mysticism in her heritage. Her Shawnee mother often told her how strong it ran through her veins. Dove couldn't say what made her glance back at the precise moment Lord Worthington was staring her way, but she wished she hadn't.

She'd recognized him right away. The advantage was hers, though, as he couldn't suspect her identity. *He knew you were a woman.* But such was all he knew. Her costume was complete. Renny helped her see to it. The spark of recognition she saw in the man's eyes was naught but her imagination, set on edge due to the evenings stressing events.

"Yes," her grandfather said, his voice hauling Dove into the present. "I do believe this is the perfect fabric for you, dear."

For the next three quarters of an hour, her grandfather, with the assistance of Madam Kershaw, chose style cuts and accoutrements while Dove pretended to care. She nodded her agreement to something about a squared bodice and gave a verbal yes to the silver armlets Madam Kershaw held and agreed they were perfect for the long, ivory gloves.

While smiling and nodding, Dove rolled the coming night around in her head once more. She would have a couple advantages at the Beaumont residence. For one, she was already familiar with the room. Second, that wonderful elm outside Lady Beaumont's window allotted her easy entrance without having to go through the house.

Yes, she would slip away from the Frasier's soiree and finish searching Lady Beaumont's chambers. This time, there would not be anyone to make trouble.

Or so she thought.

Chapter 6

They were gaping at him as if he were a stranger who strolled in off the street to join them for their morning meal.

"Mother, Ollie," Drew said as he took his seat at the head of the table, using the nickname he'd had for Olivia since she was a babe.

The larger of two scruffy mutts sitting on the other side of his little sister peeked his brown snout around her chair before returning his attention to Olivia, who he didn't doubt was slipping them scraps of food. Since when had Ollie been allowed to feed them from the table?

Mother had long ago wearied in her efforts to dissuade her daughter from bringing home strays. Still, he couldn't imagine their mother not having fits over dogs breakfasting with them. Perhaps Ollie, sixteen years old now, had worn her down on pets in the breakfast room, too.

The women, both in their simple morning gowns, faint gray for his mother, light blue for Ollie, continued to stare at him from his left and his right. His mother still held her fork, tines down, midway to stabbing a small strawberry. It was as if his appearance had turned them into a painting, 'Surprise at the Morning Meal'.

A nod to the footman standing near the sidebar had the young man, who did a poor job of hiding his own astonishment, spin around to fill a plate for the master of the house.

From the seat on his right, his slender, elegant mother, with chestnut-colored hair like his, though without the faint streaks of red, said, "Good morning, son."

She opened her mouth to say more, but then closed it again. For a woman of skilled social graces, it appeared his mother was at a loss for words.

He then received a good morning from Olivia. Drew tipped his head to his little sister, and when he raised it again, her stunned expression had not lessened. For a moment, his matched hers. Ollie, with her vibrant red hair and stubborn tilt of her chin, never had a problem voicing her thoughts. Quite the opposite. He caught his sister's widened, jade green eyes flick toward their mother, and then back to him again.

The footman placed the silver-trimmed plate before him and returned to his place at the sideboard. Drew picked up a triangle slice of toast and spooned some strawberry jam on it from a crystal bowl on the table. The sound of silver smearing over crusty bread was inordinately loud, as was his bite and chew.

After swallowing, Drew set his toast back on his plate and swung an aggravated glance at both women. "Why are you two gaping at me? Have I grown a second head, sprouted elephant ears, perhaps?"

"Dear," his mother said. "Don't misunderstand. We're thrilled you have joined us. It's just that…well…it's been so long. Are you unwell?"

"Yes," Olivia chimed in. She leaned over her plate, her eyes growing wider until the green of them fair glowed in the sun-flow through the window. "Have you come down with some sort of exotic disease?"

"A disease? Oh, for heaven's sake."

"Son, it's just that we never see you up this early."

"Nonsense. I'm often up at this time of day," he said, though the blatant lie did not slip easy from his tongue. He was not one to be up in the morning unless one counts dragging his weary tail in after a long night of debauchery.

"Well," his mother said. Her smile, a bit too bright, further shone a light on the strangeness of his appearance to share their morning meal. "We're happy you've joined us. Aren't we, Olivia."

His sister still stared at his face. "Are you sure you haven't come down with something quite unique, maybe even grotesque?"

"Olivia, dear, please, we are at the breakfast table." To Drew, his mother said, "Your sister has developed a keen interest in grotesque illnesses."

Drew sighed. "Ollie, I assure you, I am quite well."

Then, after a moment his sister said, "Do you have a rash? It could be smallpox, you know."

"I do not have a rash. Smallpox? Dear God, Ollie."

"Typhoid, perhaps. Have you a fever? Does your head ache?"

"Olivia, please," their mother pleaded to no avail.

"Yellow fever? Have you been bitten by a mosquito?"

"I have not. I assure you, I am quite healthy."

"Oh."

"This disappoints you?"

"Of course not. I am ever so happy you are well, brother. And if you should come down with something, I'd wish you a quick and full recovery, of course. It's just that I never have any good gossip to share and a dastardly disease in the family would capture everyone's attention."

Drew laughed. He'd forgotten his sister had a penchant for dramatic adventure. "Sorry to come to the table empty handed. I'll try to dig something up for you, something other than the loss of my good health."

Ollie brightened. "Something grotesque?"

"Must it be grotesque?"

"Well, it *would* add vibrancy to any story."

Drew chuckled again. "I'll see what I can do." And then his smile diminished as it occurred to him how very little he knew about his sister anymore. Although they lived under the same roof, her life had grown at a distance from his.

A riding accident had taken their father when Ollie was but three, old enough to understand he was gone, but not old enough to understand why. Drew had been fifteen.

He'd held her when she cried, comforted her to sleep. He remembered her clinging to him as if he too might disappear. With some time and effort, he'd been able to tease her into a few smiles. What a fine feeling that was. Ollie had treated him as if he were the embodiment of all things important.

Focusing on his little sister had helped keep his mind off his own pain. When had Ollie faded from his attention? Had she felt the loss of a brother, as well as her father? Drew resisted the sudden urge to take his sister in his arms and assure her he would look out for her in the future. She wouldn't understand, and he could not give a comprehensive explanation to such behavior. But since standing on the wrong side of a readied pistol, perspectives had pried open his eyes. His failings were adding up, quick and big.

Drew spent the rest of the meal catching up on the most recent happenings of the house. It was almost as if he was a guest, a long-lost relative come to visit. Family friends must know more about his mother and sister than he did.

He should not have just heard how Lord Sanguay had come to call on his mother several times over the last few weeks. Nor should he be so surprised his little scamp of a sister was blossoming into a young woman. Her fair skin was overtaking her freckles, and when had she started putting so much care into taming her wild hair? He should know these things. Drew vowed he would not allow such deficiencies to occur again.

A chuckle managed to circumvent the magnitude of his neglect. Ollie was a brassy young woman with some strange fascinations. In a couple of years, she was sure to drive some young man to distraction.

Drew's eye caught on the stone hanging from a silver chain around his mother's neck. It was an unusual stone, shiny bright blue, star-shaped with rounded points. He tipped his head toward the necklace.

"I don't remember seeing that piece before. Is it new?"

"Yes. It's a sellvyn stone."

"And what is a sellvyn stone?" Drew asked, though he had an idea. He'd bet a stack of good coin it was some sort of charm.

His mother suffered every kind of superstitious belief. All he had to do was look at her breakfast plate as a reminder. Her toast had one bite out of each corner. She always ate the corners first because she'd read in one of her books it guaranteed good relationships within the walls of her home.

Her slender fingers brushed the stone. She lifted her chin, the same willful chin his sister inherited. "It protects me and those around me from evil spirits."

Their mother's superstitions began after the death of her husband, their father. Most of the time it made Drew sad for her desperation. She'd grasp at anything offering protection for her and her children. It was not unusual for him to find some sort of shielding stone in one of his pockets. On occasion, her irrational beliefs goaded him to tease her into a smile. Such as now.

"Are those pesky spirits back again?"

Olivia grinned at his serious-sounding remark before reining in her mirth. Their mother's superstitions grew from worry, from fear of harm coming to her family. They'd both teased her a bit, but never mocked her.

"It's a lovely piece, Mother," he said. "Is this charm more powerful than the others you already own?"

She flashed a raised brow his way. "You and your sister are safe and breathing, aren't you?"

In the very recent past he stood on the wrong side of a loaded pistol. It was indeed a miracle he lived to recall the moment. Perhaps he should give more credence to his mother's superstitions.

"We are indeed, Mother," Drew said. Not only had the teasing vanished from his tone, but even he heard the note of gratitude. The satisfaction he saw on his mother's face made him glad for it.

By the end of the meal, his humor was in high spirits. Had his mother and sister always been so entertaining? Drew continued to wonder after he later bid them farewell from the doorway and wished them a pleasant afternoon for their round of visits. He'd missed out on so much, and right under his nose. Drew pivoted and made a thoughtful stroll to the study.

It was a fair-sized room, for a study. The mahogany desk was modest in size, yet carved with enough small bits of detail to see it was a fine piece of furniture. On the other side of the desk sat a gold-cushioned chair. The window behind the desk was large to let in plenty of light. He'd spent time in here as a child. Had he even stepped foot in the room since the death of his father?

This room, the shelved ledgers keeping record of the family accounts and such, he should know well. However, he did not. Drew stopped in front of his father's desk, his for thirteen years, now. It had been so long since he'd been in here, he could no longer say with any certainty what was kept in which desk drawer.

His Uncle Charles, his mother's older brother, visited on a regular basis to see to the family paperwork, keeping their financial and legal affairs in order. After his father's death, it was a blessing, having Uncle Charles to tend to the ledgers. Drew should have taken over these duties quite some time ago.

In all truth, it had never once occurred to him to do so. That, too, would have to change. He was the lord of this estate. The running of it was his responsibility. He would speak with his Uncle Charles, and soon, as the shame berating him would not be tolerant of a delay.

Furthering his disquieted state of mind was another certainty forced into the light. If Lord Beaumont had indeed taken his life that night in Beatrix's bedchambers, there was scarce a soul who would miss him for more than a brief intermission. His mother and sister would grieve. However, his presence in this household was already at such a minimum, well, not much about their lives would change were he to disappear.

Leaving the study, Drew made his way to the library. It was a large room, made cozy by the dark green and burgundy colorings, the scattering of comfortable chairs, and a red brick fireplace. Two wide windows gave good light for reading. Thick, Aubusson rugs muffled his bootsteps on the polished wooden floor.

A sizable tome sat on a table beside a wingback chair near one of the windows. He glanced at the cover and chuckled. The book was a compilation of recorded diseases. Ollie. A cloth bookmark poked from between the pages, about a third of the way through. He shuddered to think what horrid illness his sister might inquire about next.

Drew scanned the cherry wood shelves taking up most of the far wall until he found a book he hoped would contain the information he wanted. He then took the chair by the window and settled in for a read. Two pages in, a ball of gray fur hopped into his lap and he almost dropped his book.

After but a moment's exasperation, Drew gave into a grin and pet the small, silvery-gray cat with emerald eyes. "I believe you're new around here. We haven't been properly introduced. I am master of this house, Lord Worthington. You will address me as such."

The cat gave him a slow-eyed blink. Drew took it as compliance. "As you are given to popping in where you do not belong, I shall call you Bandit."

Drew stroked the cat's soft fur while his mind traveled to its namesake. Bandit. What an alluring temptress. Hmm. Siren of the sea, more like it.

The trail on which he was about to embark was fraught with possibilities, very few of them good. It was such a contradiction. On the one hand, he would become the man he should have been for some time now. On the other, well, the plan he formulated while lying awake in his bed during the early morning hours surpassed even his most outrageous escapades.

He huffed out a breath. It was beyond him how such a woman could command his attention. But he could not deny it as truth, vexing as it was. She occupied far too many of his thoughts since their serendipitous meeting, his dreams, his…fantasies.

To the cat, Drew said, "This one may indeed send me to Bedlam." The animal padded two circles in his lap before lying down and falling fast asleep. He stroked his thumb between the cat's triangle ears for a few minutes while his mind lingered long on the masked lady bandit. He had to force his attention back to the book.

Half an hour later, Drew flipped another page and shifted his body a bit in the chair so the sunlight flowing through the window once again landed upon the page. The cat didn't budge. So much time had passed since he'd last read a book, he'd forgotten how enjoyable it could be. The occasional cloud dampening the light scarce attracted his attention. A confounded voice, however, did.

"Sir?"

Drew glanced up to see Hubert, the family butler,

standing in the doorway to the library. Hubert, a lean, tidy man in his late-forties with a thin mouth and a touch of gray in his russet hair. The butler, who'd been with the family since before Drew was born into this world, sported enlarged eyes and a thin mouth agape.

"Sir...Are you ill?"

"Fine as the day I was born. Why does everyone keep inquiring about my health? And why are you staring at me as if I'm a ghoul out too far before dusk?"

"Well, it's just that I've never seen you up and about so early, not since you were a lad. It's not even quite noon."

The butler remained silent and still, as if shocked into immobility. The sight of the master of the house up and about so early had also elicited questions about his health from his mother and sister. This was his home. He should be able to rise, breakfast, and read without tossing the entire household on its head. It was damned aggravating. Though, whether the aggravation was toward others or himself, Drew refused to consider.

Before bringing his attention back to petting the cat, which'd poked his small head up at the conversation, Drew said, "Have some tea sent in, Hubert."

"...Would you care for some breakfast, milord?"

"I've already eaten."

"Already eaten? But it's not even noon."

Drew raised his head, and one hard eyebrow. He gestured with both hands toward the fireplace. "There is a clock on the mantel. I am perfectly capable of reading it. Not that it's necessary, as you've announced the time not once, but twice in the last few moments."

"Yes, sir."

At the butler's continued statuary, Drew said, "Tea, Hubert."

The butler gathered his wits, scattered by his master's unusual behavior, no doubt. Drew was happy to see him go. Hubert's shock, as well as everybody else's in the household, but served to remind him how absent and irresponsible he'd been. Not so much of a reminder, this shock at his morning appearance, as it was a hurling of his shortcomings in his face.

The cat nudged his furry little face against Drew's fingers. Drew glanced down, did the cat's bidding, and resumed his petting.

Chapter 7

Renny's hands were unsteady with nervousness as he helped Dove tuck stray strands of hair into her hood. "I don't have a good feeling about this place. Not after what happened last time."

They stood in the dark beside the carriage, parked on the same dim patch on the same side street as the night of the Beaumont's ball.

Dove shrugged into her black coat. "If anything, it will be easier. I'm familiar with the room. I saw for myself that Lord and Lady Beaumont are attending the Frasier's party right now. No one will be about but the staff, and entering through the window, I'll not even be at risk from one of them."

"Perhaps the Beaumonts have done what others have and hired a guard to patrol the grounds while they are away."

"I'll be careful, Renny. I promise."

Renny raised a glance to the sky. It prompted Dove to do the same. Clouds, heavy and dark, crept across the partial moon and dampened the light.

"My leg has been aching all day," Renny said. "I think it's going to rain tonight."

"I won't be long. Now, how do I look?"

For a moment, she worried Renny would argue with her some more, but then he sighed. He understood her motivation better than anyone else ever could. He also knew the unlikelihood he'd be able to sway her from her mission.

Renny crossed an arm over his middle and rested an elbow upon his wrist. As he stroked his shaved jaw, he said, "You look quite menacing, my lady."

Dove smiled beneath her dark hood. "I'm off then. I'll be back before you know it." A few minutes later, she was climbing through Lady Beaumont's window.

The lady's jewel box was full of exquisite stones in fine settings, but the brooch was not among the bounty. Dove carried the branch of candles she'd lit around to search the rest of her chambers. As the brooch was an exceptional piece, it might have earned a special hiding place. More so if Lady Beaumont knew of its origin.

But no, the piece was not in the woman's possession. Tonight, she would cross the Beaumont's name off her list. She was almost finished here.

Dove picked up a silver hairbrush from the lady's dressing table, carried it across the room, and set it on the bedside table. She then took the small, porcelain statue of an angel from the bedside table and moved it to the floor just in front of the wardrobe. She placed the lacey decorative pillow from a corner chair in the center of the bed. Dove glanced around. Going back to the corner, she turned the chair so it faced the wall. She picked up the branch of candles for another scan of the room. Yes, that should do it.

A flash of light gave brief and bright illumination to the room. A moment or two later, thunder rolled across the sky. Renny was right. Since his injury, Renny's bad leg could predict the coming rain. No matter, though. She was finished here and would be back at the carriage in but a few minutes. With any luck, the rain would hold out until she returned to the Frasier's soiree.

After setting down the candles, Dove leaned to blow them out. But then she stopped and stood upright again. She glanced toward the window, to the very spot where she'd received her first kiss. The memory alone warmed her body. His touch, the way his lips had brushed hers with a light tease before introducing her to sensuality, had been…wonderful.

Then he threw his stock line at her, the same line he'd used many times in the past on many other women, she had no doubt. Bedlam, indeed! The cad ruined everything by, by being himself.

Dove pursed her lips and blew out the candles with one strong, sweeping breath. She crossed the room and slipped out the window.

Branch by branch, she made her way down the now familiar tree. Lightning set the sky aglow again in a bright flicker. The thunder pounded closer behind this time, loud enough to make her jump and give her a moment's pause. Dove hurried down the massive tree.

She crouched on the last limb, ready to drop to the ground, when two big hands clasped on to her bottom.

Dove gasped.

"Up, up woman!" a man's voice hissed.

As he was shoving her upward, she had no choice but to climb. The bottom-grabber followed. She stopped and sat on a branch. A moment later, he sat on one on the other side of the trunk. Even in the moonlight broken by leaves, branches, and clouds, Dove could see it was *him*.

"Lord Worthington," she spat with more anger than shock. "What on earth are you doing here?"

"Returning the favor," he whispered back. "Lower your voice."

"Explain yourself."

"I'm saving your life. The guard is making his rounds and is almost to this side of the house. Hush now."

Lord Worthington stared down. Dove did the same. A moment later, a man stepped into sight. His gait would have appeared casual had it not been for the way his head swiveled about, keeping a survey of his surroundings. It was as if he expected the Bandit to pop out of the darkness at any moment. It was almost what had just happened.

The guard stopped. He was less than five feet below the soles of their shoes.

His head made a slow rotation one way, then lingered a moment before shifting his gaze to the other side of the property. Dove didn't move. She didn't breathe. She didn't scratch the itch on the tip of her nose. Lord Worthington held just as still.

The guard slid a cheroot from his coat pocket. Wonderful. He was going to stand there and have a smoke while Dove worried the pounding of her heart was loud enough for him to hear.

The sky lit up again, so bright she had to squint. The following clap of thunder rattled the surrounding leaves and sent a shudder through every branch. The sky having drawn his attention, the guard's head made a slow tip back. Two more seconds and he'd have an eyeful of bandit and viscount. Dove wondered if the guard carried a pistol.

Before the guard could catch sight of them, the sky decided it was a good time to shed its excess. The first few drops gave scarce warning. Rain burst from the clouds as if a host of angels were dumping giant buckets over the world. The guard dashed for better shelter than a leafy tree.

Dove and the viscount didn't dare budge until they were sure the guard was good and gone. Then they scrambled down the tree, and they ran. Dove hoped the viscount would return to whence he came, but when she glanced back over her shoulder to peer at him through the eyeholes of her hood, he was no more than a few steps behind her.

"Go away!" she shouted loud enough to be heard over the pounding rain.

He jogged up beside her and shook his head, droplets flying from his soaked hair. The pouring rain didn't hide his grin in the least.

She could try and lose him, leap a fence or two. Perhaps he'd tire, give up, and go home. She slanted a glance his way. He was tall and strong, and while she was running her hardest, the man beside her appeared to be extending very little effort to keep up with her.

Even if she could somehow outmaneuver him, there wasn't time. She needed to change clothing and get back to the party before her grandfather discovered she was gone. Her foot stomped in a puddle and sloshed water into her half boot. She cursed everything from the rain to her luck, to the clinging, bothersome gnat beside her. There was no hope for it. Dove ran to her carriage, the viscount on her heels.

From inside staring out the window, Renny must have seen her approaching through the downpour, for he shoved open the door. She leapt into the carriage. Lord Worthington right behind her. Then, Dove,

Renny, and the viscount, sat inside her carriage. If not for the pounding storm, there would be no sound at all.

Dove stared at Renny, who sat beside her. He appeared ready to faint. The dear man hadn't said a word since she and the viscount had hopped into the carriage. Renny's worried gaze shot from her, still cloaked head to toe in her sodden, Bandit disguise, to the dripping viscount, who sat across from them.

Though she couldn't be sure in the dim light inside the carriage, Lord Worthington appeared amused at this disaster. No, it couldn't be. They were soaked and cold. They'd almost been caught, which would have landed them both in prison, not to mention a boundless scandal guaranteed to devour both their families. A man would have to be brainless to find amusement in this night.

The viscount clapped his hands and hooted. "Well, that was jolly good fun!"

Dove gaped at him through the eyeholes of her hood.

The viscount tipped his head to the side. "Oh, come on now, don't stare at me in silence as if I—"

"Have a brain deficiency?" she said.

The man laughed again, confirming her suspicion. Lord Worthington was indeed a lunatic.

"Well, it would certainly please my sister if I did," he said, as if such a statement made perfect sense. "Of course, we'd have to stamp it with a more gruesome name. Perhaps, Melting Brain Disease? Yes, she'd love that." To Renny, he said, "I am Viscount Andrew Worthington, since our little bandit here has forgotten her manners and not made a proper introduction."

He dared speak of manners, this brazen rake who had the gall to put his hands on her bottom. Questions and accusations thrashed about her mind, tumbling over each other in the confusion. "Why...how did you know...?"

"Did you think I wouldn't find you, Lady Barrow?"

Dove gasped. Renny slumped back against the squabs.

Lord Worthington waved a hand toward her head. "You might as well remove your hood. I've seen your face, several times, in fact."

She believed him. Somehow, he knew her name. From there, it wouldn't be difficult to learn where she lived, and perhaps a few other things, too. Dove released a defeated sigh, reached up, and dragged the hood from her head.

"Ah, there she is. The lovely Lady Dove Barrow." He nodded to the lavender ball gown and other female accoutrements laid out neat on the seat beside him. "I'm impressed with your ability to change clothes in the confines of a carriage." With a raised brow and a hint of lewd amusement, he added, "That must take some interesting maneuvering."

Renny sat up straight. "Now see here."

"Don't take offense. I meant no insult. I am curious about one thing. Well, quite a few things. But let's start small."

Dove and Renny shared a glance tight with trepidation. Neither of them wanted to give him any more information than he already had, and he already had too much.

Perhaps his idea was to blackmail them. In her mind, Dove started a tally of what she might be able to glean from the family finances without raising suspicion. Since the beginning of her grandfather's mental decline, she tended the ledgers. However, her grandfather still had periods of great clarity where he kept up with the household's workings. The last thing she wanted to do is cause him an upset.

"What is it you want to know?" she asked.

To Dove, Lord Worthington said, "Is your driver also your lover?"

Not the significant difference in size, strength, nor class lines prevented Renny from lunging across the short distance to pounce on Lord Worthington with flying fists. The viscount reeled back. Worried for her friend, Dove jumped into the fray. Renny's string of heedless curses was loud enough to drown out the pounding rain as the carriage rocked in the tumult.

Dove didn't care Lord Worthington used his hands for no more than to block Renny's punches and try to hold off her friend. She grabbed one of the viscount's arms and yanked it away, leaving him open to Renny's assault.

"Stop it!" she shouted.

"Why are you looking at me?" Lord Worthington yelled. "I'm the one under attack."

The statement no sooner left his mouth, when Renny landed a solid punch to the viscount's jaw."

"Bloody hell!" Lord Worthington shouted.

Renny attempted a second strike. It barely touched. He sucked in two gulps of air, swayed, and fell back into the seat. In an instant, Dove dropped to his side.

"Renny! Renny, are you hurt?"

"Is *he* hurt?" Lord Worthington said, his voice up in ire. "I'm the one who's just endured an assault!"

Flashing a glare back at him, Dove said, "His heart

doesn't always function properly. You shouldn't have upset him so."

Lord Worthington's demeanor changed in an instant and he dropped to his knees on the floor of the carriage. "Lie down," he said, placing his hands on Renny's shoulders. He repeated the command in a firm yet caring tone. Using gentle pressure, he and Dove helped Renny lie upon the seat.

"Take some deep breaths," Lord Worthington told him. "Slow, Slow. Yes, that's it."

"Oh, Renny. I'm so sorry." Emotion thickened Dove's words. "Please don't leave me."

"He's not going anywhere," Lord Worthington assured her with utter confidence. "Keep breathing now, Renny, is it? Yes, in slow and deep through your nose. Exhale through your mouth. My father had the same problem. He found this method quite helpful."

Dove squeezed Renny's hand while he dragged choppy breaths into his lungs. Beside her, Lord Worthington kept a steady stream of soothing encouragements. After a long minute or two, Renny's breath returned to normal. The three held their places a bit longer as both the tension and the downpour receded.

"I believe I'm feeling better now," Renny said.

Even in the dim confines of the coach, his pallor stood out. But Renny refused to lie back any longer, and Dove didn't argue. It would upset him again. The man took pride in his ability to look out for her. However, if Lord Worthington uttered another foul remark, Dove would pummel him herself.

They helped Renny sit upright. Dove sat beside him, doing her best not to let her worry show. Drew settled in the seat across from them again. The downpour had reduced itself to steady but slowing pats upon the roof of the carriage.

Renny scowled at Drew. "Don't go thinking I can't defend Dove's honor. If you make another vile insinuation—"

"I won't."

****

"I won't," Drew repeated.

He didn't know why he asked such an incendiary question in the first place. It pounced from his mouth, as if it had been hiding behind a maddening suspicion until the opportunity presented itself. The fact that he cared at all vexed him further.

While following her over the past eight or nine days, he'd seen the two of them together. He'd watched with a commitment to learn. To anything less than a suspicious eye, it would appear they were no more than a lady and her coachman. However, Drew caught the subtleties. The discreet brush of fingers to hand. A whisper to her ear or to his. Shared smiles implying a deeper relationship.

What difference did it make to him if they *were* lovers? It was none of his business. That's not how it sat upon his chest, though. He'd observed her for more than a week. He'd hidden outside her house every evening, using discretion and his horse to follow her carriage, waiting for her to don her disguise once more.

A growing number of the upper crust was hiring guards to patrol their properties. It would take but a moment's carelessness or bad luck to land her in Newgate, lady or not. He was determined to see such would not happen. However, protecting her was not the full extent of his intentions.

With each passing day, Drew was more anxious for the moment he could speak with her again. And more agitated at the closeness she shared with her driver. Thoughts of the man with his hands on her, knowing her in the most intimate of ways, drove him to distraction.

And when those images were not disturbing him, thoughts of her still left him sleepless in his bed. Brandy didn't help. Nor did whiskey. His confounded mind always found its way back to Dove. The feel of her soft lips beneath his, imagining the wondrous things he would do to her if she were there with him between the sheets.

Little more than a week had gone by since the incident in Lady Beaumont's bedchambers. The lady bandit's kiss had been innocent, then. A thousand times over the days since, he'd wondered if her relationship with her driver had progressed, if the man had taken her innocence.

The thought of her in such intimacy with this man aggravated him beyond nonchalance, and once face to face with the two of them, trampled over his manners. But he had to know if they were lovers, and now he did. His joy at their mere close friendship was too baffling to analyze.

Raindrops continued to tap on the roof of the carriage, the storm's dwindling farewell. Clouds released the moon and more light trickled in through the windows. Lady Barrow and her friend Renny both stared at him as if he was the hangman, and they were waiting for their names to be called. He should be relishing his advantage of their duress here. However, he was not, not in the least.

"Now," Drew said, ignoring the strange mix of feelings. "I've learned quite a bit since our initial meeting. While we wait for the rain to pass, one or both of you may fill in the blanks."

They answered him with silence.

"Oh, come now. I know so much already." He leaned back and crossed his arms over the broad expanse of his chest. "Enough to turn you both over to the authorities, should I see fit."

He had no intention of doing such a thing. He'd tell them so, eventually. For now, he could use the threat to extract information. For a reason he couldn't fathom, other than it might put to rest his strange obsession with this woman, he had to know everything. Still, it didn't sit right, seeing the fear on their faces, and knowing he was the cause. His conscience pricked him further when her gloved fingers fluttered in her lap.

Dove bent forward, thrusting her words. "Renny had no choice. I forced him."

Beside her, Renny's hand clasped her shoulder and drew her back. He then leaned forward. "She did no such thing. *I* forced *her*, as matter of fact. I'm an envious man in search of easy wealth."

Renny's excuse made no sense whatsoever, as nothing was ever taken in any of the break-ins. Before Drew could state his remark, Lady Barrow shouted.

"He's lying!"

"She's lying," Renny countered.

"I'm his superior. He had no choice but to do as I bid."

"I'm a bully. A greedy tyrant. I used intimidation to get her to break into those homes for me."

The two shouted over one another, vying for blame. It was most remarkable. Friendship or not, they were talking about prison. Drew had expected finger-pointing, accusations. Never had he thought the man would risk incarceration to defend his employer. And to see a lady, a peer of the realm, lay her head on the chopping block to protect her driver, well, it was quite extraordinary.

"Stop," Drew said, holding out the palm of his hand. So much for the card up his sleeve. The threat to turn them in would gain him nothing. Better to alleviate their fears and seek to gain their confidence. "I've no intention of turning in either one of you. For more than a week now, I've known who you are and what you do, and I haven't told a soul."

"Can't you just go home and forget about us?" the lady asked.

"No. I'm only asking for an explanation. You owe me that much. After all, if I hadn't shown up tonight, you'd be under arrest right now, Lady Bandit."

She straightened and said, "And if I hadn't leapt to your rescue in Lady Beaumont's chambers, you'd be dead right now, Lord Rakehell."

After a short burst of laughter, Drew said, "Well, we're a fine cluster of miscreants, aren't we? Come now. Out with it. If you don't, you'll find I can be quite the pest until I get what I want. That, my fellow mischief-makers, is the truth."

Renny sighed and took Dove's hand. "You might as well tell him, little bird. And you," he said, swinging his head toward Drew and hardening his tone. "If you even think about bringing harm to this girl, who I've known since her birth and think of as a *daughter*, I'll

71

pound you into the ground, heart or no heart."

Drew tipped his head toward her driver. "You have my word as a gentleman." He couldn't be sure, but he was close enough to bet, he glimpsed Lady Dove Barrow rolling her eyes at the word 'gentleman'.

"The fact is," Drew continued. "It has never been my intent to harm her. I merely seek to quench my curiosity."

Dove yanked off her gloves and slapped them onto her thighs. "Oh, well, do let me entertain you with my personal tale."

While he was certain her impertinence was meant to offend him, it only furthered his attraction. What was it about this woman?

Renny patted Dove's fingers. She nodded to him and folded her hands in her lap.

"Three years ago, my parents were murdered."

"By highwaymen." Drew said. "I heard. I'm sorry."

"I don't believe it was random."

"You think they were targeted? For what reason?"

She lifted her chin. Her pride evident even in the dim light of the carriage. "My mother was a Shawnee Indian. My parents met and fell in love on one of my father's excursions to the Colonies. He returned with her as his wife. As you might imagine, London Society considered the match less than ideal."

Drew nodded. "A stringent lot, the aristocracy."

"Hypocritical, too, given their pastimes are often, shall we say, less than proper."

The insinuation hung in the air a moment while Drew fought to not squirm in his seat. His reputation as a rake was known. Never had he cared enough to give it so much as a passing thought. Why it plagued him now, this woman's low opinion of him, he couldn't say.

"My father's parents had money, title, and influence. They gained acceptance for my mother. Some of it but skimmed the surface. There are endless ways to inflict covert snubs, subtle, emotional pinches requiring polite smiles to hide the bruises." Her voice grew tight. However, the pain and the anger did not prevent her from finishing. "In the eyes of some of those in the upper classes, my mother's blood threatened to taint theirs."

"You think a member of the gentry carried their bigotry so far as to have your parents murdered?"

"Yes."

He wondered if she could see his dubious expression. Shunning was one thing. Murder quite another. "Such a radical extreme goes beyond what is acceptable, even for the *ton*. Have you any proof?"

"That's what I'm looking for when I break into their homes. My father had money that night. None was taken. No highwayman would leave so much as a farthing behind. My mother had jewelry. None of it was taken either, except for one piece."

"You're searching for a particular item."

"Yes. It's the only one of its kind."

The rain diminished to spaced taps upon the roof. Thunder and lightning played in the far-off distance.

"A dangerous thing, to hold on to something so identifiable," Drew said.

"I think the unique piece was too exquisite for someone to resist. My father had it designed for her as a wedding gift, a ruby with bronze angel wings atop it to form the ruby into a heart."

Drew set that information aside for a moment. "Why do you relocate items, yet you never take a thing?"

"I'm not a thief. But I want them to know the Bandit has been there. There were times some one of them hurt my mother because she was not of their blood, not suited to their standards. I want them all to know their world is not impenetrable."

"Doing so puts them on guard, increasing the chances you'll be caught."

"I haven't been caught because I'm very cautious. I do not enter these homes in a haphazard fashion. I plan. I prepare."

"And what will you do should you find the brooch?"

Dove hesitated, casting a bare flick of a glance at Renny before saying, "Turn the culprits over to the authorities, of course. I'll tell them everything."

She had not given him an honest answer. Whatever she had planned for the men who killed her parents, it was something she did not want her friend to know about. Drew played along and shook his head. "Not a good idea. Your reputation will be shattered beyond repair."

"You sound like Renny. I'll tell you what I told him. I don't care. You won't sway me from this, Lord Worthington. Besides, when the capture of someone responsible for the murder of London's nobility makes the news, no one will care about my method of catching them."

"You're wrong," Drew said. "Your alter ego has become quite the celebrity. The news and gossip will be so full of the Creeping Bandit, and who was beneath the hood, the capture of a highwayman will be nothing."

"Not a mere highwayman," she said, as if he'd missed the point. "A member of the aristocracy arrested for murder. You call that nothing? It will be all the talk."

"Whoever he is will insist he purchased the piece from a traveling vendor and had no idea it was stolen. There is no way to prove otherwise. If the culprit is indeed a member of the upper classes, his story will be believed. Your just cause will be lost in the scandal you're stirring."

"They murdered my parents!"

"And they should hang for such a crime. So, this is what we are going to do—"

"We?"

"Yes. You need my help."

"I need no such thing."

"Dove," Renny said. "Perhaps we should hear what the man has to say."

She swung a look his way. "Renny, you can't be serious."

"You were almost caught tonight. Going on the way we are, it's a matter of time."

"Indeed," Drew said. "The danger to you grows with every break-in."

After a moment, Dove released a quiet sigh. "And just what is it you propose?"

"You need a third person. Someone to not just keep watch, but garner information beforehand. There are things men discuss with each other to which you would not be privy."

"Such as security," Renny said.

"Yes," Drew answered.

"I hear that talk from the women," Dove said. "And pick up bits and pieces when I wander through the parties. I can get such information for myself. *I don't need you.*"

"All you've heard is some were hiring guards. Not how many, nothing of their method of patrols, times, routes, scheduling changes. The lords want their ladies to feel safe. They do not, however, share with them all the details. Some they do not even share with each other, as none of them knows who lurks beneath that hood. Also, you need a lookout. I think the point was made clear tonight."

"It would be good to have such knowledge, and another pair of eyes," Renny said.

To Drew, Dove said, "Why would you do such a thing? You know what would happen to you if you are caught."

"As you know, we in the aristocracy are always in search of new entertainments. This would be quite the adventure."

She mumbled something about his deficient brain before saying aloud, "And what do you propose we do once we discover who was behind the murders, if not call on the authorities?"

"I haven't had time to devise a plan yet. I will. Have no doubt. Give it up, Bandit. I'm not taking no for an answer. You've a new partner in this unusual investigation of yours."

At some point during their conversation, the rain had stopped. A frustrated, feminine huff permeated the carriage full of quiet.

"Fine," she said, jamming her arms across the middle of her dark costume. "Come along. But you should know, if I'm caught, I'm blaming everything on you."

Drew let loose a hearty laugh. "I would expect no less."

Chapter 8

"The window is too high."

Dove's shouted whisper was loud enough for Drew to hear. He was standing on the ground several feet below her dangling half boots. Since she was hanging by her hands on the outside of the windowsill, she wasn't too concerned about someone inside the house hearing. Most of them were asleep at this hour and she only spoke as loud as she had to.

Dove cursed the retched man for the thousandth time since she'd saved his worthless hide, since he discovered her identity, since she'd agreed to allow him to help her. Help, indeed! With help like this she'd end up with a broken neck.

The kitchen window through which they'd entered the Billings' residence was ideal, as it was not only low to the ground, but they'd found it wide open. Lord and Lady Billings were attending the opera, so the servants had taken to their rooms and retired early. But one of them had awakened after she and Drew completed their fruitless search of the lady's bedchambers.

The man must have been hungry, for he padded into the kitchen holding a single candle. The approaching light gave Dove and Drew enough warning so they could slip from the room.

In their soft-tread search for an alternative exit, they'd passed Lord Billings study. Dove peeked in.

Moonlight shone through a magnificent set of French doors. It made for a perfect exit. Drew disagreed.

He whispered to her the door hinges might squeak and give them away. She whispered back that even if anybody thought to have heard a noise in the large house, by the time someone checked the study, they would be long gone. As it was a warm night and many of the windows were open, Drew insisted they keep searching for a better way out of the house. How he thought this was better was beyond her.

They found what he believed to be a perfect exit through an already open window in a corner parlor near the back of the house. But it was a high window over a low section of ground, and even as Drew let go of the sill and hopped down, Dove had her doubts. His body was much longer, and therefore he had a shorter distance to drop. She glanced down between her straining arms. Perhaps it was a trick of the night, but the distance to the ground appeared to be as far as a full story.

"Let go. I'll catch you," Drew whispered back. "It's not so high."

"Not for someone as tall as an ancient oak. I'm going back inside to find an easier way out."

"No. It's too risky."

As it happened, her wish here didn't matter. Her arms were tiring and she couldn't heave her body back up and through the window without kicking her feet against the wall. Such a racket would no doubt get her caught. She was going to have to jump. Dove glanced down again.

"Wait," Drew whispered back. "Let me check for the guard. Don't let go yet."

As his head was faced away when he spoke his whispered words, and her hooded head was tucked with her ears wedged against her arms, all Dove heard was 'guard' and 'let go'. So, she let go.

Not only did the clod not catch her, he didn't even have sense enough to get out of the way. She landed on top of him and he fell back hard on the ground. She lay on her back atop his chest. For a good minute or so, the two of them lay there, both stunned and groaning.

"This is the first time I've ever spoken these words to a woman," Drew said to the back of her cloth-covered head, his voice pained. "But please get off me."

Dove pitched herself over and off. She lay face down with her cheek against the cool ground. Her hood was askew, leaving her but one eyehole through which to scowl at the man. "Remind me to ignore you the next time you tell me to let go because you'll catch me."

His head rolled toward her. Even in the dark with her single eye's vision, she could see his indignant frown.

"I told you to *not* let go while I checked for the guard."

"I heard you say let go."

"That hood is clogging your ears. I said *don't* let go. And what the devil are you complaining about? You had a soft landing. I feel like I was stuck with a sack of cannon balls. Good lord, woman, how much do you weigh?"

Dove lifted head and straightened her hood so she could use both eyes to give him a proper glare. "Are you calling me fat?"

"Ah, well, now I've got your attention. Women and their vanity," he mumbled as he lifted onto his elbows.

"I'm just saying I'm amazed so much weight could be packed into such a slender frame. Does that better suit your pride?"

"Even your apology sounds like and insult."

"I was not apologizing. I was placating."

"Placating? You condescending jackass."

"You know, for a lady raised in the upper classes, you have quite the salty mouth. That's the second time in our short relationship you've spat a profanity at me."

"Yes, and I've known you less than a fortnight. If our acquaintance continues, I'm afraid I'll have to search a wordbook for more."

He chuckled beside her. Dove stared at him, wondering at his thought process. Even his sense of humor was demented. The man did belong in Bedlam.

"And as much as I'd like to lie here in the dirt and be berated by a woman who cannot follow a simple instruction, we need to leave."

Dove narrowed her eyes and resisted the temptation to berate him with her fists. The man was the worst partner in burglar history. However, he was right about one thing. They had to get out of there before the guard made his rounds on this side of the house.

With slow, cautious movements, the two maneuvered themselves into seated positions. If their groans and hisses were any indication, they'd both be good and sore on the morrow.

Drew patted his hands down his body. "Good God, woman, I believe I'm going to have a bruise on the front of my body in the shape of yours."

Dove brushed the dirt off her shirt. "This could have been avoided had we gone out the French doors, as I'd wanted."

"This could have been avoided had you held on a moment, as *I'd* wanted."

"Then you shouldn't have told me to let go."

"I didn't."

"You did."

"Well, Bandit, we can sit here beneath the stars and argue the point, or we can get out of here before we are seen."

They had waited until the guard passed on his rounds before exiting through the window. But he might double back, especially if he heard any sounds, like two bodies slamming into the ground.

Dove said, "If you'd have worn the hood I made for you, at least no one would see your face. We'd have a chance to escape without being identified."

"It was too tight, and the eyeholes too small. I can't be much help to you if I can't see."

"And what would I do without you to tell me to fall from a second story window?"

"It was on the first floor, and I did not...ah! Let's go."

Drew got to his feet with relative ease. Dove placed her right foot on the ground and lifted, but when she put pressure on her left, she cried out and fell back down."

In an instant, Drew dropped to her side, his hands a gentle grip on her shoulders. "What is it?"

"My left ankle. I think I twisted it in the fall."

She expected a snide remark, another excuse to blame this debacle on her. Instead, Drew scooped her up in his arms without comment or the slightest hesitation.

"What are you doing? Put me down. I can walk. I just need a moment."

"Hush, Bandit," he said.

The sarcasm had vanished, as did his irritation. His hold, strong, secure, offered safety and protection. His deep tone soothed, and his words comforted her like a cup of tea beside the fire. It was a side to Drew she'd glimpsed once before. This was the man who cared for Renny when he wasn't well. This part of him was tender to need.

Dove gave in to a sudden and strange urge to lay her head upon the strong muscle of his shoulder. She caught a whiff of his spicy soap, and what lie beneath; Drew, a man determined to help her. He claimed it was just for fun. Was it? It's an extreme length to go for mere amusement. Could it be he held some sort of attraction to her, even cared? Or was it the long-aching immensity of her loss beckoning a wish?

Her parents' death was almost a year before she would have had her come out. One day she was young and carefree, full of open anticipation of becoming a woman. Her mother had found love with a good man amongst the aristocracy. So too would she, her mother assured her. A growing excitement colored her already happy world. In the wake of the tragedy, everything left was dingy and grim. Perhaps it had tainted some of her memories.

She took her mind back, forced herself to look past the grief and rage she used to drive her.

There were ladies who'd come to tea, and reciprocal invitations arriving on a regular basis. There were pleasant memories of several lords and ladies who treated her family with kindness and respect. Strange, for these past three years, only the snubs stood out in her memory. It was as if her pain and anger functioned as a blockade, needed to keep her from softening. For if she softened, the emotions might rise to overwhelming depths, and drown her in the flood.

"Almost there." Drew's voice a soft rumble against her side. "Does it hurt much?"

"No."

"Good. I doubt it's too bad, then."

Warmth seeped from his body into hers. She should tell him she thought she could walk on her own now, but she didn't want to. For the first time since that horrible night three years ago, Dove allowed someone else to carry her troubles. This was just a temporary respite. But she took it and savored the indulgence.

Grandfather loved her. But he'd suffered great loss, too, and maybe because of that, his mind was retreating. Renny offered comfort and kindness. However, with his heart given to bouts of irregularity, Dove was ever cautious about exposing the extent of her grief. She'd become adept at not showing any weakness. For these few minutes, in Drew's strong arms, Dove gave over to his compassion.

She closed her eyes and was close to drifting off, when in a sudden move, Drew lunged and dropped behind a hedge, jarring her from her serenity.

"What's wrong?" she asked when he'd crouched down.

The answer was in the clop of horse hooves and the wheels of an approaching carriage rolling over cobblestones. They held still and quiet, secure in their belief they would not be seen behind the hedge in their dark clothes.

Drew sat down, adjusting his hold on her, but not letting go. When the carriage passed, he said, "We'd better wait. If they're leaving an event along this way, there might be more carriages in the next few minutes, and there might not be a convenient hedge farther down the street."

Dove wiggled, her intent, to leave his arms. Not because she didn't like it, but because she did. Her mission was too important to get distracted. Drew, however, must have had other ideas, for he tightened his hold.

"Let go of me."

"No."

"No?"

She stared at him through the eyeholes of her hood. "Why not?"

"Because…because I don't want you to further injure your ankle."

Dove continued to gape at the man. Something was amiss. His response was not ready but conjured on the spot.

"I believe my ankle is fine. What are you doing?" she said when he dragged the hood from her head.

"It's disconcerting having a conversation with a mask."

Dove found it disconcerting to be unmasked. The thin cloth served not only to cloak her, but as a barrier to anything but her goal. Without it, she was no longer the Creeping Bandit, the scourge of London, but Lady Dove Barrow, a woman. She never felt it more so than here in Drew's arms.

His face was just inches from hers, like the night in Lady Beaumont's chambers. The night his kiss made her float. If he were to kiss her a second time, would it have the same effect? The question no sooner drifted through her mind than his face lowered to hers.

Panic touched her nerves, but it melted in an instant under the heat of his skillful lips. Yes, his kiss was indeed as good as before. Better, in fact, as she knew the man now, infuriating, headstrong, tender…sensuous.

He cradled the back of her head in his strong hand, controlling their positions. She let him. It was too good to argue. With the touch of his tongue, her lips parted. His breath grew heavy and his hold tightened, as if their bodies were malleable clay and he intended to mold them together.

An instant later, he lifted away from her. Dove's hand ran up his shoulder, wrapped around his neck and drew him back for another kiss. She wanted more. This she would control.

With her expressed insistence, his head descended and his lips devoured hers. And then his hand slid beneath her shirt, making a slow glide up bare skin until he covered her breast. Dove sucked in a full breath and her head surged back into the palm of his hand, so powerful was the sensation.

His mouth skimmed along her throat, her neck, kissing areas she didn't know were so sensitive. His hand roved down, lower, slipping inside the waist of her trousers. And Dove tumbled into another world. His kiss made her float, his touch…his touch made her soar.

****

The feminine, erotic sounds of pleasure escaping her sweet lips hurled Drew into madness. He wanted this woman. He burned for her with the intensity of a brilliant sunrise over night's hasty retreat. But more than mere desire was driving him to the brink of his control.

Dove infiltrated his daytime thoughts and his nighttime dreams. She took his mind where it had never been, touched him in ways no hand ever had. He cared for her beyond immediate pleasure, even beyond the carnal, which set his mind and body in direct opposition.

A part of his conscience, the part where honor still managed to brandish some influence, shouted at him to stop. She was unsullied and trusting him. However, his body cared naught for propriety or decorum. It only knew driving need. At his intimate touch, Dove called out the same.

Her fluttered mewls of desire spun him wild, a beast on a thin tether about to devour an innocent. An *innocent*. The word wielded the power of control. Drew stilled. Curses rang in his head during the fierce clash between his honor and his desire. Under the harsh rebuking of his self-directed precepts, honor won the battle.

With every drop of strength and willpower he could muster, Drew clasped her slender shoulders and backed away. He had to stop this before things progressed any further and, hidden in a hedgerow or not, it *would* go further.

Her eyes fluttered open, the sapphire color shining like a polished jewel in the moonlight. Drew opened his mouth to speak. His usual fluency of words now a dry well, as this was the first time he'd ever strained to stop. He hoped never to find himself in such a moral position again. It was damned painful.

She struggled to catch her breath between parted lips. Her gaze a mix of unquenched passion and hazy confusion. His body was also frustrated, but at least he understood why.

"We'd better go," Drew said, rougher than he intended.

Dove blinked, her fiery passion cooling to ash right before his eyes, and he mourned the loss in every way. Her head dipped. Though he couldn't see her face, Drew was sure she was embarrassed. She had no reason to be. She was a passionate woman. But of course, Dove was a lady, and an inexperienced one at that. She scrambled from his lap.

"Be careful. Your ankle."

"My ankle is fine," she said, a snap to her words.

She walked ahead with no more than a slight limp. The gentleman in him was compelled to assist her. With the carnal beast in him still afire, he didn't dare touch her. Not that Dove would allow it. The anger in her voice told him as much. Even with a sore ankle, she strode a quick pace to put distance between them. He let her.

"What happened? You're limping." Renny asked even as he rushed to open the carriage door.

"It's nothing, Renny. Just a slight twist of my ankle."

"The brooch?" Renny asked.

"We didn't find it," Drew answered.

Dove spoke over her shoulder as she climbed into the carriage. "There are still several homes left on the list."

Her voice was light, but the underlying tension was clear to Drew's ears. He wondered if her friend heard it.

If Renny learned what he'd just done, Drew would be in for another pummeling. He deserved it.

Drew stood outside the carriage as Dove slid onto the seat and lifted the simple, fawn-colored, muslin gown from beside her. As neither of them had attended any events tonight, they'd slipped from their homes and would return directly.

As with the last two explorations, they would send messages to each other through Renny as to their next search. The best thing Drew could do now was leave, and allow Dove to collect her thoughts. He had some collecting to do of his own.

"Well, I shall bid you both a goodnight, then," Drew said.

Dove and Renny wished him a goodnight, Dove's tone polite, but subdued. Her glance stopped short of him before Renny closed the door. Drew untied his horse from the back of the carriage while it rocked a bit as Dove was inside changing her clothes. His mind's view of her present state of undress further aggravated his body's torturous discomfort.

He rode for some time along the quiet, cobblestone streets, passed homes dark and still, giving his thoughts their head to run through the solitude. He'd no idea how much time had gone by before he headed back to his own house.

Chapter 9

The rapid knock at Dove's bedroom door would have awakened her, had she been asleep.

She'd thought to take an afternoon nap, as last night was a far cry from restful. The hindrance wasn't her late-night work as the Creeping Bandit. It was what happened in the hedgerow with Lord Worthington that had kept her tossing beneath her bed covers most of the night.

The man was an absolute cad, a scoundrel, a ne'er-do-well. How dare he take such liberties? *And how disgraceful of her to allow it.* His touch had transformed her into another woman. She'd become a wanton in his arms, with the potential to feed many gossip circles. However, those things weren't at the crux of her fervid discontent. What made Dove angriest was, she wanted the experience again.

It was clear to her now why young ladies were required to have a chaperone. She always thought it because of men and their desires. It never occurred to her women experienced desires, too. And she never could have imagined the power they held.

Sprawled back in his arms, subjected to his versed command of seduction, she'd cared about nothing but more of him. On top of her angry shame, the experience also left her both embarrassed and curious. She could do nothing about the embarrassment. The lingering curiosity, however, alarmed her.

The set of her mind had been so solid. From the start, she'd believed straight through to her bones there was more to her parents' death than a mere robbery gone awry. She'd had to let her grief settle a bit before she could think. Still, it had taken her a very long time to formulate her plan. Once Renny knew she would follow through with or without him, he agreed to help. There were less than a dozen houses left on her list. Soon she would know who was responsible. She couldn't have a distraction. Not now, not when she was so close.

Lying atop the counterpane on her soft bed this past hour, sleep evading her in the day as it had last night, Dove knew she would have to end her partnership with Lord Worthington. The man was a danger to her good senses.

While she had to admit, last night's debacle aside, it was good to have his help, his input, and his knowledge, to develop any kind of true feelings for Lord Worthington would lead to nothing suitable.

She'd already had the inklings of an attraction. It must be due to his handsome face, his well-muscled body. Well, there was the utter joy he found in life. The contrast to her life of perpetual sadness these past three years made him appear as warm and vibrant as summer after a long, long winter.

These were the reasons for her confounded attraction. Not anything of substance. Why else would he hold a place in her thoughts? The man was brazened and flippant, and he seduced women for a pastime.

Dove cringed at her weak and wonton behavior. Last night, in the outdoors of all things, she was all too ready to give herself over. Apparently, Lord Worthington was very good at his vocation.

Well, she refused to be added to his list of conquests. And she would not allow her heart to be broken, the only outcome possible were she to engage in a liaison with a man like Drew Worthington.

Ending their association would be nothing to the man. Once she cut him loose, his next adventure would call to him and she would scarce be a memory. For her, it was a safe decision, a sound and logical one. So why did it leave her limper than her lack of sleep?

Another knock at her door told her she could not ignore whoever was out there. It was just as well. She needed to get up and write a missive to Lord Worthington. Renny could deliver it this afternoon.

The door to her bedchamber opened and Elsa, her lady's maid, poked her head inside. Elsa was a good decade older than Dove. A sturdy woman with a head full of tiny blonde curls and a rosy countenance the friendliest Dove had ever seen.

"Sorry to interrupt your nap, milady."

"It's all right, Elsa," Dove said, sitting up on the bed and curling her legs to the side. "I couldn't fall asleep anyway."

"Well, it's good you're awake. Your grandfather is in the drawing room. He wants to see you right away."

A fission of unease scurried up her skin. She and her grandfather spoke daily, but he had not summoned her since she was a child and had gotten into mischief. Did he know she snuck out last night? Perhaps he too had been unable to sleep, roamed about the rooms. He'd done it before. Did he see her sneaking off to the stables to meet Renny? Did he notice the bundle of black clothing she carried?

Grandfather's mind wandered, and he had trouble keeping focus. When lucidity coursed through him, though, the man missed nothing.

Her maid crossed the airy room to the white and gilt wardrobe. It was a lovely piece her grandmother had commissioned for her for her sixteenth birthday. That year, she, her mother, and grandmother, had spent time and shared laughter redecorating her room in whites and lavenders. At the foot of the bed she kept her mother's cedar chest, the one that had come from the Colonies with her mother. It was where, among other things, she stored her bandit clothes.

Elsa made a determining shuffle through the wardrobe. She chose a powder blue day dress, one of Dove's newer gowns, and held it up for inspection. "Here, let's get you into something fresh. This one is quite flattering. And then I'll fix your hair into something nice and set you at your most presentable."

Yes, this was more than a simple chat with Grandfather. Something was wrong. "Did my grandfather say anything else to you?"

Elsa kept her focus on the gown as she crossed the room and laid it out on the bed. Without raising her head for so much as a glance to meet her lady's eyes, the maid fussed with the pleats at the waist of the gown.

"Just to fetch you straightaway," Elsa said, continuing to arrange and rearrange the perfect pleats.

Dove's mind gathered plausible excuses as to why she'd slipped out of the house last night. Just a short walk about the yard because, because she couldn't sleep. As to what she was carrying? Merely a shawl to guard against the night's chill. Yes, such a simple explanation would answer his questions and put a quick end to the problem.

Ten minutes later, Dove stepped into the cream and pine-green colored parlor and stood face to face with her problem. It was in the form a tall, broad shouldered rogue named…

"Lord Worthington," her grandfather said to the man posed in a casual lean against the cream-marble mantel.

Drew cut a fine figure in his iron gray trousers, waistcoat, and jacket. The burgundy color of his shirt and sparkling white cravat complemented the deep amber of his eyes. For a moment, his striking good looks distracted her. Then her grandfather's voice gained her attention.

"This is my granddaughter, Lady Dove Barrow."

Dove blinked against her shock, and the accompanying wave of dizziness. She may have even gasped. She wasn't sure. What was he doing here? Dove clutched her hands together, squeezing her fingers near to pain. Had he come to confess all to her grandfather, to tattle, as if she were a wayward child in need of a firm hand? Perhaps he believed to do so would be saving her from herself.

"But of course," her grandfather continued, oblivious to her distress. "You've already been introduced."

"Have we?" Dove managed through a tight jaw. What in blazes was Drew up to? Perhaps this was but another game he liked to play, cat to her mouse. Anger at the man's intrusiveness, at his utter gall, overcame her shock in short order. She flashed him a hardened glare. Of all the nerve, coming to her home!

"Yes," Drew said. He gave a casual nod and strolled over to her. She tugged back when he took her fingers, but his hand clasped tight onto hers as he bent and brushed a light but slow kiss against her knuckles.

When he rose, he presented her with a quick wink and a mischievous grin before his face formed a mock expression of dismay. "We met at the Beaumont's ball. Don't tell me you've forgotten me already. Alas, I'm sure my humble face is a mere spec in the crowd of young bucks vying for your esteemed attention."

Once again, Dove regretted not letting Lord Beaumont shoot the scoundrel. "The Beaumont's…"

"It was quite the thing that night, wouldn't you agree?" At her silence, Drew flashed an impish smile. "The evening will not soon fade from *my* mind."

Her grandfather nodded. "Oh, Yes. The Beaumont's threw a wonderful affair. Wouldn't you say so, Dove?"

"Yes, Grandfather," Dove managed.

"Indeed," Drew agreed. To Dove, Drew said, "Lord and Lady Darington introduced us."

"Dear," Grandfather said. "I wasn't aware you were acquainted with the Darington's."

"Yes, Grandfather. I sometimes volunteer on the committee for the Foundling Home Project."

"Did you tell me about the Foundling Home Project, Dove dear? Oh, I'm sure you did. Pardon me," he said to Drew. "My mind isn't what it used to be."

His embarrassment showed in the flush across the fair and wrinkled skin of his cheeks and the slight bend of his spine. Dove rushed to his side. She fussed with his cravat, forcing him to stand straight and lift his chin.

"Nonsense, Grandfather. You're as sharp as ever.

I'm quite sure I neglected to mention the bit of work I did for the new foundling home." She'd mentioned it several times. That he didn't recall even once broke her heart.

Her grandfather raised a green-eyed gaze to her. The gratitude in them told her this day he had clarity of mind, enough to know that some days he did not.

"The building is well under construction," Lord Worthington said. "It's going to make a fine home for the children."

"She's volunteered her time and efforts for other charitable causes too." Her grandfather nodded and smiled. The blush of his embarrassment from a moment before now a glow of pride. "My granddaughter has a heart of gold."

Dove patted the perfect lay of his white cravat against his white shirt and stood back. "As many have volunteered, I had but a small part in helping to make the new home a reality. It's the Daringtons who have shouldered most of the burden."

"Ah, modesty," Lord Worthington said, an impish gleam livening his expression. "An admirable quality. Lady Barrow, you are a paragon of upstanding scruples."

It would have been easier to shovel rain than it was to keep from smashing the nearest vase over his instigative head. Dove shot a glance toward the green, porcelain vase atop the round end table but a couple feet from her eager hand. Returning her glare to him further tempted her anger. His lips were clamped together, succeeding in but a partial dampening of his laughter.

Restraint from the well-deserved attack was only

gained by jerking her head away from the rogue. For if she kept her eyes upon him, Dove was sure to commit an act of violence.

Her grandfather beamed. He hadn't an inkling of Lord Worthington's facetiousness. For his sake, Dove corralled her anger. Sarcasm wasted no time taking its place.

Facing Drew again, she said, "As I'm sure are you, Lord Worthington. A paragon of scruples, that is. All the ladies speak of your ever-virtuous intentions. Quite remarkable, as so many men of the *ton* practice their amorous pursuits with great vigor. I believe it was Lady Beaumont who said your reticence with women might someday send you to a monastery, or Bedlam."

The strike hit its mark. His humor and arrogance departed in tandem, slipping away through his narrow-eyed glare. Good. The scoundrel needed his smug feathers ruffled.

"Well, a fine man you are, sir," her grandfather said. He then waved toward the jade-colored sofa and Hepplewhite chairs with the matching seat cushions. "Shall we sit? I'll have some tea and biscuits sent in straight away."

"…Thank you, Lord Barrow, but I can't stay," Drew said.

To Dove, Drew managed to smile and scowl at the same time. She had to force her lips together to keep her laughter from escaping.

"As I was telling your grandfather before you arrived, *Lady* Barrow, my mother is throwing a masquerade." Drew slipped a hand into his coat pocket and took out a rose-colored envelope. "Your invitation somehow escaped from the stack and was just found. In apology, I wanted to deliver it in person and beg your forgiveness, as well as your attendance."

Her grandfather gave a hearty clap. "A masquerade! It's been ages since I've attended a masquerade. What do you think, Dove? Shall we?"

The last thing Dove wanted to do was to attend an event with Lord Worthington. The man was beyond the pale. But her grandfather stood before her, bushy white brows raised high over eyes widened with excitement, clasping his aged hands, awaiting her decision as a child might in hopeful askance. How could she tell him she didn't want to go? She couldn't.

"Of course, Grandfather. We will attend."

Her grandfather bellowed laughter, much louder than proper decorum would dictate in the company of a guest, and his face blossomed with joy, ironing out some of the wrinkles. "Oh, a masquerade! No time to waste. I must go to my study straight away and sketch some ideas for a costume. Dove, my dear, we're going to have a wonderful time!"

He scurried toward the door without so much as a farewell, breaching polite and appropriate etiquette. Another sign his mind was slipping. Not only was he abandoning a guest, he was leaving his granddaughter unchaperoned, alone with a man to whom she was not related. There was a time he would never have done such a thing.

Her grandfather jerked to a stop at the doorway and spun back to face them. For a moment, Dove believed he had caught his error in propriety.

To Drew, her grandfather said, "And as to the other matter we discussed, Lord Worthington, I believe that too is a fine idea. My permission is granted." With that, he was gone.

The air still stirred from his exit when Dove swung around to Drew. "Permission for what? What are you about, Drew? How dare you come to my home like this? And why have you delivered an invitation? What trouble are you brewing for me now? I demand to know what my grandfather meant by—"

Holding a hand toward her, palm out, Drew said, "If you're going to throw a long series of questions at me, at least take a breath so I might answer one or two." With a cavalier grin, he added, "And I must say, it is *you* who are the brewer of trouble. I merely sweetened the pot."

Dove scarce heard him over the worry buzzing in her head at her grandfather's parting words. The miscreant was up to something. She couldn't fathom what it might be, but she had a good, solid sense she wasn't going to like it.

Dove took but a scant moment to recover, as unease laid waste to her patience. She *had* to know what was going on. She strove for calmness, but her voice still ground tight.

"What is this other matter my grandfather mentioned? To what did he give his permission?"

"Well, at least the answer to those two questions is one and the same." Drew quirked a brow. The twinkle of mischief was back in his eyes. Not a good sign. "I've spoken with your grandfather and asked his permission to court you."

"*What*!"

"Before you grab for the vase, yes, I know just what you were thinking back there, hear me out. It's a matter of logic. It will be much easier to communicate and plan if we are courting."

Dove shot a glare at him fierce enough to cow a lesser man. He didn't even flinch. "Before your wayward thoughts carry you off, you should know I wouldn't marry you if I were an ancient, poverty-stricken maiden in desperate need of protection."

Drew slapped a hand against his chest. His tone so conciliatory one could almost doubt the insult. "You wound me. Do not panic, though. I've no intention of marrying you either. You are no doubt far more trouble than you're worth." He took a sharp pause before continuing. "You're considering the vase again."

"I've surpassed considering and I am now in the planning stage."

"Do stop, Bandit."

"Do not call me that here!" she spat in a low hiss.

"Forgive me, *Lady* Bandit."

The appeal of violence against this scoundrel grew by the minute.

"Calm yourself, woman, and listen to reason. I've got it all planned. Once we resolve this matter of your parents' murder, one of us will cry off."

"I will."

"One of us will."

"I will."

"It would be much more believable if I cry off," he told her.

"Of all the pompous, condescending—"

"Seeing as a great many women have attempted, and failed, to bring me up to scratch, it would be easier for society to believe it was I who ended the courtship."

Dove punched her fists against her hips. "You are by far the most arrogant, ego-bloated, conceited, big-headed..." Dove stopped at the sight of his quaking shoulders, of his face, reddening at his effort to restrain his mirth. It struck her then. His audacious statement was but a jest. At her silent, gape-mouth stare, he burst out with laughter. A moment later, so did she.

She laughed until tears rolled from her eyes. A muscle twitched in her side. Her hands clutched her ribs and her laughter continued to flow. How long had it been since she'd laughed? So long ago she couldn't remember. God, it felt good.

"You are incorrigible," Dove said, once she caught her breath.

"So I've been told."

"Courting, of all things."

"Oh, I'm quite serious about courting you. No, before you argue, consider what I've already said. Our system of communication makes setting a plan slow and inconvenient. Add to that, we're running poor Renny into the ground."

That part of their working together had been bothering her, too. Renny said it wasn't a problem, said he felt hale and hearty. Still, she hated giving him the chore of traveling back and forth with their messages. But he was the only one she trusted with her secret. Well, he and the viscount. She gazed at Drew now with an objective eye.

The man was far too handsome for his own good. For the good of many a female, too, if what she witnessed of his rendezvous with Lady Beaumont was any indication. Dove believed it was. She would have to be a fool to think otherwise.

Earlier he'd been jesting, but Dove guessed more than a few women had set their caps toward him. She wasn't ignorant. Drew probably had intimate knowledge of more women than she had fingers, perhaps even toes. Lord, she'd borne personal witness to one of his affairs.

Had almost become one of them.

Too often, the man exhibited the disposition of an adolescent. Dove had to admit; lately she was finding that quality more amusing than annoying. And he *had* come to her rescue, risking a great deal to help her since. There were things Society would forgive. Assisting the Creeping Bandit would not be one of them. It hadn't stopped him from stretching his neck out to protect her.

Her career as the bandit would have ended with the Beaumont's guard, had Drew not appeared and shoved her back up the tree. All hope of finding who killed her parents would be gone. She would be in prison, her mission a failure.

His points about pretending to court her were good. It *would* make their communications much easier, and Renny wouldn't have to sneak messages back and forth anymore. There were other reasons too, as to why she wanted to spend more time with Drew.

As if out of her control, her mind traveled back to his passionate kiss, his touch, the wondrous feelings he could stir in her. But she would not think on those things now. She should not think of them ever.

"Fine," Dove said. "We will pretend to be courting. And once we have found the brooch, and the persons responsible for my parents' murder, *I* will cry off."

"As you wish," Drew said, conceding with a nod and a genuine smile. "A true gentleman would have it no other way."

An airy laugh slipped past her lips. Whether his response was out of merriment or self-mockery, she couldn't tell. Nor did it matter. When he wasn't conjuring her wrath, the man did indeed amuse her.

Dove walked him through the foyer and bid him farewell at the open door. When she would have gone inside and closed the door, she instead leaned against the jamb.

Drew ambled down the straight, brick walkway toward the street where his shiny black curricle with yellow-spoked wheels was parked. A balmy, afternoon breeze ruffled his hair and caressed her face with the same breath. It carried the sweet, dreamy fragrance of the jessamine lining the walk.

Drew was almost to the low gate. Still, Dove stayed where she was.

The man was never rushed, and almost always calm. Come to think of it, even in the face of death, Drew kept a cool head. It was as if he didn't bother to worry over life's twists and turns, because he knew how to ride them without falling off.

Just outside the short, iron gate, a plump, calico cat crossed Drew's path. He bent and gave the cat a scratch beneath its offered jaw. He said something to the little thing, but Dove couldn't make it out. All she could hear was his voice, soft, kind. The sight tugged at her heart. He cared to spare a moment to pet a cat, this notorious rake?

Drew straightened, and the cat rubbed figure eights between his feet. He held still until the cat finished its show of affection and trotted off in the opposite direction. He then made a quick and nimble climb into the small curricle.

Before picking up the reins, Drew swiveled his head toward where Dove still stood in the doorway. He waved and gave her a broad, boyish smile she couldn't help but return. The man could charm a cross dowager back to her youth.

Dove didn't go inside until his curricle had rolled out of sight. She closed the door and leaned back against it. Maybe it wouldn't be so bad, pretending to be courted by Lord Worthington, for a while.

Chapter 10

"What's this?"

Drew raised his head from the ledger he was studying to see his uncle standing one step into the study.

Charles, his mother's brother, was two years older than Drew's mother, putting him at fifty. He was a petite man with narrow shoulders over a slightly broader body. More than a few strands of gray showed in the deep brown of his thinning hair. His eyes, a dour blue, were as sharp as they'd ever been.

Charles was a man of conservative garb and simple tastes, for the most part. The glimmer of a small stickpin in his cravat drew attention to the modest diamond. He wore it often. Sometimes he wore a gold signet ring. Never both pieces at the same time, but always one. His home was much the same as the man. He liked things with subdued embellishments, with no more than small touches of elegance.

"Uncle Charles," Drew said. "Good. You're here. I have a couple of questions for you."

Drew sat up and stretched his neck left, then right. He'd spent the entire morning in the study, his father's study, as he still thought of it. But it was his now. This morning he'd set upon the duties of lord of the manor, starting with the family finances. A glance at the porcelain-faced clock on the mantel told him he'd been in here for close to three hours.

Three tall windows along one wall and the white and gold flocked wallpaper gave a warm feel to the study. Much of that warmth, he was sure, still lingered from the love and kindness of his father. Even after all these years he could still see the man sitting behind this very desk, strong, capable, tending to the family business.

"Drew, what are you doing with the ledgers?" Charles said. He crossed the room in crisp strides. "I hope you've not gone and made a mess of things. There's an order to bookkeeping, you know."

That his uncle thought him so incapable was yet another spear to Drew's already battered dignity. "I assure you, I have not 'made a mess of things'.

Charles rounded the desk to peer over Drew's shoulder. He gave a quick, fretted inspection to the exposed pages. "What is it you're looking for? All you need do is ask me. Have you made any marks?"

"I'm not looking for anything, nor have I altered your marks. What I am doing is familiarizing myself with the financial workings of this household. It's past time I took over my proper duties, don't you think?"

Charles took a step back, gaping at Drew as if he were but ten years old and had decided to be a grown up. Circling the desk to the front, Charles stared down at his nephew for a moment before saying, "You want to tend to the ledgers, manage the family finances?"

It was nothing short of irking, this surprise at him wanting to take his rightful place. However, in all fairness, Drew could not in good conscience fault his uncle for the opinion, as he'd never shown even a passing interest in minding his responsibilities.

"Yes, Uncle. I do. I am ever grateful for the time and work you have put in here to keep everything running. You're also owed an apology from me, for having left the burden on your shoulders for so long."

His uncle's eyes widened a bit before the man shook his head. "It hasn't been a burden. You, Olivia, and your mother are my family." Charles cleared his throat, frowned, and gave his nut-brown waistcoat a good tug. "Drew, if this is a whim—"

Drew ground his teeth together before cutting off the sentence. "It is not a whim, I assure you."

"These matters of finance must be approached with the utmost gravity."

Charles paced before the desk, his brow furrowing deeper. Drew leaned back in his chair and raised a steady gaze to his uncle. "You have my word; I am quite serious about this."

Charles ceased his pacing and stood in front of the neat desk with the open ledger to stare down at Drew. "Has something happened I should know about? Are you in some sort of trouble? Are the funds you're provided not enough for your…amusements?"

Having to argue those points mocked his gathering pride. He was a man, a grown man, a peer of the realm, no less, and his uncle was treating him as if he were a burdensome miscreant.

Aware the fault was his own and he was working to better himself did not ease the severity of his self-reproach. Drew couldn't help but worry he'd damaged his esteem beyond repair. With his uncle rubbing the blight of his irresponsibility in his face, anger chewed at Drew's calm.

"I am not in any trouble, Uncle Charles," Drew

said, his voice tightening. "And the funds I am provided are quite sufficient."

"I don't understand, then. Why do you want to spend your time buried in these dull ledgers?"

Surprised as much as his uncle, Drew slammed the flat of his hand upon the desk hard enough to jiggle the ledger. "Because it's what I'm supposed to do!"

Charles plopped down in the chair on the other side of the desk. His eyes wide, his mouth worked a second or two before closing in silence. It was a rare thing for Drew to raise his voice, and never did he show such a flash of temper.

Drew scrubbed his hands through his hair and took a breath. "I'm sorry, Uncle Charles. Please forgive my outburst. It's just, well, let's say I've had an epiphany of sorts.

"An epiphany." A thought lifted his expression. "Is it a woman?"

Drew laughed. He pictured his staunch uncle's face were he to tell him the woman who'd saved him from certain death and inspired him to be a better man, was also the Creeping Bandit. He tempered his grin and said, "Isn't it always a woman?"

His uncle found no humor in the response. The man had never married. Perhaps looking after his sister's family gave him purpose other men found with their own. Nevertheless, conducting the business of this household was Drew's responsibility. One he would no longer neglect.

"Look, Uncle Charles, the fact is, I have been beyond remiss in my duties to my family, to this home, as well as my title. It's past time I took the reins in hand, don't you think?"

He smiled at Drew with warmth, something his uncle not often did, as he was a rather stern man. "I've thought so for some time. To be frank, I did wonder if this day would ever arrive. It does my heart good, this change in you. So, are you thinking of taking a wife?"

"A wife?"

The word no perched on the edge of his lips yet hesitated at outright dismissal. Why would he marry? He had life by the tail. His every need was met. If he had want of a woman, he had a bevy of choices. Though he hadn't sated his lust since Beatrix's husband put an instant stop to their trysts. Since the night death had tapped him on the shoulder, the only woman to occupy his thoughts was Dove. But she was an innocent and he would not ruin her. He did have *some* ethics.

"No, Uncle Charles. I am not taking a wife."

Someone would have her, though. Dove was beautiful, elegant, exotic. Their faux courtship was to be short-lived. Before the Season was over, someone would offer for her. Someone desirous of marriage, of Dove. Some other man would have all of her.

"It was just a question, Andrew. I didn't mean to anger you."

Drew left his thoughts and followed his uncle's gaze. Atop the desk, his hands were bunched into tight fists. He imagined his feelings must be making a show upon his face.

Drew splayed his fingers and made an effort to shake the image of another man taking Dove to wife, to bed. The effort failed. A crackle shot through his brain, exploded in his breast, and lodged in his heart where the woman had taken up residency. Instead of outrage or resignation, the aftermath left his core with a strange degree of warmth he'd never experienced.

Drew rested his elbows on top of the mahogany desk, his father's desk. He took a slow, fresh scan of the study. The chair in which he now sat was where Drew used to sit upon his father's lap drawing pictures on foolscap, staining his fingers with ink. He glanced at the thick, Aubusson rug where years later, baby Olivia had crawled toward their mother's outstretched arms.

To most in the gentry, this room was the man's domain and children would not dare to cross the threshold, lest they disturb the master of the house. His father always welcomed his family in here. Drew had the oddest feeling the room missed the sound of children's laughter. Or maybe it was him.

He had been remiss not just as master of this household, but of his life, of his future. Drew had splashed about in the shallows of frivolity as if he would forever be a rummaging youth, as if it was the best life had to offer. All the while, he was missing the more solid pleasures of adulthood.

He scanned the room again. His father's study. No, Drew amended, *his* study.

He would care for it as his father had. With love, attention, and pride. No longer did he want to dodge his responsibilities, but rather, explore and embrace the next wondrous phase of his life. He wanted to fill this house with children, Dove's children. Not long ago, the thought of such bindings would have horrified him. Now all he wanted was for it to happen, right now, yesterday. His body desired her. His heart craved her. His soul knew she was his destiny.

"Andrew, what on earth has put such a silly smile on your face?"

Drew's eyes shifted again to Charles. "You're right, Uncle."

"About what?"

"It is a woman." And soon she would be his wife.

Chapter 11

Dove stared down at her costume laid out in neat form upon her bed and very obvious in the many lit candles. Elsa, her wide-eyed maid, stood beside her.

"It's quite the thing, isn't it, milady."

The woman's tone implied she couldn't decide if Dove's choice was amusing or a bit too brazen. Given the current mood of the *ton*, the latter was a more appropriate accounting.

"That it is," Dove answered, echoing the sentiment. She was having second thoughts about wearing it. Third thoughts, too.

The idea was audacious and sprung from the mischievousness of the child she once was and had believed long gone. A bubble of laughter rolled past her lips as she pictured Drew's expression when he saw her. The delight she took in the image overrode her doubts. The rascal deserved to have his feathers ruffled.

"I would have helped you put it all together, if you'd asked."

"Thank you, Elsa, but I rather enjoyed doing it myself."

Elsa bent and dragged a finger along a seam, inspecting the stitching. "Well, you did a fine job with this. You'll no doubt be all the talk of the masquerade. Your viscount is sure to be impressed."

My viscount. She'd be lying if she said she hadn't

been thinking of him so. Even worse, liking it. For three long years, her heart had flailed in great depths of grief, her life kept afloat tied to a progressing vessel of vengeance.

"We'd best be getting you dressed now," Elsa said. "It's almost time to leave. Your grandfather is so excited; he won't want to miss a minute of the party."

Dove glanced toward the window. The night was clear and promised to be entertaining. She stared down at her costume again, a bit giddy. For the first time in a very long while, she was attending a party for reasons other than taking note of the home's layout and listening for information to facilitate her mission.

It was such a relief, however brief it might be, having her mind in a lighter place. Her grandfather had talked of little else since they'd received the invitation to the masquerade. By agreement, both had kept their costumes a secret from one another. The revealing was close at hand. Yes, tonight, was just for fun. Adding to the excitement, she had a flutter in her stomach, knowing she was going to see Drew.

Although they were just imitating a couple in the hub of attraction, Dove conceded at least some of it was real. Temporary, of course. She would do well to keep in mind what a poor match they were for one another. Drew was too glib, too flippant. After all, what kind of man would find amusement as the Creeping Bandit's aide?

What kind of woman would be the Creeping Bandit?

No, it was not the same. She had a serious mission supported by solid reason. Drew was a light-hearted man who searched for nothing more substantial than his next bit of pleasure. Life with a man such as he would be filled with…*laughter, cheer, merriment?*

Infidelity, more like it. While many in the *ton* accepted their husbands having mistresses as the way of things, that would not be the case for her. If she were ever to pledge herself to a man, his vow would have to be of equal sincerity. She wanted what her parents had.

Dove slipped out of her shoes, and out of her senseless musings. She could not let her attraction to the man get the better of her. Even if her feelings were developing into something more significant, his were not. Drew didn't love; he played. Something else it would serve her well to remember.

Oh, she appealed to him all right, as did about any female who crossed his path. His reputation alone made such clear. This she must keep at the forefront of all thoughts of Drew. She was not special to him; she was just current.

The acknowledgement dulled some of the sparkle from her anticipation of the evening. It was for the right of things, though. Better to traverse disappointment now than to have her heart broken later. And a man like Drew would no doubt break her heart.

Dove glanced out the window and into the mass of darkness appearing to stretch into forever. For three years, she hadn't considered a future past justice for her mother and father. She'd not given a moment's thought to what would become of her after. Though, whatever lay in her future, it would not include Drew. She gave her head a cleansing shake before facing her maid.

"Have you seen my grandfather's costume? He hasn't let slip so much as a hint as to what he'll be wearing."

Elsa shook her head 'til her yellow curls swished across the plump apples of her cheeks. "Oh no. He's been very secretive about it to all of us. His man Shettlyn is the only person who knows, and the stubborn old goat hasn't said a word. Told us he'd sworn an oath of secrecy. He wouldn't even break when Cook threatened to deny him his evening biscuit. And Shettlyn is a man who loves his sweets."

Dove giggled as Elsa helped her out of her gown. Shettlyn was loyal, even more than she'd imagined, to turn down one of Cook's delicious biscuits. "Grandfather is very excited about this. He's been like a little boy all week."

"I know," Elsa said on a chuckle. "The two of them were up late last night putting the finishing touches on his costume. When I passed by his room I heard your grandfather laughing."

Dove smiled at the image. It was as if her grandfather was regressing, becoming childlike instead of aging. Maybe getting lost in the joys of a youngster, the innocence, the playfulness, was how his mind coped with his grief.

It had begun after the murders of her parents. A year later when her grandmother, his wife, closed her eyes for the final time, the pace of his regression accelerated. Thinking about it now, over the course of these past three years, she and her grandfather had exchanged roles.

In small bounds, Dove had taken over the handling of their affairs. There were no other males in the family. In fact, there was no other family. Those who dwelled within the household, as well as some of those outside, deferred to her rather than him. Grandfather never noticed. Or if he did notice, he didn't care.

On the one hand, it was a sad thing to see him regress so. He'd been a sharp and conscientious man who'd taken pride in his position as head of the household. He was a wise and kind patriarch. Level-headed, responsible, yet not inflexible. On the other hand, Dove often envied her grandfather's escape from the deep suffering of their loss. At least these years of his life would be happy.

Thirty minutes later, Dove stepped into the parlor where her grandfather waited. The moment they set eyes on each other, they both burst out laughing. She had to hold onto the back of a wing chair to keep her balance.

"Grandfather," Dove said, when her laughter calmed. "You are the grandest carrot I have ever seen."

"Do you think so?" he asked, rotating a slow circle for her inspection, his orange-sleeved arms waving through the holes in the sides. "I was a bit worried the greens atop my head might be a little overdone."

Dove stared at his costume. Bright orange with a few artful creases, it tapered to a point between his shins. She hoped the leg holes were big enough for him to maneuver his steps without trouble. The greens at the top were indeed excessive, but it suited the joviality of the costume. His face beamed through the large hole cut into the front.

"Grandfather, you will be the finest root vegetable to ever attend a party."

He bent, as much as his carrot costume would allow, in the most regal bow a giant carrot could manage. He then waved an orange arm at Dove.

"And your costume, my dear, is very clever.

Timely, too. Lady Ashbury is sure to grab for her vinaigrette when she lays eyes on you."

"You don't think it's in poor taste, do you?"

"Not at all! You'll be a smash! I can't wait to see everyone's face when you walk into the Worthington's ball dressed as the Creeping Bandit."

"Me too, Grandfather." *One face in particular.*

Chapter 12

Drew scanned the full and boisterous gathering of their costumed guests, searching for his sister.

The little imp had absconded again without letting him know where she was going. Ollie was still a bit too young to attend the ball, but she'd pestered him until he said yes to chaperoning her, as their mother was overwrought in attending to her duties as hostess.

The one condition upon which Drew insisted was that she stay at his side the entire time. He couldn't have been clearer, or more inflexible, with this rule. Olivia was too young and inexperienced to understand the potential perils a young girl faced in certain situations. One careless moment, even if innocent, could cause her ruin.

If she needed a moment of privacy, she was to tell him first. It was the only time she could be out of his sight, and he promised her he would have one eye on his pocket watch. He'd repeated the rule with stern emphasis. And she'd acquiesced to his mandate without argument.

This was the second time within the hour Ollie had vanished without a word. If the impertinent chit didn't start behaving, he vowed he would lock her in her bedchamber for the duration.

Someone dressed in a multi-colored jester's costume scurried across the busy room, and Drew cringed. It was the same sort of ridiculous costume his mother had wanted him to wear. The battle was a narrow win, but he did emerge the victor, thank goodness. Bad enough he was walking about outfitted as a Viking warrior.

The tunic and trousers weren't terrible. He didn't even mind the cloak fastened at his shoulder with a decorative metal brooch. The horned helmet perched atop his head, however, was ludicrous.

Even though he told Ollie and his mother such helmets were worn for ceremonial purposes rather than combat, they insisted he wear it. With the two of them arguing the same position, and after his hard-won victory over the flamboyant regalia of a court jester, he lacked the fortitude of his namesake costume, and succumbed. The helmet was still better than flitting about as a jester. And the horns might come in handy.

If his little sister didn't show within the minute, he might just use one of those horns on her cheeky little arse.

"Drew."

Drew narrowed his gaze from the gathering to one, Lord Derek Durham, the Marquis of Durnhaven. He couldn't help but chuckle. Derek was dressed head to toe as a wizard. He wore a deep blue, floor-length, cone-shaped coat adorned with bright yellow stars and quarter moons. The pointed hat atop his head was of the same design. A thick, yellow cotton cord trimmed the bottom of both his coat and his hat.

Drew chuckled. "Derek, I see you've come to cast some magic spells upon unsuspecting ladies."

Confidence hefted a dark brow halfway to his cone-shaped hat. "As if I need magic."

Drew would have liked to respond with a good set down, but women flocked to Derek like hungry hummingbirds to nectar. On any other man, the retort would have sounded arrogant. One couldn't say such of Lord Derek Durham. The man was merely aware of the fine looks nature had bestowed upon him. And more than happy to use them to his advantage.

"Tell me, have you seen Olivia?"

"Your little sister? Can't say I have. What is her costume?"

"She's dressed as a fairy princess, sparkling star-tipped wand, and everything," Drew said, scanning the room again. A scowl darkened his features. "The little imp is in my charge tonight. I gave her firm orders to remain at my side. I think the girl listens with her ears too full of fluff and stubbornness to know what's good for her."

Derek's laugh burst forth at the statement, followed by his feigning empathy. "And it is quite unheard of for a Worthington to step out of bounds. No, don't turn your glare on me. I suppose I could make the rounds for you, see if I can spot her."

"Thanks. You're one of the few men I know I can trust. She might be chumming about with Elspeth Havisham."

Derek winced. "The Havisham chit is of a strong marriage mind with her cap set toward me. I've spent the last three balls dodging her copious eye flutters and unwarranted twitters. The last thing I want to do is hurt her feelings, but if the simpering girl doesn't desist her pursuit, I'm afraid I'll have to resort to candor. You're sure Olivia is with her?"

Forgoing his usual humorous jab, Drew said, "Last

I saw. Please, Durham. Ollie has a penchant for trouble and she is my responsibility."

"Very well. But if I am forced to abide Elspeth and her excessive charms, you're going to owe me a sizable debt. Oh, I've an idea." Derek's glance roved the crowd. "Have you seen Lord Foxboro?"

"Foxboro?" Drew said on a distracted note while searching for Ollie's fairy princess costume. The chit was begging to be locked in her chambers for the night. He was a blink from doing it, too. "No, but I do believe my mother invited him. Why?"

"Word has it he's got an eye for your sister. Perhaps they're together."

The speedy jump from concern to outrage snapped Drew's head from the crowd to Derek. "Foxboro! That gambling fool has a notorious reputation for trifling with the feelings of young innocents. The scoundrel finds it an amusing boost to his self-regard. If that cad comes within flirting distance of Ollie, I'll challenge him to a duel this very night."

"Don't order up your dueling pistols just yet," Derek said.

Did the man dare to snicker?

"We don't even know if Foxboro is here," Derek continued. "I'll head this way, see if I can find your sister. Do be a pal and cross your fingers she is not with Elspeth. The girl is insufferable."

"Thanks," Drew said as Lord Durham departed. Before spinning around, he said to his friend, "I'll head the other direction." *Foxboro!*

Drew took no more than three steps when a carrot waddled into the room. Vegetables were indeed popular this year. He'd already seen a stalk of asparagus, a plump tomato, and some sort of leafy green. This carrot costume was quite well done, and he spared it a moment's glance. He then caught the joyous face poking from the large hole near the top. It was Lord Barrow, Dove's grandfather.

His eager gaze swept the room, searching the many faces of his costumed guests for her. Some held full or partial masks on sticks to cover their faces. The masks didn't deter him. All he required was a glimpse of Dove, as he well knew the unique sway of her hips, the distinct incline of her head when someone held her attention. Even a glimpse of one of her delicate hands was all he would need. A mere face covering would not prevent him from recognizing her.

Then the woman of all his thoughts and desires rounded a tall, potted plant to stand beside her grandfather. Even hooded, he knew it was she.

Drew's head almost exploded.

The carrot turned away from her to engage in conversation with a man dressed as a Cossack. In four angry strides, Drew stood before his Lady Bandit. He clasped one of her slender arms clad in a garment no one should see on her, ever, yanked her close with as much subtlety as he could bear, and bent to bark a whisper into her ear.

"Are you mad?"

"Unhand me, you…" Dove stretched back far enough to take in his full costume through the eyeholes of her hood. "You Viking barbarian."

The laughter in her voice as she stared at his horned helmet further provoked his already inflamed ire. "What were you thinking, coming in public dressed so? I can see you grinning through your mouth hole.

Stop it. This isn't the least bit funny."

"On the contrary. It's hilarious. All of London's elite is searching for me, and here I am right under their noses, costume and all. And when did you become so serious?"

"When did you become so reckless?"

It did appear their traits were rubbing off on each other. It could take him days to think *that* through. Right now, all Drew wanted was to see her stripped from her incriminating costume and dressed in something less likely to land her in gaol.

Or just stripped.

The errant thought plunged into Drew's brain and seeped with slow deliberation through every extension of his long-suffering body. He caught her scent— honeysuckle and woman. No, not any woman. It was Dove's own individual perfume invading his senses with her drugging allure. Were he to be blindfolded, Drew had not a doubt he could find her in a crowd. Taking in her scent, remembering the give of her body beneath his touch, distracted him from everything but his want of more.

Could he slip away with her? Whisk her up to his chambers and spend hours teaching her all the wonders a woman could know? He no longer had to worry such a night would ruin her, for he had every intention of making her his wife. *Yes.*

His breath caught in the tightening of his chest as carnal images taunted him with brutal mercilessness. Yes, he could have her this night, without guilt. Though Dove did not yet know it, they were already bound.

Three violinists in periwinkle blue cutaway tailcoats and sand breeches stepped upon a low platform at the side of the room and struck up the night's music. It slapped Drew's attention back to the matter at hand. As he stared down at Dove attired as the Bandit for all the world to see, his desire receded before the humorless march of his concern.

Aware his domineering position could draw attention, and ignite a spectrum of gossip, he released Dove's arm and straightened. Drew strove to keep his voice low, but it took no effort to maintain his pique.

"Have you forgotten Lady Ashbury has seen you in this costume?"

Dove also kept her voice just loud enough for him to hear over the stringed instruments and the chatter. "She's already told everyone the Bandit is a large man. Arms as big as her thighs, I believe she said."

"She could recognize you."

"Drew, there are at least two other Bandits here tonight."

He'd seen them. Both men. Both large, prowling through the ball, one with his hood drawn back from his face and hanging from his head like a sleeping cap. Beneath the other hood, he knew, was his own Uncle Charles. Neither of them could be mistaken for Dove's lissome form.

"That's not the point—"

"What on earth happened to your hand?" Dove asked.

Already aware of what she was talking about, Drew glanced down anyway. The thumb on his left hand was swollen, the dark bruise lessening as it spread toward his wrist. "I struck it with a hammer yesterday when I was working on the new foundling home."

She stared, wide-eyed in her surprise, through the

eyeholes of her hood. Her shock gave chafe to the insult. "You've been working on the foundling home, personally?"

His frown spoke before his words. "I am capable of charitable volunteering, you know. I happen to possess a benevolent nature and skill with a hammer."

"Your skill left a bruise on your thumb."

Her lips quirked through the mouth slit. He didn't know what he wanted more, to kiss her or shake her. "You're trying to distract me from the subject at hand."

"How is it working?"

"It's not. Coming here dressed so—"

"Drew, dear, there you are."

At the sound of his mother's voice, Drew's attention shifted. Lydia Worthington stood before him, dressed as a lantern. No glass, of course, but the four stiff, black fabric casing poles surrounding her implied it. The faux casing met in a point above her head. Around her body within the casing, his mother wore a pale cylinder. Atop her head and beneath the point of her lantern costume, she wore a cone hat of red, orange, and yellow gossamer that flickered like flames every time she moved her head.

"Oh, my," Lady Worthington said. "Another bandit. And who is this beneath the hood?"

"Mother, this is…" to Dove he said, "Do remove your hood for an introduction."

Dove hooked a thumb at the bottom of the hood and slid it up high enough to show her face, giving him partial obedience. If she kept up this insolence she was going to end the evening over his knee. *Or beneath his lips.*

"Lady Dove Barrow," Lydia Worthington said.

"Have you already met?" Drew asked.

His mother cast a reprimanding glance his way. Her hat of gossamer flames blazed, matching the show of fire in her eyes. "No dear. I'm only familiar with her name because Lady Benton informed me my son was courting her."

Drew cringed. As the courtship had been no more than a sham, he'd not mentioned it to his mother or sister. At the time, he'd assumed he would have all matters settled before the gossip circulated wide enough to reach his mother. Now that his feelings had changed, had solidified, he considered it wise to inform Dove he wished to make the courtship one in earnest before bringing the news to his family. Damned gossips. "Um, well, mother…"

"It's all rather sudden," Dove said.

Lydia cast a warm smile on Dove. "I do hope we can have tea soon and get to know each other. As my ill-mannered son hasn't seen fit to extend an invitation," she said, shooting a brief, narrow glare his way before returning to Dove. "Please accept mine."

"I would enjoy nothing more," Dove said.

Lydia faced her son, the warmth drained from her smile. She leaned in, as if to place a kiss on his cheek. In his ear, she said, "I should have heard this news from you. We'll talk later."

With that, his mother pinched the skin of his upper arm hard enough to leave a bruise. Drew stifled a groan and marveled at the strength of his mother's fingers while dreading the message they sent. He was going to pay for his lapse in propriety.

"I must circulate," Lydia said, back to her light, airy self. And then she scanned the area around her son with concern. "Drew, where is your sister?"

"Ollie is in the washroom. She should be back in my presence at any moment." *Where he would chain the little rascal to his side.*

"See that she is, Drew. Lord knows what mischief she might find tonight. I couldn't convince her to wear my copper charm of protection around her neck. She said it clashed with her costume." Lydia Worthington then took Dove's hands in hers for a warm squeeze. "This week, please come to tea."

"I will," Dove answered.

"Your mother seems quite nice," Dove said when Lydia Worthington was gone. "She isn't pleased with you, though."

Drew rubbed his arm where she'd pinched him. "I'll make it right with her." His gaze slid from his mother's retreating form, her gossamer flames flickering as if to throw sparks at him with every step, back to Dove. His ire returned in full, as if it had never receded. Of all things, dressing as the Bandit!

The right corner of her lips lifted the same degree as her right eyebrow.

"Now, Dove," Drew cast a fierce glower on Dove, who, at his tone, slid the hood down over her face. "Back to the matter at hand."

A clap on the back heaved him from his scolding, again. Drew reined in his irritated scowl and faced his friend, Burke Darington, Earl of Blackwood. Beside Burke was his beautiful wife, Rose. Or rather, before him stood Mark Antony and Cleopatra.

Rose wore a dark wig over her blonde hair and a golden tunic decorated with a variety of colorful, paste jewels. Her blue eyes were lined with kohl in dramatic fashion. Gold bands formed as snakes, coiled around the slender circumference of her upper arms. Burke wore a metal cuirass over a long tunic. Hanging from the cuirass were long, fat strips of fabric. A military cloak completed the costume.

"Nice horns," Burke said on a chuckle, nodding toward Burke's Viking helmet.

"Nice knees," Drew shot back. He couldn't help but be amused at his friend's silliness. It still amazed him how such a stern and joyless man as Burke had once been could now be the epitome of bliss. Rose could take all the credit for that, her love for him, his love for her. And all they overcame to have each other.

"Rose," Dove said. "It's so nice to see you."

Rose stretched her neck forward to peer at Dove's eyes. "Dove, is that you beneath the hood?"

"It's me."

Looking between the two of them, Drew said, "I wasn't aware you two were acquainted."

"Dove has volunteered her time on the Foundling Project," Rose said. "She's accompanied me several times to the old home where the children still reside to spend time with them and helped plan for the new home. Some of the physical works you've been doing were her ideas."

"You needn't look so stunned, Drew," Dove said at his gape. "You're not the only one with benevolent skills."

"Yes," Rose said. "Dove is wonderful with the children. They're always excited to see her."

"It makes me happy to spend time with them," Dove said.

A tick in Drew's chest ignited his imagination. He

could see her with children, children who looked like her, like him. *Their children.*

"We'll have to catch up later, Drew," Burke said. "My Cleopatra here was so busy getting into her costume, she forgot to eat." The scolding expression he directed toward his wife was softened with an abundance of love, his reprimand a sign of his caring.

Shaking off a bare hint of bedevilment, Rose laid a placating hand on her husband's arm to stall him. To Dove, she said, "I'll be going to the foundling home tomorrow afternoon. If you'd like to go, I'll pick you up and we can travel there together."

"Yes, I'd like that," Dove answered.

"It's time to feed my child," Burke said, giving the small round of Rose's belly a gentle tap. His other arm wrapped over his wife's shoulder, ready to sweep her away. It was clear he would not have her well-being delayed another minute.

"I'll see you tomorrow," Rose said over her shoulder, as Burke was already leading her away.

"When did you start volunteering to work with the children at the foundling home?" Drew asked.

"About a year after the death of my parents. Renny suggested it. He was worried about me. He thought being around the children would lift my spirits, and he was right."

"You enjoy children?"

"Very much. Someday," she continued, but in a low, conspiratorial tone as she leaned into him. "I plan on having a brood of little bandits." She giggled at her jest. Drew did too, before growing serious again.

"As I was saying. Appearing in public dressed in this costume was not wise, Dove. In fact," Drew started, when something caught his eye.

At the far end of the room, one of the curtained glass doors leading out to the terrace had been left half open to allow a breeze of fresh air into the crowded room. Near one, he spotted Derek, escorting his young sister out into the night, alone. The door closed behind them.

"Bloody hell!" Drew ground out. He took one long stride before wheeling back to Dove to issue a command, emphasizing it with a jab of his finger to the spot where she stood. "You stay right here."

"If that's your idea of sweet talk, it's sorely lacking."

His jaw tightened and he reversed his stride to stand before her once again. "We are *not* finished with this conversation, Dove." In a harsh whisper, he said, "Stay!"

Without waiting for a response past the spark of ire in her eyes, he gave her his back and strode a determined pace toward the terrace doors, where he had every intention of pummeling Lord Derek Durham.

****

Dove gaped at Drew's stalking form and wondered what had riled him, as she'd never seen him so ill tempered. Perhaps someone else had aggravated him before she arrived. The man was in quite the state. Of all the nerve, telling her to stay put as if she was under his authority. And then to stalk off without a proper parting word. Drew was behaving as if he was the barbarian of his costume.

Her grandfather was deep in conversation with his old, dear friend Lord William Trent, dressed as a Cossack, and another man who appeared to be outfitted as an oak tree. As he was well occupied, Dove headed in the opposite direction Drew had gone. She would *not* be standing there like a loyal pet when he returned.

In her usual routine, Dove wandered, she visited some, and she made a surreptitious search for easy access to the house. The practice was so natural for her anymore. She couldn't help it. Sometimes she wondered if the habit would cease when this was all over.

She made her way toward the long buffet tables, thinking to join Lord and Lady Darington. Several round tables were set up nearby for the guests to sit and eat. Each was covered in a starched, white cloth with centerpieces of small boxes of purple and pink hyacinths. She spotted the Daringtons sitting at a table near the center. Dove took two steps toward them and stopped.

Lady Ashbury and two of her friends, all three dressed as butterflies with different colored wings, sat at a table quite near the Daringtons. From her horrified expression and demonstrative hand movements, Dove assumed the woman was yet again telling the embellished story of her encounter with the Creeping Bandit.

How she would love to march over there and tell the others the truth, how she'd been the one caught in the room that night. How she, being at least two stone lighter and half a head shorter, had been more frightened than Lady Ashbury, and had dashed from the room approximately two seconds after the lady entered. Of course, the gratifying scenario of truth-telling remained tucked in a fantasy. The satisfaction would not be worth wringing her own neck.

Perhaps Drew's point held some validity. Lady Ashbury was the only person outside of Renny and Drew who had ever seen her dressed for her mission. Well, and Lord Beaumont.

But from what Drew had told her, Beatrix's husband believed the concocted tale of how he'd wandered into her chambers, half in his cups, where he fell and hit his head on her dressing table. Lord Beaumont was convinced his memory of the Bandit was naught but a hallucination. Still, he *had* seen her.

All it would take would be a spark of recognition from Lady Ashbury or Lord Beaumont, and she'd be finished. Dove pivoted away and left the area. She would have to keep an eye out so as not to run into either one of them while she was here in her Bandit costume.

It was time she checked on her grandfather. He wasn't in the grand parlor where she'd left him, but neither was Lord Trent. She found the two of them in one of the smaller salons. Seated at a polished, teakwood card table, the two men were playing a card game. Grandfather was laughing, his face beaming through the face hole in his carrot suit.

At her approach, his smile faltered and confusion smudged his joy. This heartbreaking occurrence happened sometimes. He recognized her as familiar, but it took a moment for him to place her. Lately, the slippage of his memories into loss was accelerating. Dove choked back her tears and returned his smile.

"Dove, dear," Lord Trent said.

He stood, adjusting the astrakhan hat topping off his Cossack costume, and placed a kiss on her cheek. Lord William Trent was the same age as her grandfather, but his robust appearance shaved years off his face. His gray hair held more than a few traces of the rich brown of his younger days. His broad chest hadn't quite the girth it used to, and his movements were less swift. But his indigo eyes twinkled with wisdom, kindness, and clarity of thought.

"Lord Trent," Dove said, wrapping her arms around him for a hug. In his ear she whispered, "Thank you for entertaining my grandfather."

He whispered back, "Ronald has been my dearest friend since we were boys. I'm happy to have this time with him."

After releasing her, Lord Trent motioned toward one of the empty seats and said, "Dove, would you like to join us for a game?"

"Oh, posh, Wills." Her grandfather waved of his orange-sleeved arm. He shifted in his chair and the greens atop his costume hat swayed. "She's a beautiful young woman at a party full of eligible young men. She shouldn't be spending her time with two old codgers like us."

"Don't be ridiculous, Grandfather," Dove said, taking the empty chair. Lord Trent sat on her other side. "I'd love a game of cards. What is it you two are playing tonight? Loo? Whist?"

Her grandfather laid his hand on top of hers, comfortable in all the ways of warmth, and gave her a squeeze. "Dove, dear. Go, have some of the ladies make introductions. It's time you look forward to your next stage of life."

Dove met his gaze. In that moment her grandfather was there, all there. His care flowed into her, but concern lurked beneath his clarity. The love around

Dove's heart tightened until it hurt.

"My season grows late, Dove."

"Oh grandfather, please don't say such things."

He thumbed a tear from the corner of her eye. "Don't cry for me, dear. I've had a wonderful life, well, most of it. You've been a treasure. You *are* a treasure. Don't let anyone ever convince you you're anything less. I need to know you'll be all right."

"We both will," Dove said.

Her smile was tinged with too much sadness to impart any confidence in her statement.

"Go, Dove," her grandfather said, leaning back in his chair. His tone took on a jovial air. He flicked an impish grin toward his friend before saying, "Let these two old men enjoy a game of cards."

"Who are you calling old man, old man?" William feigned a frown, and both men chuckled.

"That's true," her grandfather said. "I *am* three months younger than you."

William faced Dove. "Your grandfather is right. We're fine here." He sent her a wink and a nod, telling her without words he would stay with his friend while she was off and about. "Go enjoy yourself."

"Very well, then," Dove said as she stood and forced a bright smile. Both men rose. "You boys play nice now, and I'll be back to check on you later."

"Play nice? Now what fun would that be?" William said, a mischievous grin holding remnants of his youth and drawing a laugh from her, as well as her grandfather.

Dove left them to their game, wandered out of the room, and toward the front of the house. She said hello to a couple of people, but mostly she walked, and worked to focus her attention on anything other than losing her grandfather. As she'd done these past few months, to assuage her pain, Dove firmed to her mission.

Drew's home was on her list. In fact, she'd skipped over it the last time she was out, in deference to his aid. He was sure to argue his mother's defense. He wouldn't sway her. Sooner or later she would have to search for the brooch in Lady Worthington's chambers. It occurred to Dove, as she slid a covert peek toward the grand stairway, tonight would be the perfect opportunity.

Drew was otherwise occupied, for the moment, at least, with whatever had drawn him outside. She wouldn't have to tell him until it was over. Maybe she wouldn't tell him at all. Keeping this search secret would circumvent harsh words and feelings. Since likely the brooch wasn't there anyway, what would be the point of stirring up such a hornet's nest if she could settle the matter tonight?

Dove took a casual glance about the costumed crowd. Eyes were more occupied than usual, with everyone inspecting everyone else's costumes. It wouldn't be like last time, as she was *expected* to be dressed as the Creeping Bandit. Yes, she would not find a better opportunity than the present.

Dove was up the stairs in less time than it took to shift a suspicious eye.

****

Drew stormed through the terrace door like a tornado homing in on a specific target. If Derek thought he could seduce his young sister and get away with it, he had another thing coming-Drew's ready fists.

At his violent intrusion, both Derek and Ollie spun toward him in guilty display. The torches ensconced at intervals along the balustrade near which they stood gave sufficient light to show the surprise on their faces. Derek must have thought he was quite clever, slipping away with her while her guardian was searching elsewhere. Well, the disloyal rogue would find himself far less nimble of mind once his brains were good and rattled.

While Ollie had the good graces to maintain an expression of alarm, Derek gathered his wits in short order, and had the utter gall to look him in the face and chuckle.

Standing there in his ridiculous wizard costume, Derek said, "I found your sister." His quipping grin was Drew's undoing.

"You brazen reprobate," Drew spat, lunging toward the man, his fists already raised.

Ruffles of pink taffeta and glittered slippers leapt between them.

"Drew!" Olivia shouted, one pink-gloved hand up with splayed fingers to block him. Her red hair was braided in a coronet, fronted with a silver-glittered tiara. The other hand gripping her sparkling, star-tipped wand rose to him as if she wielded a cudgel. "Have you gone mad?"

"Out of the way, Ollie. You're too young and innocent to understand why this libertine escorted you out into the night alone."

Over Olivia's head, Derek said, "Drew old man, you've not got the right of things."

"Don't I though? A man with a reputation such as yours escorts a young innocent out to the night's deserted terrace, *unchaperoned*. I know exactly what you're about, Durham, and you'll not get away with it."

Ollie stamped her decorated slipper on the flagstones hard enough to dislodge some of the glitter. "Drew! Lord Durham did not bring me out here. *I* brought *him*."

Drew shot a glare at his sister so fierce it sent her back a step.

"You brought him out here, did you?" Drew said, his voice a low menace. "Well I feel *so* much better."

"Clear the filth from your thoughts, brother, and listen to me!"

"I'll clear my head and listen to you, all right. As soon as I thrash the depravity from his!"

With those words, Drew rounded Olivia so fast she hadn't time to argue anymore and Derek hadn't time to react. Drew pounded a fist to Derek's face hard enough to send the wizard-attired lord flipping backward over the balustrade. A flash of Derek's pointy-toed shoes caught in the torchlight. Two seconds later, a rustled thud told Drew the man had landed in the row of shrubbery.

Before satisfaction could settle in, a female scream from behind Drew seized his attention. It did not come from his sister.

Drew wheeled around to find Elspeth Havisham with the spread fingers of both her hands crossed over the wide gape of her mouth. Elspeth, standing beside his fairy princess sister, was in the full attire of a gypsy girl with a coral blouse, a floating, patchwork skirt, arms full of bracelets, and a colorful scarf tied about her head. While Ollie's countenance bore pure anger, young Lady Havisham was the personification of horrified.

"Elspeth?" Drew said.

"If you've killed him," Elspeth shouted, her hands flying from her face to form fists that pounded the night's cool air. "I'll see you hung for this!"

From the short drop on the other side of the wall arose a rustling of bushes, indicating he had not killed Lord Derek Durham. At the sound of a pitiful groan, Elspeth spun toward the steps leading down to the gardens and was gone in a flurry of whirling, patchwork skirts.

"You've ruined everything!" Ollie shouted.

"What did I ruin?" Drew demanded, confusion mixing in to dull his anger. "What in blazes is going on here?"

His sister stomped toward him, her slippers losing a bit more glitter with every hard step across the paving stones. Once posed before him, she slammed one fist against her hip. The wand in her angry grip pointed straight at his chest.

"Elspeth and I have been working on this plan for weeks! I was to get Lord Durham onto the terrace to point out the constellations. Everyone knows he's an interest in such things, so it wouldn't seem the least bit odd. We would 'coincidentally' run in to Elspeth. The man hasn't spared her more than a moment's visit and she's been moon-eyed over him for ages."

Olivia crossed her arms and shot Drew a glare fierce enough to rival his own of a moment before. "And now, because you think I'm a ninny and Lord Durham is without any morals whatsoever, you've ruined our careful plans and their probable happy marriage!"

"Oh, well, be at ease, Ollie, no harm has been done here tonight," Drew told his sister, ready to settle her mind and this matter with the facts. Once she understood the way of things, her anger would subside. With an indulgent smile, he said, "I've spoiled nothing. Lord Durham has no intention of proposing marriage to the girl, no matter your clever ruse. He finds her unappealing."

"Oh!" Ollie stomped the heel of her foot on the toe of his boot, sending up glitter which then rained from the shin of his pant leg down.

"Ah! Ollie!" Drew shouted, hopping on one foot while he rubbed sore toes through his boot. If his mother and sister kept up their assaults, he'd be crippled by the morn.

"Shut up, Drew! You know nothing of romance, so just shut up!"

She punctuated her last words with jabs of her wand. It was as if instead of a fairy princess she was a wicked, malicious queen casting a spell. Quite a nasty one, too, if the daggers shooting from her eyes were any indication. He'd never seen her so angry.

Olivia spun away, a fairy princess spewing sparks and sparkles, and fled down the concrete steps, he assumed, to offer aid to Derek.

Drew supposed he should go see if his friend was all right. But with what he could hear of the two young women fawning over him, and with the way they all three must feel about him at present, it was best he let tempers cool before making an apology to Derek. Perhaps his friend would understand, as they were both unwitting victims of the girls' machinations.

Drew shook his head and rolled his eyes

heavenward. The evening had scarce begun and already disasters were flourishing. In the span a mere few minutes, he'd been pinched, stomped, scolded, he had aggravated four women, a new record for him, and punched a friend in the eye. This party was off to a rousing start.

As there was nothing more for him to do out here, Drew reentered the party to further attend his discussion with Dove and her foolish decision to come to the masquerade dressed in her Bandit costume. At least on that he knew he was right.

****

Lady Worthington's chambers were elegant in the colors of peach and white. Unusual, too. At least three different, cloth-covered plates around the room held some sort of stone. An odd weaving of purple netting with square, yellow beads all strung from a long piece of sun-bleached driftwood, hung on the wall above her white, iron headboard. The strange piece of art was as wide as her mattress and reached almost to the ceiling.

Aside from those oddities, the rest of the spacious room was as she'd expected. Long, peach-colored drapes covered both windows. Oriental carpets cushioned the floor. A sizeable armoire in the French provincial style sat against the wall opposite the windows. In the corner was a petite writing desk with a cushioned chair.

On the right side of a small, rectangular Chippendale table near the desk sat a simple tin plate. In the center of the plate was a cone-shaped pile of orange powder. The top was blackened, as if it had been burned. Another oddity she did not understand.

The other side of the table held Lady

Worthington's jewel box. On stealth feet, Dove headed straight for the box.

It was well-crafted, shiny rosewood with polished, silver trim. Dove raised the lid. Drew's mother possessed some fine pieces, though not as many as one might expect for a woman of her age and station. A gold ring with a jade stone, an array of earbobs, and several necklaces of varying value. A shallow bowl held a variety of stones set with gold bails to hang from a chain.

She made a second pass through the box, making sure. The brooch was not there. Dove exhaled an audible breath.

Though she'd told herself the brooch wouldn't be found in Lady Worthington's possession, she conceded it had been a concern. She feared any connection of the crime to Drew. No matter she didn't want her heart to open a place for him, no matter he lacked the proper amount of solemnity, and no matter his sordid reputation, Lord Andrew Worthington had become entwined within her emotions.

A sigh gave way to a reluctant smile. Silly, really, given the nature of their relationship, and their individual temperaments. She'd been fighting it. Her blossoming feelings for this man to whom she should not be attracted met every day with denial. Her parents' union drifted through her mind, and joy shooed her hesitancy. No one could have guessed the two of them any better than a terrible mismatch, and they were the epitome of marital bliss.

Her mother, a Shawnee Indian from the Colonies. Her father, a member of London's aristocracy. While Dove was raised in her father's world, she grew up hearing stories of her mother's upbringing, life in the tribe.

She knew the story behind every one of the few pieces of Shawnee memorabilia placed about their home. There were three wood carvings of different animals, a wolf, a bear, and an eagle. Her father had brought back several arrowheads for his father. Her grandfather loved them so much he had them displayed on a velvet cushion in a glass case in his study.

Her mother's cedar chest at the foot of Dove's bed held two blankets, one made by her mother, the other by a grandmother she'd never met. Her mother's parents had both died long before she was born. But from the moment they met, her mother and father had each other. They *had* each other. Their backgrounds could hardly have differed more, yet they'd found true and lasting love.

Could she and Drew find such happiness together?

Dove ventured to dream it for a moment. She dared to envision a marriage of her own like the one her parents had. Could she have it too, a love match in a world where marriages were made for reasons having little if anything to do with tender wants? Could she have it with Drew?

The beat of her heart, like the rhythm of the Shawnee water drum of her mother's people, still kept in the music room, pounded a steady declaration of her longing.

Did Drew feel the same? He desired her. She knew enough of men's ways to believe that, understood her own body's draw to his. Dove's face heated with the memory of his intimate touch, of her shameless desire for more, and the powerful urge she'd had to put her hands on him.

What future she and Drew might have beyond desire, she couldn't say. Maybe they would have none. Perhaps her aspirations were born of ill-considered fantasies never meant to come to fruition. An illusion to warm the chill of her loneliness. Or perhaps, with the end of her search which was at present in sight, her mind and life might experience a new freedom, the haunts of her past releasing her to embark on a new course.

Before she could proceed to the future, however, she had to conclude her business with the past. After lowering the lid on Lady Worthington's jewel box, Dove made a slow rotation to take in the room, and she made a fresh decision as well.

At first, it was to be just for tonight, not moving things about the room as she normally would. If Lady Worthington were to find her chambers in such specific disarray, she would know the real Creeping Bandit had been there. After all, that was the point of rearranging items. But Drew would know, too. And he would know just who was responsible. This night she would forgo the act. In fact, it would be her new habit.

Tweaking their noses, bringing attention to what she was doing, did naught but increase the chances she'd be caught. It was a foolish thing to do right from the start. Worse, now, as the upper crust had grown edgy and on high alert for the Bandit. Drew had been right about that. The bit of satisfaction she got making her mark was not worth escalating her risk of capture.

If the *ton* were not on their guard, completing her mission would be much easier. Leaving things as she'd found them wasn't just sensible, it was right.

Of late, it was weighing on her conscience, upsetting innocents. They didn't deserve to feel so invaded. When she'd begun this mission, anger and grief had restrained her compassion. She couldn't say when her feelings changed, but they had and she'd no choice but to change with them.

"I thought I'd find you here."

Dove spun toward Drew's voice. He stood in the doorway, large, imposing, handsome in every way. He held his Viking hat in his hand by one of its horns. His hair was mussed in a most adorable fashion. By his expression, she guessed he was just a little more amused than he was perturbed.

"If it's any consolation," Dove said, slipping off her hood and patting her pinned hair. "I didn't find the brooch."

Drew quirked a grin. "Ah, well, yes, learning my mother is not a thief and a murderer does put your audacious intrusion in a better light."

Dove resisted her embarrassment at being caught, and made a defense by saying, "You must have known all along sooner or later I would have to look."

Drew spoke as he took lazy strides, stopping two or three feet before her. "Yes, I suppose I did."

"Are you angry?"

"I should be, but I'm afraid the events of this evening have left my energies too depleted for any more anger."

It was Dove's turn to grin. "Already? What mischief have you been up to so soon in the evening, Lord Worthington?"

"I was led down a wrong path."

"So, none of this trouble you found tonight was

your fault?"

Drew huffed a breath upon which rode an airy chuckle. "Well, I couldn't by all rights go that far. However, I can assure you, at the very least it was unintentional."

The mock frown he donned so belied his contrite tone, Dove's laughter sprang sudden and natural. Before it had subsided, she said, "I'm sure you are beyond innocent of any wrongdoing."

He tipped a solemn nod.

"Drew, is that glitter on your pantleg? Just what is it you have done tonight?"

By the time he finished his recounting of the incident on the terrace, ending with how he sent his wizard-attired friend tumbling back over the balustrade and into the shrubbery, the feeble barrier of Dove's fingers against her lips could no longer hold back her laughter.

"It's not funny," Drew said. Though the merriment dancing in his amber eyes said different.

"Are you quite sure he's all right?"

"It's no more than a three-foot drop to the ground. And the bruises and scratches I inflicted on Derek tonight will award him a great deal of sympathetic tending from Ollie and Elspeth, I've no doubt. He'll be waited on hand and foot for the duration of the party while my good name will bear endless defamation."

Drew sighed and continued. "I, on the other hand, am sure to suffer further rebuking from my sister, *and* my mother, who is already perturbed with me for not telling her about our 'courtship'."

Wringing false gravity from her mirth, Dove said, "You know, for someone who never sets out to find trouble, you certainly do land in it often enough."

After a self-deprecating chuckle and a slight shake of his head, Drew's intensifying gaze settled on her. His countenance set a thoughtful form. The gold of his eyes darkened, sending a strange and wondrous tingle through her limbs. His voice lowered and became distant.

"But on rare and spectacular occasions, the trouble I find is a boon in costume. Did you know the sighting of a dove represents the beginning or ending of a life?"

Dove gaped at him, a little stunned at the sharp turn of subject. "Yes, of course I know. It's a name from my mother's people. A dove is a link between heaven and earth. You've been reading about my name?"

Drew nodded. "I am capable of reading, you know."

Drew stepped closer until no more than an inch separated them and dropped his Viking hat. It landed on the carpet with a dull thud. He lifted his hand and stroked the back of his fingers along her cheek. The touch simple, yet powerful enough to vibrate waves of warmth through her entire body. Her hood slipped from her gloved fingers, glided down, and caught on one of the horns of his hat.

"A link between heaven and earth," Drew said. His voice still had a remote quality, but his gaze focused on her with great attentiveness. "With a little bit of the devil thrown in for good measure?"

He was teasing her, but without rancor. Drew stood quiet and still. Caught in the intensity of his regard, Dove was also motionless. It was as if the entire world perched on the edge of what was fated to come next.

As he lowered for a kiss, Dove tipped her head

back in welcome. Like the fingers trailing a heated path down her throat, the initial kiss was light, a sprout of sweet grass brushed with a warm, summer breeze. Yet it held the power to bar any objections the rest of her world might throw.

His hand wrapped around her neck, drawing her nearer with gentle insistence, requesting and receiving more. Dove clutched his shoulders, meeting his body with hers, craving to be closer, closer.

The earth could have crumbled to dust and she wouldn't have known until it fell away, taking her from Drew's hold, from his kiss. He was heat and pleasure. He wrapped her in carnality, drenched her in want.

In a sudden tilt, her feet left the earth and Drew was holding her in his arms. He carried her out of his mother's chambers, past spaced sconces of candlelight and down a long corridor to another room. His room. He stopped just outside the door for a long, slow kiss. With her arms around his neck, she clung to him as if she feared the precious moment to be ephemeral.

Backing a bare breath from her lips, Drew carried her over the threshold. He kicked the door behind him and it closed with a resounding click.

A small fire behind the grate was the only light in his chambers. It bathed the spacious room in soft flickers of orange and red. Dove noticed little else as he set her on her feet beside the massive bed.

With quiet deliberation, Drew removed the pins from her hair. They made a soft clink on the wood floor, almost unheard above the low crackle and pop of the fire. Running his fingers through her locks, he marveled at the silkiness, the rich color, so dark in the firelight it hinted at blue. It fell to her waist in a wildness that doubled his intense draw to her.

How many times over these past weeks had he thought about having her like this, all to himself in the privacy of his chambers? Too many to count. Unlike the past claims of his wants, as they were nothing anymore, at times he could almost believe he'd go mad with his desire for Dove. Before proceeding, however, he had to know she understood what was happening, and that she wanted him, too.

Honeysuckle scented his room, bestowing physical equality to Drew's imaginings no less intoxicating than the finest brandy. He let it calm the roar of his body before cupping her perfect, exotic face in his hands. He sucked in a deep breath. The stunning sapphire of her almond-shaped eyes against the unique tone of her skin harmonized with the firelight, sang to him songs of future and intimate fortunes.

Dove salvaged all that was good in him. She called to the forefront the best of what he was, and gave hope to all he now knew he wanted to be. He could almost laugh at the irony, the infamous Creeping Bandit, his beacon of nobility. Yes, Drew had no doubt she was his personal link to heaven.

His fingers traced the line of her cheekbone, her jaw, making sure her gaze was on him, and he had her full attention. "I want you, Dove," he said, his voice roughed with yearning. "Here. Now. Do you understand what I'm saying?"

Dove nodded. "Yes, I understand. My mother was open with me about such things. Drew, I'm here because I want to be. I want this," she said before clasping her hands around his neck, urging him down in her demand for another kiss.

Her awareness of what was happening, coupled with her amorous response, set him afire. She possessed his body. She owned his heart. She enraptured his mind until he was near to losing it.

Drew gentled his advancements. Her understanding of the mechanics could not prepare her for the unfamiliar onslaught of sensations. This reminder of her innocence helped him fetter his return, lest he frighten her with the mad scope of his passion.

He forced himself to take his time, letting the kiss grow ardent in restrained increments. Dove responded in kind to each subtle escalation. She showed no sign of fear or reticence, so he advanced further.

Drew slid his hands inside her Bandit coat and over the dark clothes keeping him from her slender form. His thumbs brushed against the tips of her breasts. Shock stammered her sharp gulp of air, and his desire escalated.

In the next instant, her coat fell to the floor.

Drew ran his hands down her back, slipping them beneath her shirt, relishing at long last the soft warmth of her skin against his eager touch. He lifted the hem.

Since the garment was a bit large for her, he didn't have to waste time with the buttons. Dove raised her arms for him, and her shirt landed atop her coat.

Dove's face warmed at the sudden baring of her breasts. No man had ever seen her so. But she would not let her embarrassment rob anything from this beautiful moment. Resisting the urge to use her hands to cover herself, she lifted her chin and let him look.

Drew had seen breasts before, many. But these were Dove's, his Dove's, full, tinted with her exotic hue, hypnotic in their lush beauty. He caressed them with the reverence they deserved. And then, because instinct and desire would not be denied, he bent for a taste.

Dove's knees melted. Had Drew's arm not wrapped around her waist to catch her, she would have sunk to the floor. Sensation crackled through her body. Her mind dimmed. She clutched the hair at the back of his head and leaned into him.

Her lack of inhibition struck a spray of cracks in Drew's control. He marshaled his efforts to keep hold. Desire, though, coupled with her willing enthusiasm, would not be long fended.

He knelt before her, lips trailing kisses down to the waistband of her trousers. One hand wrapped around her ankle and lifted her foot high enough to remove her Bandit's boot and her dark stocking. He did the same for the other foot. After releasing the gusset tie at the waist of her trousers, he dragged them down her legs inch by slow revealing inch, then shoved them aside with the rest of her clothing.

Dove stood nude before him. Her confidence bounded about various emotions. Never in her life had she been more vulnerable. Nor had she ever experienced such selfish want, and this utter sovereignty to take it. And take it she would. Gathering her courage, she met his gaze with her own.

At the raw desire emanating from his expression, uncertainties played at her spine. She routed her concerns, refused their influences. Desire beat so steady a pulse she could do naught but learn all he would teach.

Drew leaned in to place a reverent kiss low on her belly, to breathe in her intoxicating aroma, and used the moment to steady his breath and the wild pounding of his heart.

To have Dove here, beside his bed, naked and willing, set him afire as no woman ever had. Or ever could. Words floated through his head. He should assure her she was not merely another conquest. She should know before they went any further he intended to make her his wife. But his desire for her drove him senseless. It took all his concentration to not become a wild beast and frighten her into fleeing.

Drew sat back on his heels. He allowed his eyes to feast on the alluring tint of her skin, on the perfect shape of her every curve. He rose to stand before her. As he struggled to find command of his voice, she took initiative and unfastened the brooch at his shoulder.

Dove didn't know if she was supposed to undress him, as he had her. Nor did she care if it was the proper thing to do. She would see this man unclothed as he was seeing her. Her determined fingers worked at the clasp. His cloak slipped to the floor, and she set the brooch on the bedside table.

He rose to stand his full height before her. Tall and strong, a danger to her heart, a promise to her body. His gaze touched her everywhere, but his hands remained at his side. Again, she would do what she wanted. This night she would take for herself. Dove opened his buttons and removed his shirt.

The enticing expanse of his chest fascinated her. She wished to touch him, so she did. Soft, earthen hairs over hard muscle, sculpted arms and shoulders rounded with strength from his time spent boxing, a tapered waist heating a trail into his trousers. He gave her free reign to touch what was bared to her. She took her time, relishing the power to quiver his skin with a mere brush of her fingertips. Her curiosity grew over what was still covered.

Drew yanked off his boots and socks. He could wait no longer. Her lack of inhibition was maddening. Her curious, unreserved touch ferried him to his brink.

After removing his trousers, he straightened and clasped her close. Dove lifted her arms. With the flat of her hands against his chest, she exerted enough pressure to keep him at bay. Had she changed her mind? His harried body tensed in frustration. To withdraw now would kill him. But if she wasn't ready, then withdraw he would.

Then Drew understood her meaning. Her mind had not changed, at least not yet. Dove was curious. Once again, he reminded himself how this was all new to her. Keeping still, he studied her as she stepped back to make a visual quest of his body.

Where her hands didn't touch, her eyes explored. The paired perusals catapulted his body into an advanced state of arousal. Every inch of him was raw. Even the bare brush of her breath seared his skin.

Dove retreated a tad, creating a bit more space for a better look. Her seeking eyes lowered, and then widened, curiosity giving way to trepidation. It didn't escape Drew's notice, as if anything she did ever would. He took her face in his hands again, lifted, captured her gaze with his.

"It'll be all right. You don't have to be afraid of me."

Defiance lifted her chin from his palms. "I'm not afraid."

She was. Her false bravado was good, but not

sufficient to hide from him the slight tremble of her lower lip, or her attempt to control it. But she would not allow fear to rule her. Dove was a woman who made her own destinations. With all his heart and soul, he loved her.

Drew lifted her, relished the warmth of her bared skin against his. He followed her down on the bed.

Dove slid a thigh along his leg. He covered part of her with his body, so different from her own. Powerful, masculine. His lips were on hers while his hands explored. With every caress, she discovered a new awareness. When he touched her in a most intimate fashion, he wrested from her sounds trotting on currents of ragged breaths.

Drew shifted until he was atop her. "Dove," he whispered, wanting to forewarn her. All his mind could conjure was her name. He said it again, an incantation to christen the night. And then his body took hers in one swift move.

Dove tensed and bit into his shoulder. Though a tremor rocked him, Drew managed to hold still. Whispers rode kisses from his lips to her ear. He promised the pain would soon pass. And he waited. His body was taut, and damp with need. But he would wait through all of eternity until she gave him a sign she was ready.

Dove relaxed in small degrees, letting the rich feel of him filling her overcome the shock. Her instincts confused her. Her hands had circled to the front of his shoulders to shove him away. At the same time, her legs wrapped around his so he would not leave. He shifted the tiniest bit, sending decadent waves pitching through her body. Dove nuzzled her face into the crook of his neck and circled her hands around to clasp him as close to her as possible.

Her stirrings gave blessed acquiescence to his body. Now, now he would make her forget there'd ever been pain. Drew kissed her until she writhed beneath him. She met his strokes, tentative at first, but not for long. Their lovemaking grew in mutual escalation until their worlds exploded into a million pieces, and reassembled as one.

Chapter 13

Drew kissed the top of Dove's head, lying warm and still upon his chest. Perhaps she'd fallen asleep. He was near to drifting off, too. Their lovemaking left him both depleted and dazed in the most wondrous of ways. Another part of him, the heart of his heart, wanted to leap from the bed and shout from the window his love for this woman.

His hand caressed her bare hip. He dragged his thumb over the sleek protrusion of her hipbone. No man had ever touched her there. There, or anywhere. No other man ever would. She was his Dove. All his.

A brief and airy chuckle escaped him. He'd once thanked his lucky stars he had the fortitude to keep a woman from settling into his heart the way Rose Darington had settled into his friend, Burke's. Burke had come close to losing his mind when he believed Rose guilty of deception, and worse. Now Drew understood what made love so worth overcoming any obstacles chance might throw between them. Nothing would ever keep him from this woman.

Dove stirred, snuggling into him with a sigh. Drew had no doubt he could spend the rest of his days in this bed with her, and never want for another thing. The image gave him both peace and fire. He closed his eyes. Dove would give him all that and more.

"I have to go," Dove said.

The sudden break to his musings alarmed him. She was a lady, and she'd been innocent. He needed to make his intensions clear and see she understood her virtue had not been stolen.

"Dove, you've nothing to be ashamed of. Here, look at me. I want to talk to you."

She rolled onto her stomach and tipped her head back until she faced him. Her cat's smile elicited one from him, as well as relief.

"I'm ashamed of nothing," she said. "I wouldn't change what happened between us if I could. It was…glorious."

My, but she did please him.

"But my grandfather is down there alone. If he's looking and can't find me, he'll worry. Sometimes he gets…confused."

The reminder of the party going on below stairs struck him with his own obligations. Following a sigh, Drew said, "Yes, and I've left my sister unattended. It's beyond my imagination to guess what trouble she might be into now. And my mother will have my head if she finds out I'm not watching her. But Dove, we still need to talk."

Dove sat on her heels and faced him. Her hair swung in wild disarray over one shoulder and settled across part of her right breast. The other was exposed to him in full.

At the sight of her so, Drew almost forgot anything else in the world existed. She didn't grab the bedding to cover nudity because she was not ashamed. Dove was the singular, most magnificent woman ever to grace existence. And she was his. He wished he could make it official this very night.

"Marry me," he said

Her dark brows lifted, but her eyes showed no sign of surprise. "We're bypassing protocol, again."

Drew's palm cupped her knee. "I'll speak to your grandfather. I want to start posting the banns as soon as possible."

Her head tipped a little to the right. The surprise she lacked before arrived at last. "You're serious."

"Of course I am. I love you."

Dove dragged the counterpane up to cover herself. Worry covered him. Perhaps she did not care to share more than this singular experience with him. Then the bud of a smile tugged at her kiss-swollen lips.

Relief gave him a smile of his own. "Did you think I was but dallying with you?"

"If there is any truth to your reputation."

He sat up, the counterpane tangling across his lap, and traced the contour of her jaw with his finger. "My reputation is about to undergo a drastic metamorphosis."

"You won't miss it?" she asked. "The women, the late nights, bouncing around the gambling establishments with your pals?"

"I stopped missing all of it the moment we met."

Her obvious pleasure stretched, and then retracted. "What of your taste for variety? I'll never be anything more than what sits here before you."

His finger crooked into the top of the counterpane in between the swells of her breasts. She held it tighter, refusing him entrance. Drew raised his solemn gaze while his single finger prodded at the top of her covering. "One doesn't continue to shop for trinkets once he's unearthed Heaven's treasure."

"I think you..." Her words lost focus when he ceased his delving efforts and settled for caressing her breast through the covering.

"You were saying something?"

She clasped his hand in hers. "I think you might well be sincere."

He covered her hand with both of his. With a squeeze, he said, "Dove, I have never been more serious about anything in my life. Tell me you'll be my wife, bear my children, grow old with me."

Her eyes puddled. When she nodded, so did his. "Yes. I will marry you."

As he leaned in to kiss her, Drew tugged at the counterpane. This time, Dove let it fall. Almost immediately, she grabbed it back.

"Drew, I've left my grandfather alone too long already. And if you're chaperoning your sister, well, you've a house full of men downstairs."

Drew could have wept for her truthfulness. It didn't even matter if Ollie's anger had passed or still raged. She was his responsibility. And he had to respect Dove's dedication to her grandfather.

"You're right. It's killing me, but you're right." Drew leaned back to drink in a final look before saying, "Cover yourself, woman, before I forget my obligations."

Dove giggled and raised the counterpane. "Renny will be ever so pleased to learn of your proposal. He's warmed up to you, you know."

"Your first thoughts are for Renny, not your grandfather?"

"Oh, grandfather will be pleased, of course. More and more often of late, though, grandfather lives in another world. I've known Renny my whole life. He knows me well. He worries for me, more so these past few months."

Drew took his time brushing the hair from her candescent shoulder. "Have you two always been so close?"

"We've always been friends. After my parents were killed, my grandparents were steeped in their own grief and I often turned to Renny. Not long after the murders, my grandmother fell ill and never recovered. When a year later she died, well, that's when grandfather's mind began slipping. Renny was a great support to me. He was the only person I trusted enough to tell of my plan to become the Bandit." Dove gave him a little grin. "Until you leapt into my life."

"If I remember right, you leapt into mine."

"It's not as if I had a choice."

In a heartfelt, solemn tone, Drew said, "You had a choice. You put yourself in danger to save my life. I plan on spending the rest of mine seeing to it you never regret it."

"You have Renny to thank, too. Initially, Renny tried dissuading me from becoming the Bandit and searching for my mother's brooch. When I made it clear to him I would not be deterred, he insisted on helping me, even though he knew better than anyone what I was up against. To be honest, though, I don't believe I could have done it without his assistance. And you and I never would have met."

"I'm glad you've had Renny at your side." His stare roved over the covering she held across her nudity, picturing the beauty of what he knew lie beneath. Then a question lifted his gaze. "What do you mean, he knew better than anyone what you were up against?"

"Renny was their driver that night."

"He was with your parents the night they were murdered?"

"He was. That night is going to haunt the poor man for the rest of his life."

Drew stroked his shaved jaw for a moment. "Why was Renny allowed to live? He could identify the killers."

"They were all dressed in black, and they wore hoods, the same as my Bandit's costume. It's where I got the idea. Not that their disguises mattered. They shot Renny anyway, once in the chest."

Dove frowned and took a breath before continuing. "He fell from his driver's perch. The hard landing broke his leg. It's why he walks with a slight limp now, more so when the weather is damp. He doesn't remember anything after being shot. They must have believed they'd killed him. They almost did. If a wagon of chimney sweeps hadn't come along, Renny would have died that night, too."

Dove paused to take in another shaky breath. After Drew bent to place a kiss on her forehead, she told him the rest.

"It's a true miracle Renny survived. No one thought he would. His injuries alone were serious enough to end his life, and then a fever nearly took him. For days he was delirious, when he was conscious at all. The priest had come, and the other servants took turns saying their final goodbyes. I stayed with him almost every minute. Tending to Renny was what kept me sane. At least with him, there was still hope, thin as it was."

Dove stopped talking and her face grew taught. Drew took her hand. A moment later, she continued. "At one point, he looked me straight in the eye. I watched him fade, Drew. He was so close to death, part of him was already gone."

"Dear God."

"When Renny was at last well enough to demand to know the fate of my parents, he was steeped in guilt because he hadn't been able to protect them. But there were three of them, all armed. The poor man hadn't stood a chance. He told us he'd shot one, though Renny said he was sure he just grazed his upper left arm. He said the man staggered back and fell, but stood up again."

"Did he hear any of their voices?"

"One man's voice. He didn't recognize it." Dove blinked and shook her head. "Drew, we both have to get back to the party."

Drew nodded. "You're right. We can't both go down at the same time."

"Of course. You go first. I won't be long behind you."

Drew snatched his trousers from the floor and slid in his legs. As he was buttoning his shirt, he said, "Are you...Are you all right?"

She gave him a low nod, a tad bit of shyness at such verbal intimacy. "Yes, I'm fine. I need a moment of privacy. I...I want to wash."

"You'll find everything you need over there," he said, nodding at the ceramic pitcher and basin on a washstand in the corner. A shelf below held fresh, folded towels.

After repining the brooch to his cloak, Drew said, "How do I look?"

"Thoroughly ravished," Dove answered, appearing far too pleased with herself.

Drew laughed out loud and combed his hair back with his hands. Before bending to give her a kiss, he said, "We're going to have a wonderful life together."

"Yes, I believe we are," she said, and then her joy faltered. She shifted a worried gaze toward the low fire at the hearth.

"What is it, Dove?" With a touch of his fingertips beneath her chin, he had her facing him again. "Tell me."

"I'm a little concerned about…"

"Yes?"

"About your family."

"My family? I don't understand."

"Drew, you know how certain people of the *ton* feel about mixed blood. My mother was a Shawnee Indian from the colonies. Anyone can look at me and see I am not quite like the other women. Your mother was pleasant enough in public, but what will your family think of you marrying me?"

"First, I love you're not like other women. And my mother will, too. What you saw down there was not a public display, that was my mother. She would not have invited you to tea if she didn't want you. I'm sure she finds you fascinating. As will my sister. They're both drawn to the uncommon, so your heritage plays in your favor and will serve to endear you to them. Second, you will soon come to learn my family, well, often treads in unusual waters." He chuckled. "Perhaps you are the one who will have second thoughts."

"What do you mean?"

Drew sat on the edge of the bed and stuffed his feet into his boots. "You were in my mother's chambers."

Dove gave him a thoughtful nod. "Stones on plates, a pile of orange powder, part of it burned, some odd weaving hung on the wall above her bed. What are those things?"

"My mother is very superstitious. She's always had a bit of the belief in her. It expanded in every direction after the death of my father. Each of those stones in her room represents some sort of luck or protection."

He nodded to his bedside table. A porcelain plate held a dull black, fist-sized stone.

"It's called infinite. It's supposed to protect me from illness. My sister has one next to her bed, too. I'm not sure about the orange powder, but the weaving with the yellow beads hanging on the wall over the head of her bed is supposed to catch evil spirits that might wander in whilst she sleeps, and disperse them to whence they came."

"My goodness."

"Yes. I've no doubt mother will find you nothing short of enchanting. If anything, I'll be praised for bringing you into the family. Did your mother pass on to you any stories of her people, of your heritage?"

"Yes, of course."

"Wonderful!" he said, laying a hand on her leg. "My mother and sister will be intrigued. I'll be lucky to get a minute alone with you. Ollie, Olivia, has an interest in all things mysterious. At present, it's horrid diseases."

Dove laughed. "Diseases?"

Drew laughed, too. He bent to say against her lips

163

before taking them in a kiss, "They will love you as much as I do."

Before the kiss was finished he was near to yanking off the clothes he'd just donned. With a significant amount of effort, he backed away and growled, "I think we'll spend the first year of our marriage in this very bed."

She giggled. "If you insist."

Drew stood tall beside the bed. "I'll come to your house tomorrow and speak with your grandfather."

****

Dove could swear the wood floors were made of puffy clouds as she made her way down the long, sconce-lit corridor not more than ten minutes after Drew. She was different. Her woman's body all but floated, her heart both light and full, and her future lay in wondrous miles ahead.

Perhaps it was foolish to believe the vows of such a known rake. She did believe him, though. Drew had requested her hand in marriage after they'd made love, not before. At the point of his declaration, he could have bid a fond farewell and called an end to a challenge. Instead, he promised her his love, his name, and his life.

As she neared the stairs, Dove patted her hair, pinned neat and back into place. Something wasn't…her hood! It would not do for her to claim she'd lost it, only to have the servants find a part of her costume in Drew's bedchambers. Or worse, his mother or sister might find it there. She rushed back to his room.

A slow inspection followed her initial quick scan. Dropping to the floor, she peered under the bed. She didn't spot so much as a single ball of dust. She ran a view of the floor again from her low position. Nothing. Climbing atop the bed, Dove rummaged through the mussed sheets. It wasn't there, either. She stood and gave another fruitless search to the room. Where could it have gone?

Then she remembered dropping it on the floor of Lady Worthington's chambers. If her Bandit's hood were to be found there in her private rooms, what followed would be nothing less than suspicion thriving on scandal. Spinning on the toes of her half boots, Dove hurried back to Drew's mother's room.

Her hood was indeed on the floor, the hem hooked on one of the horns of Drew's Viking hat and dangled like a limp, black flag. She'd have to leave his hat there, as carrying it down would risk setting the gossips all a twitter. When she saw him downstairs she would give him a discreet reminder as to where he'd left it.

Dove bent to snatch up her hood. When she straightened, something caught her eye. Something she hadn't seen when she'd searched the room earlier. A thin, braided string loop of purple. It poked out from beneath Lady Worthington's pillow, lying noticeable against the pure white of her bed linens. Just a string, likely no more than a remnant from a torn night rail.

Her attention shifted to the hood in her hand. A sudden sense of dread churned in her stomach and she wished she'd chosen another costume. The one she wore, her Bandit costume, had always been her cloak. But now it was as if she'd been taunting fate, and this night it endeavored to seize her.

Yes, with Lady Ashbury and Lord Beaumont in attendance, wearing it to the costume ball was a foolish and perilous act. However, the sick pit in her stomach throbbed to a new, worrisome fear.

Shooting a brief glance at the purple string, Dove's fingers tightened on the hood. She wished she could crush it to dust, erase it, go back in time and never have chosen to wear this costume for the party. If she hadn't worn it, she wouldn't have had the nerve to search this room and let a mere thread raise suspicion. She stared back at the string.

No, she was being irrational. For three years, she could see nothing bright in her future. Now that happiness was in sight, fear of losing it created doom where there was none. It was naught but a string, a silly purple string attached to nothing.

Spinning away from the bed to face the door, Dove stuffed the hood into the inside pocket of her coat. She wouldn't put it back on tonight. Perhaps she would never put it on again.

Most of the houses on her list were searched and crossed off, with no success. More like than not, the brooch was long gone, even dismantled. It was quite possible the stone had been removed and cut. Smaller gems would be easier to sell. It would also make it impossible to link them to the crime, lessening the chance of the villains getting caught. Renny had once made that argument when trying to convince her she was risking her neck for something she likely would never find.

Dove hadn't cared about risking her freedom, her future, or even her life. Little kept her grounded to this world anyway.

Her grandfather's mind was slipping at such an alarming rate, in another year or so he might not even know her name. As his manservant tended to him and his personal needs, grandfather called for Shettlyn more often than he did her. Grandmother was gone, her parents were gone. She tempered her grief in front of Renny so as not to upset the flutter of his heart. For the last three years, the only constant she'd had was anger and grief. But another door was opened to her now.

She would be one of the fortunate women, getting to marry for love, bearing children with a man of her own choosing instead of something arranged. If what Drew said was right, even his family would accept her. The world could be hers. Was she willing to risk everything life was offering to continue her mission, searching for nonexistent proof? No, she wasn't.

Her mother and father had loved her and lived for her happiness. Perhaps it was time to accept what she could not change. Her parents were gone, and could better rest in peace were she to settle into a happy marriage than go on the way she'd been. Renny would agree, and he'd be right.

With her search of Drew's mother's chambers, she'd cleared his family of any involvement. That would have to be enough. A fresh start in this world was offered to her, and she was going to take it. She all but flew out the bedchamber door.

Dove was several steps down the corridor before she stopped.

No. She'd already searched Lady Worthington's room. She'd already decided it would be her last. She took two more steps before stopping again, and pivoted back.

Since this was the Bandit's last night, and since she was marrying in to the family, if she didn't look, she would always wonder. Her entrance to this family would come without a sliver of a doubt. She trotted back to Lady Worthington's chambers.

Crossing the room to the bed, she pinched the loop of the braided string, and gave it a slight tug. Since she'd expected nothing more than a thread, the weight surprised her. And dread returned. It crept up her spine and wrapped around her throat. Dove did her best to ignore it. Fear. Baseless fear, that's all it was. She tugged again.

From beneath Lady Worthington's pillow slipped a velvet bag.

Like the string, it was purple, about the size of her hand. Painted on the bag were several white markings within a white circle. The markings, like the bag itself, were unfamiliar to her, so she spared them little more than a glance. Dove pried open the drawstring and tipped the bag. Into her palm slid her mother's brooch.

Her breath caught on an emotional hitch so thick she had to force her lungs to take in more air. The room could have shrunk, or spun, or grown ten times its size and flipped upside down for all her chaotic senses could tell. The world had changed in an instant, and it could never be right again.

In an effort to keep from succumbing to anguish, to the implications of finding it here in the Worthington household, Dove focused on the stone. The ruby shone clean, cared for. The bronze angel wings lay atop the stone and formed the ruby into a heart shape. The brooch was as she'd last seen it, hours before her parents were murdered.

She gazed at her mother's treasured jewel while the memories assaulted her. Her father, kissing her mother on the cheek simply because he was passing by. Her mother's beautiful voice as she sang at the pianoforte she'd practiced so hard to learn. Meals seasoned with laughter and shared stories. Two caskets blurring before her tear-drenched eyes as they were lowered into the ground in side by side graves.

Dove's fingers closed around the brooch her father designed and her mother so cherished. Her fist full of proof rose to bear down against her aching heart, as if the pressure could staunch the torturous flow.

"Dove?"

Her name from Drew's lips invaded her surge of memories. It beckoned her, but couldn't wrench her from the encompassing torrent, couldn't prod her voice into a response.

"I forgot my hat," Drew said. "That purple bag."

Of course, he was referring to the bag she'd dropped on the peach-colored counterpane. His voice had taken a different tone from his usual carefree self. One of unease. It pierced the love and tragedy dizzying her emotions, stirred into a frenzy by what she'd found, by what it meant.

Dove opened her eyes, releasing the tears gathered behind her lids. Through the blur, she made out Drew, standing in the doorway. She blinked. More warm tears glided down her face and her vision cleared. The pitying question in his gaze mingled with apprehension. He didn't ask it, and her voice was still too choked with emotion to speak.

"One of my mother's charm was in that purple bag," Drew finally said. He paused to swallow. "She's been sleeping with it under her pillow for some time now. I don't know for how long."

"Three years."

Drew shook his head. "You're mistaken. It's not your mother's brooch. You want so much to find it, perhaps-"

"Have you ever looked inside the bag?"

"No," Drew admitted. "My mother has so many charms and talismans, I long ago lost interest. Dove, it can't be the same brooch. Perhaps it's but similar."

Dove lowered her hand until it stretched out before her, and unfurled her fingers in a slow revelation. Drew shook his head, though with sagging vigor. He couldn't deny the truth, but he could refute the implication.

"My mother would never be a party to anything so horrid as murder, not for anything. It's not in her."

"Then how do you explain this!" Dove shouted, jabbing the evidence like the dagger of proof it was.

He approached her, staring at the pendent as if by will he might change the very specific design into something else. Denial drained from his gaze as he raised it to hers. An instant later, he glanced away. It appeared to her, he was giving himself a moment to think. Let him think. It wouldn't change the evidence. His mother had some form of involvement in the murder of her parents.

"I remember she told me it was a gift. It's supposed to keep nightmares away." Meeting her gaze, he said, "She doesn't know of its origin. I'd swear it on my life."

"Who gave it to her?" Dove asked. The pain in her voice boosted the accusation. She didn't care. Drew hadn't a part in the murder of her parents, but he knew who did. "Who gave my mother's brooch to your mother?"

"Dove…"

"Your mother's lover."

"My mother has had no lover since my father's death. She's been keeping company with a man, but only for the last few months."

"A relative, then."

Drew twisted his head away from her. He cursed low before facing her again.

"Tell me," Dove demanded. "Tell me who gave this to her. I have a right to know."

"She once mentioned her brother, my Uncle Charles, had given her a charm to chase away bad dreams. She said even its bag bore ritualistic symbols. She showed the bag to me." Nodding at the purple bag on the bed, he said, "That bag."

Dove folded her fingers over the brooch and shifted a slow glance at the bed. "Something she might sleep with under her pillow. That's where I found it."

"He didn't have anything to do with the murder of your parents. My uncle's reputation is stellar. He couldn't have known of its origin any more than my mother does."

"The crime was in the papers. It was all the talk for a long while. The brooch was described in detail, on numerous occasions."

"My mother doesn't read the papers. She doesn't even discuss the news much in her social circles if it's something terrible. She finds the whole of it too disturbing."

"And your uncle?"

Her question was answered in Drew's hesitation. "He could have purchased the brooch from a traveling vendor, one who cared naught from where he obtained his merchandise. Perhaps my uncle believed the piece was similar in style. A replica, even."

"A vendor would have sold a stolen piece elsewhere. Not in the very town where the crime was committed. Not where so many of London's elite, the people most able to afford such a piece as this, were aware of it."

Dove ran her thumb across the ruby. "And if it was a mere replica of this famous piece of jewelry, which it is not, a vendor would have said so to enhance the sale, and your uncle would not have had your mother hide it beneath her pillow. No, your uncle had to have known about it, perhaps taken part in the crime."

Drew rubbed a hand on the back of his neck. "Let me speak with him and try and straighten this out for us. Perhaps—"

"Perhaps nothing! Do you think I can't see which way the wind blows? He is your family, and you will defend him even if he outright confesses."

"That's not true."

"You stand here before me in denial and expect me to believe you would not turn a blind eye to your uncle's deeds, no matter the evidence against him?"

His eyes hardened, became flinty. "I expect you to trust me to do what's right."

"What's right for your family, you mean." Dove stormed by him on her way to the door. Drew grabbed her arm before she could pass. She yanked and twisted. His hold wasn't painful, but it was unyielding, as was her resistance.

"I should never have told you what I found," she spat. "Now you will alert your uncle, give him time to forge a viable lie, or make a clean escape."

"I'll allow him to do neither of those things. Stop thrashing about and listen to me. If my uncle was indeed involved in the murder of your parents…"

"Yes?" Dove stopped her struggles and held his gaze, daring him to do what was right, no matter the cost. Pain tightened his features. She didn't care. His anguish was nothing compared to hers.

"I'll take the situation in hand."

"How?" she demanded.

"I don't know. I'll think of something."

"Would the gallows be in your realm of possibilities?"

"Dove, try to understand. I can't let my mother suffer the scandal. And my sister, Ollie, has not even had her come-out yet. The gossips would be relentless. This would ruin her. Please, be reasonable."

She had met Olivia once, at a tea. The girl was kind to her. The last thing she wanted to do was cause harm to anybody, especially an innocent young girl. If it became known Olivia's uncle was guilty of murder, her chances of making a good match would indeed be obliterated.

However, Dove could not let her parents' murder go unavenged. Her mind on this matter had always been so clear, so irrefutable. Right was always on her side. Now, nothing she did would be all the way right, and any way this went, innocents suffered.

Drew's hands clasped her shoulders, strong, capable hands, drawing her in. She twisted away, but he wrapped his arms full around, holding her in place.

She shoved her curled hands against his chest. She might as well have been shoving at a wall. Dove twisted in his arms, anger and frustration boiling over.

173

"Let go of me!"

Drew tightened his grip, desperation tinged the hard pitch of his voice. "No. Not until you listen to reason. Trust this to me, Dove."

The crushing weight of her despair urged her to give in to Drew's comforting arms, to let him take her burden and see to its end. For three years, it had constrained every aspect of her life. Three lonesome years. Her grandfather's mind was childlike, when he was there at all. Renny was with her, but his heart condition kept her from burdening him. It was so tempting to let Drew take on this responsibility. Too tempting.

No, she couldn't. She wouldn't. It was too much trust to hand over to a man with divided loyalties. And she would not allow the injustice to continue one second past what she could help. It was already so very far overdue.

Dove twisted, yanking from Drew's grip and strode to the door.

"Where are you going?" he asked.

"I'm going to kill your uncle, now."

Before she could set foot outside the room, Drew grabbed her by the waist and hauled her back in. He shouldered the door shut, spun her around, and pinned her against the door with his body.

She fought him using every scrap of might she could muster. "Stop using your size and strength to bully me!"

"I'm not bullying you. I'm protecting you."

"You're protecting your family, not me!" She kicked at him, but he was ahead of her, and entwined her legs within his.

"Dove, you're not thinking straight. If you go down there and commit murder, you'll be ruining countless lives, including your own."

Dove's fists tightened. She would kill Drew, too, if she had to in order gain retribution for her parents. It had been her whole focus, her every thought, her every breath.

Her legs were trapped, but her lower arms were free enough to pound her fury against his chest.

Drew didn't stop her. He spoke, something kind, she assumed from his tone. All she could hear were her own strangled cries and the roar of reckoning in her head. She would have her vengeance. All else be damned!

The tips of the bronze angel wings clutched in her hand dug into her palm, poked through her skin. A trickle of blood ran down her wrist and into the long, black sleeve of her shirt, a warm, crimson statement on what she would become. A killer. No, not a killer, an avenger.

She fought harder against him. One leg slipped free and Dove kicked as she slammed her fists wherever she could strike him. Drew took it, all her anger, her frustration, three years of restraint let loose. Her verve raged on until exhaustion descended upon her.

Dove wilted, gulping elusive breaths. She held loose, weary fists against his solid chest. In part, to keep steady. More so, though, to keep some semblance of distance between her and the luring comfort of his embrace.

"Dove, look at me."

When she raised her eyes to meet the amber depths of his, he said, "You would do your parents a further injustice going down there and killing him. Granted, I never met them, but I know the love and kindness they created in you. They must have been very special people to raise a woman such as yourself. If you go and commit a public execution, you'll disgrace their memory. I'll help you get justice for them, Dove. I promise I'll find a way. At least give what I've said a moment's thought."

As much as she wanted to ignore Drew's words, her defenses were too worn, her emotions too raw. Besides, he was right, damn him. Her parents wouldn't want her to do such a thing, to ruin her life, the lives of innocents. But they were murdered! No solution was pure. Every choice ended in more suffering and loss.

The weight of her burden tipped her head until it fell against Drew's chest. Clutching fistfuls of his cloak, she fell against him and gave into the last emotion she had left this night, and wept.

Drew wrapped her in his arms. He was warm and strong, and she let him hold all of her.

When at last her tears subsided, he kissed the top of her head, and Dove raised her watery gaze. The same tormented love churning her insides dwelt in the dimmed amber of his eyes. He *did* care for her. It showed in his empathy, in his willingness to carry her pain. It was in the clutch of his hand at her back, the tautness of his body. This situation was terrible for him, too.

Drew rubbed a slow circle on her back. "I'll see to this matter. I promise you. Please, Dove, trust me."

Had her mind and body not been so depleted, if her heart hadn't already belonged to this man, she might have responded with different words. She might have walked out and done what she always knew she would do when she discovered anyone who had anything to do with that terrible, murderous night. But would-haves shuffled behind reality when faced with a plea and a promise from the man she loved.

"I will trust you," she said. For the first time since that horrible night three years ago, Dove allowed someone else to carry her misery.

She would give him time to find a solution. She'd waited this long. A little more time wouldn't make a difference. While Dove believed Drew's mother hadn't a part in the murders, his uncle, at the very least, had information. He'd had his hands on the brooch during the brief time between her parents' death and Lady Worthington's possession of the piece.

If Drew failed, however, she would reclaim the matter and do as she'd always intended. She would kill the man. Discreetly, though, not in a public forum where she would give validation to those who believed her mother a savage, and her father a blind fool for marrying her. She would not dishonor them so.

But no matter how the tragedy played out, the future Dove saw less than an hour ago was gone. Drew's family had torn hers apart. This moment of faith was not a preamble for years of love and trust to come. It was a noble farewell.

Chapter 14

The chill breeze did nothing to cool Drew's temper.

Beneath a ceiling of low-lying pewter clouds, the afternoon rang with pounding hammers, the rough sawing of boards, the clanking arrival of a freight wagon loaded with more supplies, shouts, as well as a few laughs from the twenty or so men working to build the new foundling home. The framework was almost complete. Construction was moving along at a smooth and steady pace and was expected to be ready for the children in a few more weeks.

On any other day, Drew was the first to throw out a jest or a bawdy joke to rouse laughter from the other men. Today, he at most mumbled a distant greeting as he stalked past them. The dour expression no doubt stamped upon his face was enough to keep the men from striking up any banter with him. He paid less than scant attention to the murmurs at his back.

Drew pounded another nail, imagining the head of the nail was the blasted head of his Uncle Charles.

He'd endured a galling, futile wait at his uncle's townhouse this morning, having been told by the perplexed butler his uncle was sure to return at any moment for their arranged meeting. For three quarters of an hour, Drew had paced the small study with growing tension and shrinking patience.

Had Charles suspicions about the nature of this meeting? Perhaps the grim glances he couldn't help but slant his uncle's way during the remainder of the costume party were not as surreptitious as he'd thought.

They'd exchanged several missives, via one of Drew's footmen. It had taken him two days to pin down Charles on a time. His uncle had claimed a variety of reasons why they couldn't meet. Or, as Drew now believed, excuses. Once Drew made it clear in his final note he would be on his uncle's doorstep this morning, and Charles had best be there to meet him as it was a matter of great urgency, his uncle agreed.

Not only was the man not in residence upon Drew's arrival at the designated time, but he'd left no message explaining his absence, or to say when he would return. The haughty butler deposited him to his uncle's stark study before spinning on a stiff, polished heel and disappearing. Drew bided the unwelcome rudeness of both his uncle and his uncle's butler in a festering stew.

During his wait, Drew couldn't help but notice the black coat, part of the Bandit costume Charles had worn to the masquerade, hanging on the coat rack in the corner of the study. He'd paused in his pacing more than once to stare at the damned thing. Could his uncle have taken part in the murder of Dove's parents, wearing this very coat?

Drew's stomach roiled at the thought. He paced some more.

Due to the overcast day, just a modicum of light crept through the single, unadorned window. Dark-paneled walls gave a sense the small room was even smaller. A watercolor hung behind the simple, oak desk, Hyde Park on a sunny, Spring day. His mother had gifted the painting to him years ago. The single, pleasant decorative item in sight, with its whimsical feel and vivid colors, stood out in the dour room like daisy in a mud puddle.

Papers sat in a short, neat stack at the left edge of the desk. A plain, black inkwell perched on the upper right of the blotter. The oval rug on the floor was thin, but not frayed. Drew soon had the brown and gray checkerboard pattern memorized.

He stopped before the coatrack again. The question dogged him every time he passed it, this article of clothing poking at the corner of his eye.

With a twinge of dread twisting his gut, Drew lifted the sleeve of the cropped riding coat. The garment was not something his uncle would wear, as the man didn't ride. In his youth, he'd suffered several broken bones when a horse threw him, and gained a lifelong fear of the saddle. If Charles had to go somewhere, he either walked or took a carriage.

A speck of hope used logic to pry its way into Drew's brain. The men who'd attacked the Barrows' had all been on horseback. It couldn't have been his uncle with those other two men. Or, could Charles's fear of riding be a clever ruse?

Drew inspected the fabric. It was not well-worn, which would support his uncle's certain claim he'd purchased it for the sole purpose of his costume. One of the elbows, however, bore a scraped patch, as if he'd taken a spill and slid along the ground.

Had his uncle fallen while wearing his new coat, perhaps sometime after he'd left the costume ball? Charles never drank enough to tumble so far in his cups to lose his balance. Of course, he could have stumbled and fell. It happened.

Recalling something Dove had told him about the night of the murders, Drew ran his fingers up the right sleeve of the coat. Then he did the same for the left. Near the top outside of the sleeve he found the damning threads. He carried the coat to the window for a better look, hoping he was wrong. He wasn't. A short line of stitching closed a tear in the upper arm. It was in the exact place where Renny said he'd shot one of the men who attacked Dove's parents.

Leaning on his shoulder, Drew sagged against the dark-paneled wall. His gaze darted about the small study without seeing any of it. An ache pounded against his skull as the room closed in on him. This evidence, combined with the brooch he'd had in his possession right after the crime, could not be excused away. His uncle was a killer.

Why? Why would Charles do such a thing? And what could Drew ever say to Dove? He wondered if, once she gained this further confirmation, she would go through with her threat to kill Charles. Drew didn't believe such a cold-blooded act was in her nature. Regardless of her declaration, Dove was a benevolent soul. But rage and grief were a mighty toxic combination, with potency enough to poison even the purest waters.

From the doorway, James, his uncle's stick-thin, pompous butler said, "Would you care for some tea while you wait, milord, or perhaps something more…" With a quick sniff and a trace of disdain, he finished his sentence. "Indulgent."

The offer was proper etiquette on behalf of his

absent master, not the due civility toward his master's guest. James had developed a magnificent talent for managing simultaneous acts of dutiful decorum and condescension.

While it should have bothered him from the first, enough to put the man in his place long ago, Drew had never spared the lack of respect so much as a tick. It consumed him now. Perhaps it was because Charles wasn't there to accept his wrath, and James was. At present, the foolish butler was goading a beast in a paper cage.

"Where is my uncle?" Drew all but shouted the angry demand at the man as he jerked upright from his slump. Rage and frustration exuded a deliberate threat in his hard, directed glare. Drew claimed a small bit of satisfaction when the butler paled at his drastic change of demeanor. "I demand you tell me this instant."

James's narrow fingers tugged against the bottom of his pristine white waistcoat. His chin raised, however, his insolent tone wavered in the face of fury where Drew had never seen anything but nonchalance. "My lord does not inform me of his every move, sir."

Perhaps it was the truth, perhaps not. It didn't matter. He was going to have to postpone confronting his uncle. However, he could no longer stay here and wait. If he spent another minute pacing the confines of the room, he'd tear it apart with his bare hands.

James was forced to take a hasty step back when Drew marched toward the study door. Drew stopped sudden, whirled around and stomped back to the desk. He shoved a hand in his pocket and whipped out the small purple bag with the white markings, the one that for three years held Dove's mother's brooch. He slapped it down in the center of the desk before storming out of the house.

Drew would return after dining with his mother and sister, and have a full explanation if he had to beat it out of his uncle. A scenario he more than half hoped for. In the meantime, he had to expend some energy. Working on the new foundling home was just what he needed. And so here he knelt, pounding another nail to within an inch of its life.

"Slow down, Drew. You're making the rest of us look bad."

Hammer held high, staring at a nail already well-pounded, Drew glanced up at his friend. Like him, Burke Darington was dressed as the hired hands, in serviceable trousers and a simple lawn shirt. Their clothing and work boots were brushed with sawdust. Burke's shirt had a tear at the hem.

They were two of the very few members of the gentry who enjoyed dirtying their hands and the physical exertion of working for something meaningful. And it did feel good, doing more for the worthy cause than signing his name to a bank draught.

"Of course, when Durham notices you over here," Burke continued as he motioned with his head to the right. His voice held more than a touch of humor. "You might want to keep hold of that hammer."

Drew followed Burke's line of sight. Lord Derek Durham was assisting two other men as they unloaded boards from a freight wagon. The dark bruise smudging Durham's cheekbone was visible even from this distance.

Having honed his boxing skills for years at Gentleman Jackson's, and at present filled with unexpended fury, Drew held definite advantage should Derek have a notion for some fisticuffs. Of course, Derek was the injured party, and had a fair portion of his dignity to reclaim. The man was close to Drew's size and strength. If Derek should decide to retaliate for the clouting Drew had given him, it wouldn't be an easy fight for either one of them.

Drew glanced at Burke. In an instant, he faced his work again, as he cared naught to see Burke surrender in his feeble effort to restrain his mirth. The nail was already embedded, deep. He gave it another pound anyway.

After a chuckle, Burke said, "You punched him clear off a terrace, as I heard it."

Drew twisted his head toward his friend. "You of all people should know better than to be swayed by gossip." Before Rose was his wife, she'd been accused of a horrid crime. It was an awful time for them both. Believing the worst of her had almost cost Burke the best thing that ever happened to him in his entire life.

Burke conceded with a nod. "Right you are. But this bit of gossip is supported by Durham's black eye, as well as a few scratches from your shrubberies."

"Yes, well, as it happens, it's true," Drew said. "A simple misunderstanding. I'm sure Derek has already forgiven me."

A small, self-deprecating smirk tugged on Drew's face at the memory of Durham in his wizard costume, flying backward over the balustrade. It *had* been quite a sight. No wonder the events of the evening were in circulation. It was too juicy a tale to keep contained.

If the story had spread to Burke's ears, it had without doubt spread throughout the *ton*. All parties involved would have to laugh off the incident, lest the gossips make any more of it. He didn't know about Durham laughing it off, but it would be easy enough for Drew. The memory of a back-flipping wizard would always give him a grin.

Then, the intrusion of wrenching heartbreak wiped away every trace of humor.

Drew let go of his hammer, his fingers releasing the tool a few inches from the ground. It landed in the dirt with a soft thud. He breathed in deep the warm smell of sawdust. In a slow, straightening move, he stood upright before his friend. Drew's face must have given sign to the troubles roiling inside. Burke's expression switched from prodding humor to serious in but a second's time.

"Drew," Burke said, surprise evident in his voice. "There's more to this than a misunderstanding between you and Durham. I've never seen you look so…miserable."

The simple reason was because he'd never been so miserable. For a flash, Drew wished he'd never met Dove, wished he could go back to his carefree ways. Wished his heart would lose all entanglements. No, no, none of that was even close to true.

His life before Dove had been vacuous, void of meaning and depth. Even the pleasures, in retrospect, had begun to lose their luster, had in fact become dangerous in the reckless rile of his amusements. Amusements now absent of any appeal. And during his long disregard for honor, the losses he'd paid for his larking about had mounted.

How much laughter had he relinquished at the table with his sister and mother, precious moments he could never recoup? Even when attending the same gatherings, he spared the two of them little more than polite exchanges on his way to something he found more enticing. He'd taken for granted what few loved ones he had left.

Soon Ollie would be grown and married. Perhaps, once his sister was settled into a home of her own, his mother might remarry. Lord Sanguay had come to tea at least twice over the past couple of weeks, and had escorted his mother to the opera one evening. His mother's volume of joy always rose when Lord Sanguay was due to arrive. Yes, perhaps she would indeed remarry.

How much time did he have left of just the three of them before the opportunities for making these memories were gone? Not much, not enough, as life marched on whether you're paying attention to it or not. If it wasn't for Dove, he would not have heard the ticking clock until it was too late.

Scrutinizing his life through a lens of brutal honesty, Drew could not deny he wasn't far off from becoming a softened wastrel, a cork-brained millstone fastened around the neck of his family. Bookmakers had a more familiar relationship with him than his mother and sister. As things were, his future held a profound loneliness he cared naught to contemplate. If Dove hadn't risked her life to save his, he wouldn't even *have* a future.

One smile from her made his heart sing. The very idea he may have seen the last of Dove's smiles, might never again enjoy the experience of teasing her into her musical laughter, made Drew ache to the very depths of his soul.

"Come on," Burke said. "Let's take a walk."

Both men were silent as they left the construction site and blended into the surrounding woods. For a while they walked at a slow pace about the birch and oak trees, and scatterings of scrubby underbrush. Leaves dappled the cloud-dimmed sunlight.

Every so often, one of them stepped on a thin twig, causing it to snap. The sounds of construction dulled with distance and the chirp of birds took its place. Except for the sounds made by their boot steps, Drew and Burke remained quiet.

The men slowed. The trees thinned out, making a gradual break into a clearing. Burke leaned against an ancient oak. Drew shuffled about and suffered through several false starts, as the enormity of his troubles hefted their weight upon his voice. His friend waited with patience.

Drew glanced at Burke. The man was indeed his friend. Drew had been there through Burke's troubles, had seen the man at his lowest point, and stood by him. If there was anyone in this world he could trust with the secrets he held inside him, it was Burke Darington. And if there was ever a time in his life when he needed a friend, it was now.

"Burke," Drew started. "Some things have happened."

"Some things having to do with Lady Dove Barrow?"

Drew stopped beside a cluster of slim, white-barked birch trees. Did Burke know of Dove's secret identity, of what they'd been doing? No, he couldn't. Perhaps he believed it was no more than a simple matter of the heart, a quarrel between sweethearts.

Were it only so.

"How did you know my troubles have anything to do with Dove?" Drew asked.

Burke sighed, and looked at Drew with eyes that had seen much, and knew much. "Because you look the way I must have when I thought I'd lost Rose."

With a sad smile to accompany his nod, Drew said, "Yes, I suppose I do."

Drew remembered seeing his friend in utter agony. Burke was as strong and unshakable as any man Drew had ever known. Yet, the turmoil in his heart during those dark times had hurled him into near madness.

Burke took two steps and clasped a hand on Drew's shoulder. With a steady gaze, he said, "You were my friend when I needed one. I'm yours now." Standing back, Burke asked, "What has you so troubled? Maybe there's something I can do to help."

Drew huffed out a breath. He glanced around at the quiet woods. A bird fluttered somewhere in the leaves. A squirrel had stopped several yards away. It was raised up on its small haunches, holding still and staring at them with alert eyes. After a moment, it scurried away, and Drew brought his attention back to his friend.

"I'm not sure where to start."

"I've always found the beginning to be a good jumping off point."

A broad shaft of sunlight broke through the clouds and into the clearing, opening a space between the two men. Burke leaned back against the oak and waited.

"Like all of London," Drew said after short pause that ended in a firm decision. "I'm sure you're familiar with all the gossip about the Creeping Bandit."

"Of course. He's caused quite the uproar amongst

the *ton*. In fact, just yesterday Rose and I were discussing..." Burke's expression sharpened. "Drew, don't tell me *you're* the Creeping Bandit."

Drew's sudden, airy chuckle was full of self-mockery. "No," he said, meeting his friend's wary gaze. "I'm the Bandit's assistant."

Burke took two steps to sink down upon a large rock, his elbows on his knees and gaped up at Drew as if he were a new life form never seen by a human eye. After a good stare, he said, "I'm listening."

By the time the two men walked out of the woods, Lord Burke Darington, third Earl of Blackwood, knew the whole story. From Drew's first meeting with the Bandit in Lady Beaumont's bedchambers, and how Dove had saved his life, to this morning's finding of the bullet-grazed coat in his uncle's study. What was more, Burke was ready to help.

The two men were still discussing options when they exited the woods and stepped back into the construction site. A raised commotion of movement and voices gained their attention. Men were dropping their tools, running toward horses and wagons, the foreman shouting instructions, other voices sharp with alarm.

Drew grabbed hold of one of the younger workers as he ran toward the supply wagon, already filled with men.

"What's happened?" Drew asked.

The young man pointed toward the eastern sky. Dark smoke billowed into the clouds, a mass of it, blotting out the sky with its density.

"A rider just told us. It's the foundling home, sir. It's on fire!"

"Rose is there today," Burke said from beside him,

terror freezing him for a moment. "Dove is with her."

The two men were on their horses and racing down the street before the wagon full of men got to a good roll.

Chapter 15

When Drew and Burke leapt from their horses at the edge of the frenzied crowd, the fire was thriving, and not long from claiming victory.

Black smoke bulged and billowed in great huffing expulsions from two of the upper windows of the two-story foundling home around robust blades of flames. What portion of the roof they could see was ablaze. Some of the stones from the walls had already collapsed at the upper east corner of the building, as the wooden support beams were burned away and the fire had weakened the ancient mortar.

The charred air was so rough it scratched their throats and took up too much space in their lungs. Its unnatural density gritty and painful. Getting a sufficient breath was difficult, as smoke vanquished dwindling scraps of clean air. And they hadn't yet gone through the front gate and into the courtyard of the doomed home.

A score of men had formed a line and were passing buckets full of sloshing water down the row, through the open gate, and to the fire. They were fast and efficient, but their efforts were near to fruitless. The building was not far off from its final throes.

"I don't see Dove anywhere!" Drew shouted over the fire's chomping roar and the human shouts of chaos around them.

Like Drew, Burke's gaze scanned and rescanned the crowd. "Rose, either!"

A skinny, frazzled young woman ran over to them. Terror shone bright in the whites of her eyes, accentuated by the surrounding skin darkened with soot and panic.

"Hester," Burke said when she stopped in front of them.

She answered Burke's question before he could ask it. "They're inside, both Rose and Dove! One of the girls, Ellen, didn't make it out. They ran back in to get her."

The two men sprinted past children who sat in the street outside the gate, coughing, weeping. One little boy cried into the smoke-stained fur of a panting dog. They plunged into the black and orange inferno without a second thought.

In the great room, a wooden chair lay tipped on its back engulfed in flames a few feet away from several other chairs, still standing around a table and untouched by the fire. Half a dozen or so long tables with chairs took up a good portion of the large room. They too had not yet caught fire. Debris from a hasty exit was strewn about the floor, a shoe, a rag doll, a carved wooden horse, among other things.

The low flames in the hearth were well contained within their bricks. Down here, the only thing ablaze outside the hearth was the single chair. The fire must have started upstairs, as it was just beginning to catch on the first floor. The fiery beast roared above them, though, and would not be long in its consumption.

He and Burke split up and ran through the downstairs rooms calling for Dove, Rose, and Ellen.

They dashed back into the main hall at the same time, having failed to find any of them. Drew glanced again at the debris on the floor. Something was…odd, not right. However, with Dove, Rose, and Ellen still missing, there wasn't time to reason it out.

Through the vicious snapping of flames and splintering timbers, rang Burke's desperate shouts. None were answered.

A broad length of flaming ceiling beam broke loose and crashed onto the stairs. It bounced once, flipping over and down, before landing on the floor near where they stood. With a resounding crack, it snapped in half and released a million orange and yellow-red sparks in a furious burst of brutal heat. The men leapt back, shielding their faces with their arms.

"They have to be upstairs," Drew shouted.

At the first landing, where smoke was already thickening, Burke said, "Get down on your hands and knees."

Three more steps up and both men were coughing. They took out their handkerchiefs and pressed them to their mouths. It helped no more than a little. Drew shot a watery-eyed glance upward. Intense heat and smoke foreshadowed what was coming, blackening some of the wood-paneled walls ahead of the fire.

Dear God, they're somewhere up there.

Drew's terror strove to overwhelm him. If something were to happen to Dove… The frantic pounding of his heart impelled him to move.

Drew and Burke called out as they crawled up the stairs. The inferno crackled louder, grew hotter, scorching their skin, their eyes, their lungs. Several times the men had to pat out glow-red embers landing on their clothes. They didn't retreat. They continued to crawl upward, calling the names of the women they loved.

Close to the top of the stairs, Dove answered him.

"Keep shouting, Dove!" Drew yelled, and then coughed out smoke and soot. "I'll find you!"

Seconds later, he did. She and Rose, coughing, clinging to each other, scurried low past the banister at the top of the stairs. Flames blazed across the wooden handrail running along the narrow corridor, catching on the rail going down.

Drew gathered Dove in his arms and covered her nose and mouth with his handkerchief. Burke did the same for Rose. Before wrapping his other arm around his wife, Burke let his hand pause on the slight protrusion of her belly where their second child grew.

"Come on!" Burke shouted. "We have to get out of here, now!"

"We haven't found Ellen," Dove said.

Without hesitation, Drew faced Burke in the mounting smoke, "Get them out of here. I'll find the girl."

"I'm going with you," Dove and Burke said at the same time.

Drew's answer was immediate. "No. You've both got a family that needs you."

No one needed Drew. If he died in this building today, no one's life would change much. This was the second time death mocked him with the punishing fact. If he survived this, he vowed, sparing a bare second to lay his cheek upon Dove's head, it would be the last.

"I'm not leaving you," Dove cried, surprising, pleasing, and terrifying him, all at the same time.

Drew clasped her face and kissed her, quick and hard as the bellowing flames crept toward them. A loud, frightening shift in the roof spat sparks and small balls of flame down on them. The shoulder of Dove's gown caught a tiny flare. Drew patted it out and shot Burke a hard glance and nod. It was all the explanation his friend needed. Drew shoved Dove into Burke.

Burke latched his arms around the two women. Dove struggled, but she was no match for his strength. She cried out once, the word 'no' penetrated the fire's crackling tumult. Her worry for him wrenched his heart as she disappeared. He hoped he lived long enough to prove himself worthy of it.

He spun around as malignant smoke chased the three of them down the stairs, death's emissary thwarted, this time.

Drew rushed to search what he could of the upstairs, the fire endeavoring to shrink his options, feasting on everything combustible.

Some of the rooms so blustered with frenzied flames and its fatal offspring of black smoke, he could scarce see a thing beyond the doorways. Even from his place low on the floor, Drew could not enter. He hoped the girl was not in one of those. If she was, no one could save her now.

He crawled through two rooms the opposite direction from which the women had come, before he found the young girl of about thirteen or fourteen-years-old. She was sprawled on her back across the floor, unconscious, a thin trickle of blood running down the side of her head. The poor girl must have fallen in her terrified haste to get out.

The linens on all four of the narrow beds were

afire, as were the humble cloth curtains. On a rack against the wall hung several simple dresses. They too were burning.

The girl coughed once but did not open her eyes. Drew scooped her up in his arms as something in the pocket of one of the hanging dresses popped and expulsed an extra flame. Smoke watered his eyes, and burned in his nostrils, his throat, and his lungs.

A loud, ominous crack yanked his attention toward the roof. Drew enfolded the girl as close to his body as he could and rushed from the room to the stairs.

He was on the landing, almost there, close enough for his burning eyes to catch flashes of the outside through the opening of the front door, when, with a vicious snap, a chunk of the ceiling gave way. By the time he saw it falling, it was too late.

It swung down and struck him on the back hard enough to throw him forward. He landed face down on the stairs. The debris weighed enough to trap him there.

The girl was still unconscious in his arms, protected beneath him, as he struggled against the heavy wreckage.

In hopes of loosening the trappings enough to crawl out, Drew hunched his back. There was a bare hint of flexibility. He slipped his arms from beneath Ellen, placed his hands on the step, and shoved up harder. Its weight was too substantial.

In desperation, Drew thrust upward again, straining, pushing, giving it every bit of his effort. The rubble shifted a little bit.

He collapsed, holding his weight on his elbows so he wouldn't crush the girl. After huffing out a thick cough, Drew tried again, heaving upward with all his strength. In an instant, the unconscious girl slid down quick from beneath him.

He managed to grab her leg with one hand, but the debris shifted again. Part of it crowded down on his shoulder. The bulk of fallen roof weighed more than he'd thought, and in its movement, became a crushing encumbrance. The way he was now trapped, he couldn't stretch his other arm far enough to grab her with both hands. Nor could he get any leverage.

A thin, flaming piece of timber dropped and landed on one of her legs where her skirt had ridden up to expose bare skin. Drew swatted it off before it could burn her with any severity. However, in that instant when he didn't have hold of her, she slid farther down the stairs. He lashed out his arm. All he could grab was her foot.

He squeezed his fingers, but her shoe loosened and was slipping from her foot. At the bottom of the stairs lay the flaming remains of the board that had fallen near him and Burke earlier. It had set the wooden steps near the banister afire. Should she slide down those last few steps, the blazing hunk of rafter was in her direct path.

Drew struggled to free himself, and at the same time, to not lose his grip on the girl.

Using the one arm trapped beneath, he made the best use of what little leverage he had. The debris gave a scarce hint of movement. He needed the strength of both arms if he had any chance at all, but he couldn't let go, not even for a second. If he did, the girl would plummet straight into a fiery death.

Drew wrested in helpless anguish as Ellen's heel popped from the back of her shoe.

"Ellen!" he shouted. "Ellen, wake up!" Her eyes

fluttered. She coughed and her eyelids lifted. A bare second later, they closed again.

"Ellen!"

Sweat dripped into his eye, stinging where he already burned to near blindness. A coughing fit racked his body for several seconds. He tightened his damp grip, yet her foot slipped farther.

"Let go!" a man's voice shouted. "I've got her."

Drew raised his head enough to see Derek Durham gathering the girl in his arms. He let go of Ellen's foot. Derek hefted Ellen and handed her to Burke, who emerged from the thickening smoke. Burke then passed the girl to someone else. Was that Renny? Yes, it was.

Renny took the girl and in an instant, disappeared down the stairs. Burke and Derek worked to lift the heavy chunk of roofing off Drew. The men sweated and heaved through their coughs, then altered their positions. A quick series of three thunderous cracks resounded from above, followed by one long, piercing creak.

"It's no use. Get out, while you still can," Drew told the men as it became clear all three of them would die if Burke and Derek stayed another minute.

"Save yourselves. Go!" Drew shouted again when the men wouldn't leave, the last word more cough than voice.

But he wanted to live. He wanted to make things right with Dove, right with his family, right with his life. He wanted to watch his progeny grow, to leave behind more in his life's wake than a vague memory of distant pleasures in the minds of women who had loved him with their bodies, but had no room for him in their hearts.

Then Dove was there, helping the men with all the might she could summon from her slender arms, and his panic soared through the burning roof. His life had been pointless. Her life was everything.

"Get out of here, Dove, go, now! Burke, Derek, get her out of here!"

All three of them ignored his commands and continued their straining efforts to free him.

A length of ceiling beam engulfed in blaze crashed on the landing right behind him. It broke in half and produced a bellowing *whoosh*. Flames expelling horrendous heat burst from its hellfire core. Drew was sure the soles of his boots were melting.

The reverberating cracks from above, spitting down sparks and flaming rain, was a portentous promise of more to come, and soon.

An ember dropped on his calf and burned through his pant leg. Drew gritted his teeth and kicked as much as he could until he shook it off. The fire was surrounding them, closing in at an alarming pace. A narrow path at the bottom of the stairs between the wall and the blazing debris was the last slim means of escape. With the fire's voracious appetite already consuming the handrail and part of the steps below, time had run out.

Drew pounded a fist. "Get her out of here!"

Perspiration ran tracks down Burke's sooty temples as he heaved and strained along with Derek and Dove. Hard coughs racked all of them now, with minimal respites in between.

"We've almost got you out," Derek said through his laboring efforts.

As they shifted the debris, a fire-hot ember broke

away and landed on Drew's back. He cried out in pain as it burned through his shirt and seared his skin. By arching up and twisting, he managed to scrape it off against his trappings.

A series of hard crashes on the floor above made them all jump. Stones from the wall. The building was falling apart, and still, the three of them refused to leave him and save their own lives. "Damn you, Burke, get out of here. *Get her out, now!*"

"I'm not leaving you!" Dove cried.

Not mere words, not empty passages of dramatic prose, or half-hearted sentiments as he had so often used to get what he wanted. She didn't have any ulterior agendas. He had her heart. That was the whole of it. Dove remained in this blazing deathtrap working as hard as the men, risking her very life, because he had her heart as much as she had his.

Drew swore to the powers of fate and destiny his faithful servitude to this woman and to forsake all the meaningless pursuits of his past. *Just give me the chance.* Oh, how he wanted to live!

"From this side!" Burke shouted to Derek.

Derek rounded Drew to stand on the same side as Burke, and together the men shifted the smoldering hunk of roof beam to a slight lean. Dove crouched down, grabbed Drew's arms. and let him hold onto her for leverage. With Drew using his feet to shove against the steps, he slipped free. As soon as he stood, Dove and the men slapped at Drew's back to extinguish several small, smoldering patches.

Drew shot a quick upward glance from his place on the staircase where he had an unobstructed view of the second-floor ceiling. The fire was finishing off what was left of the supports. At any moment, the entire roof was going to come down.

A crash, followed by several more, pounded the floor above. Stones from the wall crashing onto the second floor as the mortar weakened. The fire livened and roared with impending victory. More cracking, another crash, this one hard enough to rattle the floor above them. The walls were caving in.

Dove and Drew raced down the last steps just ahead of Burke. Derek was right behind Burke. They rushed out the front door, coughing, singed, and ever grateful for their escape.

They embraced gratitude a moment too soon.

The wooden awning over the front door had caught fire above the chain-hung sign reading 'Foundling Home' in white paint, now blackening in the fire's assault. The flaming board holding the sign let out one terrible snap. Derek, the last of them to leave the building, looked up just as the board swung down in a hard drop. Derek cried out when the heavy sign struck him across the face and knocked him to the ground.

The back of his head slammed onto the concrete stoop. Derek's eyes rolled back before closing.

"Stay back," Drew shouted to Dove before rushing back, Burke with him. Drew flung away the sign, and his stomach roiled at the sight.

The edge of the sign had cut a long gash across the left side of Derek's cheek. In fact, it had cut all the way through, the bleeding gape wide enough to see the inside of his mouth. The chain had been so hot, it burned into the skin below the cut. Extensive scarring on a face so many women had pined for was imminent and would be horrible. The man's life was about to undergo a drastic change.

Burke pressed his handkerchief across the wound. Drew and Burke hefted Derek away just as the mortar around the upper stones had had enough. The building was collapsing.

As more stones gave way, plummeting inward as well as out, the crowd scurried farther back. Even the men with their water buckets had to concede their loss and retreat to the outside of the wall.

As they all coughed the smoke from their lungs, Drew and Renny helped Burke get Derek and Ellen into the Darington's fine carriage, the one Rose and Dove had used to get there. The Darington's driver was nowhere to be seen, probably searching the crowd for the women in his charge. So Renny took the reins and rushed them off to get needed medical attention.

Ellen had regained semi-consciousness as they were lifting her into the carriage and, while coughing and rather confused, didn't appear to suffer any permanent damage. Once she was settled into her seat, she mumbled something about 'the man'.

"He's right here," Burke told her, nodding toward Drew who stood at the open door of the carriage. "He's the man who saved your life."

Her head wobbled Drew's way. Her line of sight passed by him. Then, Ellen's dazed eyes returned. With her head wound, Drew figured, she was having difficulty focusing. She must be having trouble thinking, too, as she appeared somewhat puzzled.

"Rest now," Rose told her. She knelt on the floor of the carriage, helping Ellen get settled in. The girl lay her head back against the squabs. She remained awake, but her bewildered expression did not abate.

Derek lay unconscious, slumped in the corner of the seat opposite Ellen. A bloody cloth laid across his ruined face. Drew had no doubt the man would live, but he would bear horrific scars of this day, and be forever disfigured.

Burke helped Rose exit the carriage. Instead of looking back to what she couldn't help, Rose took to organizing. Burke did the same. The two spoke to each other for a minute or so. Then, walking in different directions, put whatever plan they had devised into action.

Drew stared at the carriage as it rolled away. Then his attention swept the surrounding aftershock of disaster.

The crowd no longer rang with hysterics. Except for some murmurs and a fair amount of coughing, an eerie quiet settled over the scene. Even the two dozen or so children, sitting on the ground, did little more than gape in shock at their home as the flames devoured what was still left of it.

A section of rock and flaming wood collapsed inward. The fiery crash shot cannons of sparks and enraged the flames to new heights. The building's mortal bellow drew screams from some in the crowd. Everyone scurried farther back, the adults grabbing children as they ran.

With each portion crashing in or falling out, a mass of blazing embers erupted, a volcanic affirmation to the fire's triumph. At its peak, it roared with success. All anyone could do now was stare as the inferno gave ghoulish illumination to the afternoon's smoke-stained sky.

Flames shot from the lower windows now. Scraps

of burning curtains bucked on tides of blazing heat. Peering into the front door where mere moments before they had made their escape, was like looking straight into the teeming coals of Hell.

Dove slipping her hand into his shifted Drew's attention from the fiery destruction of the foundling home to the woman he loved. Soot coated her clothing and skin, her dress torn and singed, the gleam of her dark hair dulled from smoke and falling from its pins in the aftermath of her heroics. She was the most beautiful woman he'd ever seen.

"You were out, safe, and you risked your life going back in for me," Drew said, with something akin to wonder.

"You were first," Dove said. Her tremulous smile reticent but offered to him nonetheless. "You risked your life going into that deathtrap for me. You had no reason to do such a thing."

He clasped her sweet, sooty face in his filthy palms. "I had every reason. My impetus was the same as yours. I love you, Dove. And you love me. Don't try to deny it, not after what happened here today."

Her mouth opened slightly, to offer the very denial he forbade, he was sure. She couldn't do it, though. The lie was too big, too illogical to give it voice. Drew almost laughed with the joy of it.

"Yes," he said. He brushed back a fallen, smoke-grimed lock. "That's what love is. It gives everything." *And it overcomes.*

Drew said the words to her, but it was yet another epiphany for him, another valuable lesson he learned because this woman owned his heart. He would risk his life every day if that's what it took to have her. He would do it without hesitation.

"Yes, it's true. I love you too, Drew. I can't help it. I didn't want to, but I do. I love you."

He did laugh now, as his happiness was too great to contain. *She went back in for me. She outright said it. Yes, she loves me. Her life would change if I had died in there.*

Drew's chest tightened, and then burgeoned with life and love, and all the glorious seeds they yielded. For the first time, he looked to the future beyond a single night's pleasures. A lifetime worth of days and nights were there, every single one of them with his Dove.

All those women he'd known before her, they weren't filling a place in his life, they were holding it. His debauchery was naught but killing time, waiting for Dove to soar into his world. Or rather, he recalled with a chuckle over their first meeting in Beatrix's chambers, leap into his world.

With his thumb, Drew caught and wiped the tear sliding down her face, leaving a damp, sooty smudge across her cheek. Her forehead wrinkled. Her face grew taut. His blithe side strove to convince him it was the swell of emotion, the day, the mutual acknowledgement of their love. Contributing factors all, but not the root of her angst.

He clasped her tense shoulders, willing his firm hold to convey his conviction. "We'll settle our troubles, Dove. We'll work it all out. I'll see to it."

"But Drew, your uncle. I know you don't believe me about—"

"I believe you." Yet, in the days and weeks to come, would his belief matter? Would she ever be able to look at him without thinking about what a member of his family had done to hers?

Dove coughed against the back of her hand, and then raised an unwavering chin. "What has your uncle to say? I always wondered, when the moment came, if the killer would be rebellious or feign repentance. Did he say anything of the other two men who were with him that night?"

Drew shifted his glance away from her and toward what was left of the foundling home. More stones tumbled from the collapsing building as the blaze wrought its final consumption. He faced Dove again. His beautiful Dove who had suffered so much, who had saved his life, twice now. At the very least, she was owed honesty, and he would give it to her.

"I have not yet spoken to Charles."

She tipped her head down before he could read her expression and stepped back.

"Dove, it's not for lack of trying, I assure you. I'd arranged to meet him at his home this very morn. He wasn't there when I arrived. For close to an hour I paced his study, waiting for him to return." Drew coughed before continuing. "Whilst there, I found his jacket, the one he wore as part of his Bandit costume the night of the ball. There is stitching in the shoulder. It repairs a tear."

"Where Renny shot him the night of the murders." Her head snapped up, her excitement growing as she spoke. "We can take it to the magistrate. It's proof of what he and those other two men did!"

"It's a hole in a coat. It proves nothing."

The angry compression of her lips eased just enough to ask, "And my mother's brooch?"

"Again, all he would have to do is claim he purchased it from a traveling vendor, and had no knowledge of its origin."

Her stiffening posture sent a clear signal he was losing her. The low, furious tone in which she spoke to him, yet another.

"That excuse reeks of lies," she spat.

"Yes, it does. But along with his status and clean reputation, it's functional enough to suit his needs. We need more before we approach the magistrate. I'll go back and speak with Charles."

"And will anything your uncle says lend justification to what he's done?"

"No, of course not. He'll pay for his crime," Drew said after a brief fit of coughing. However, he was at a loss as to how he could accomplish such without causing severe damage to his mother and sister, and Dove was too perceptive not to see his impasse.

She crossed her arms, a blockade he could feel. "Will he?"

Drew hated the doubt, so sharp in her eyes. What he hated even more was he felt it, too. Though he was certain his uncle was guilty, the avenues it could go from here, well, none of them were good. Every solution ended in tragedy for someone he loved. Good God, his mother might even be implicated in the crime, as she'd had possession of the brooch these past three years.

Dove had risked everything in her pursuit of justice for her parents. And she would have it, one way or another, even if it meant exposing herself as the Bandit to do so. She wouldn't think twice about becoming a martyr to righteousness. The scenarios grew worse with every considered angle.

Drew was far from certain he could even prove his uncle's guilt. As he'd said to Dove, the brooch, the hole in his coat, could all be explained away with a variety of excuses. Charles wouldn't even have to worry about his lack of an alibi. Three years had passed since the murders, so his uncle couldn't be expected to remember where he'd been on that specific night.

Charles's reputation was heretofore untarnished, and the evidence against him simple enough to refute. Justice was no closer than it had been before Dove found the brooch. Except, they both knew the truth.

Even if he did establish his uncle's guilt enough to satisfy the magistrate, even if he got a confession from the man, nothing had changed regarding the devastation such a scandal would cause to his mother and sister. But not to act would be to betray Dove, to betray justice, and his own new-found honor.

Reacting to his hesitation, she spun away from him.

"Dove!"

She whirled back, the volatile mix of emotions clear in her watery glare. Behind her, the building roared to a destructive crescendo. More blocks of stone fell inward, careening through the second floor and crashing to the floor of the main hall with a blazing wallop violent enough to prompt a few screams from the crowd. Dove was so isolated in her personal tumult, she didn't so much as flinch.

It was there on her face, in her tormented eyes, the pain and anger, all of it at present directed toward him. She loved him, she did. Her actions today proved it. But what was between them was insurmountable.

A hand on his arm drew his attention. It was Rose, as smoke-stained as the rest of them. Vague traces of her blonde hair showed scarce through the layers of soot.

Rose coughed and then said, "Drew, can you take any of the children with you? We're dividing them up so they'll all have someplace to stay for a few weeks until the new foundling home is finished."

"Yes, of course. We have plenty of room. My mother and sister will welcome them."

"Good," Rose said, with a quick smile of relief before rushing back to her business of organizing.

Drew wheeled back to speak with Dove. He didn't know what he would say, and as it turned out, it didn't matter. Dove was gone.

Chapter 16

Dove tied a pink ribbon in Marion's wavy blonde hair. The ribbon matched the ruffle-skirted dress she wore and loved. The little girl swished her small hips and giggled at the way the ruffles fluttered. Then she did it again.

"Hold still just a moment longer, sweeting," Dove told the child. She finished tying the bow and sat back on her heels on the floor of her bedchambers. "There, all finished. Go look in the mirror and tell me what you think."

Marion skipped over to the long mirror supported by a stand in the corner. She swished her skirts again before giving a reverent touch to the ribbon in her hair. Like everything else the child wore, the ribbon was a donation.

Old satchels and wooden crates full of used clothing started arriving the morning after the fire to all the homes of those who'd taken in children. The generosity was remarkable and appreciated. Everyone who had fled the foundling home were left with nothing more to their names than what they had on their backs.

As the child gazed with delight at her reflection, spinning around one way, and then the other, a wonderful idea poked its head into Dove's mind. A call for donations in forms other than money could be arranged on a regular basis, perhaps an annual event.

The clothing of the children of the upper classes could be put to beneficial use instead of moldering away in some attic trunk. She would discuss this with Rose later.

The little girl spun around and raised her vivid green eyes to Dove. At six years-old, Marion had already seen too much. From what Dove learned at the foundling home, the child's mother was an east end doxy who had not the means nor the inclination to care for a child. Marion had lived at the foundling home since her mother abandoned her at the front gate when she was two-years-old.

"There," Dove said, coming to her feet. She put her hands on her hips and smiled at the little girl. "You look just like a princess."

Shyness colored the child's fair skin with a blush. She was ever grateful for any and everything, even the smallest compliment, and as sweet as a treat.

"Thank you, milady."

"I told you, call me Dove, just like when we were at the foundling home."

The child beamed a tooth-gapped smile. "You know, that's the best name I ever heard. Like a bird."

"A dove is a sign of peace," her grandfather said from the doorway of Dove's bedroom. "Hope, goodwill, and family, too, as well as a few more wonderful meanings."

They'd taken in four of the displaced children, two girls and two boys between the ages of six and nine. These past days, with the children, her grandfather had been happier than she'd seen him since the murders. More in control of his mind, too. Perhaps once the new foundling home was finished, she should take him on her visits. He loved playing games with them. They both enjoyed tucking them in at night, telling them stories. Except for her personal misery, the house was filled with noise and cheer.

She was grateful for the distraction.

For a moment, after having escaped that burning building, knowing Drew had risked death to come for her, she thought nothing could stand in the way of their love. It was naught but the foolish fantasies of the girl she once was. Some things could not be overcome.

"Marion," her grandfather said, stepping into the room and patting the girl's head, careful not to upset the ribbon. "Cook has made some Banbury cakes dusted with cinnamon."

The child clapped her small hands together. "Those are ever so good!"

"Well, you'd best hurry down before they're all gone."

Marion dashed from the room so fast her fresh tied ribbon was in danger of flying from her hair.

"Don't spoil your dinner," Dove cried after the girl.

"Oh, let her spoil her dinner," her grandfather told her. "She's on holiday!"

Dove couldn't help but laugh. It trickled through her misery, drawn out by the high mood of her grandfather. But then her grandfather's smile faltered. He stepped close enough to take her hands in his. Today his grip was strong, his eyes clear and sure.

"What is it, Grandfather?"

With his face focused on hers, he said, "He's a good man."

Dove didn't have to ask who he was talking about. Drew had penetrated her life all the way to her home.

But her grandfather didn't know the whole of it, and she couldn't tell him.

"Dove, did I ever tell you about the days following your father's return from the colonies with his new wife, your mother?"

"I know they were very much in love. Mother told me she felt it from the moment she saw him."

"Your father, too. It's a good thing. Life wasn't so easy for them here, not for a while."

Dove nodded, withdrew her hands, and sat on the edge of her bed. "Society. I saw traces of their disapproval here and there. Acceptance of their marriage was never complete."

Her grandfather sat beside her. "Yes. The aristocracy doesn't take kindly to mixing blood. Nonsense, all of it. If I had my way, why, it would be required."

Dove swiveled a wide-eyed stare his way. She'd been ever aware of his liberal side, it was the part of him to which she'd always felt the most connected. It was why he'd accepted her mother so much easier than others had. This viewpoint of mixed blood being a requirement, however, was extreme even for her grandfather.

"You heard right," he said in answer to her stare. "Required, until there was so much a mix of culture and background running through everyone's veins, no one could look at anyone else and feel either superior or inferior."

"Because we would all be the same," Dove said. It was a sad truth, but he may well be right. Too many people searched out nonsensical reasons to dislike one another. "Perhaps it is the only way there will ever be peace."

Her grandfather glanced about the room as if viewing the world of his thoughts. Instead of bolstering his opinion, his thoughts appeared to sadden him. On a sigh, he said, "Perhaps. But then we'd lose the beauty of diversity. If only people could withdraw their heads from their privilege and see all the wondrous assortments the world has to offer."

She laid her head on his shoulder. "Grandfather, you are a kind and wise man."

"Not that it matters a whit, but thank you, dear. My opinions on social issues count for naught. Society will do what Society does."

Dove sat up and smoothed the fine turquoise muslin of her skirt. She would hear more about her parents while her grandfather was willing and able to talk about them. "Those early days must have been difficult for my mother, even with the love of my father and his family."

"Yes. She was far from her home, from everything familiar to her, thrown into a culture of vast differences. Even your grandmother, rest her soul, took a while to adjust to her. But she did. And many of the other ladies did, too, thanks to her."

"How did Grandmother get them to accept her?"

He chuckled then, and raised gray eyebrows over his sparkling green eyes. "Your grandmother had a talent for phrasing. She pointed out how fortunate we were to have in our family this exotic treasure from another land. Then, at a ball, at the precise moment she had all the right ears in her attendance, she dropped the name of a certain revered duke, Hollindshire, it was, saying His Grace was most interested in meeting this woman from a foreign land."

"Was it true?"

"Oh, Lord Hollindshire was in residence at a mansion on Park Lane. Your grandmother was convinced he would without a doubt be interested in a discussion with our daughter-in-law, once he knew of her. But no. As far as I know, the man was never aware of your mother's existence."

Dove chuckled at her grandmother's loving deception.

"Soon after, invitations arrived by the bucket load. It was in style to have your mother at one's home."

It was easy to imagine. Her grandmother did have a way with speech. Father used to say she could sell manure to a stable boy. Still, Dove had no idea the woman had stepped so far out of bounds, bragging on a duke's nonexistent interest to gain her mother's acceptance.

Once her laughter subsided, Dove shook her head. "I had no idea. Grandmother was quite clever, wasn't she?"

"Indeed. Do you remember how you used to hate going to bed?" he asked.

"Yes." Dove furrowed her brow, searching her memory. "But then I didn't hate it anymore. I don't remember why."

"I do. One night you were being stubborn about it. Your grandmother managed to convince you bedtime was the best time because that was when wonderful dreams visited, and anything you wanted could be true, every wish, every fantasy. Within seconds of hearing that, you rushed to jump into your bed."

"That's right! I remember being excited to go to

bed every night, because sometimes I had dreams about flying."

"Yes! That was your favorite dream. Sometimes you dreamed about flying over the city, other times you dreamed about flying above the trees."

She chuckled at her grandmother's loving manipulation. No, it wasn't difficult to imagine the woman altering a great many opinions of her daughter-in-law from a savage to a coveted foreign ambassador.

"So that's how my mother was granted her social entrance."

"And yours, too. Oh, there were still, are still, people who will never accept such a difference mixed into the ranks. Your mother suffered some barbs and snubs. And she had much to learn. In the beginning, life for her here proved difficult and burdensome, what with all the many rules of etiquette. But she was almost always happy, even in the early days."

"How could she be? It sounds as if those times consisted of nothing but conquering obstacles. How could anybody know happiness living that way?"

"Your mother was *steeped* in happiness because she was in love. She was in love with a good man who loved her back. Such a powerful foundation can overcome much, Dove."

Dove shifted her attention to stare out the window. Sunlight played on the clean pane of glass. The brightness of the afternoon a deep contrast to the painful shadow encasing her heart.

"Not every difficulty in life can be overcome," she said.

"No, Dove, not everything. However, if you don't give it a chance, you'll never know. If you don't give *him* a chance. Step back and sort through your quarrel with independent thought. See if it is as insurmountable as you now believe."

How she wanted to unburden herself, to tell her grandfather everything. But to stir up that horrible time after the murders again, no, she wouldn't do such to the poor man. It was better he thought her heartbreak was over some silly lover's spat.

Dove blinked back her tears and forced a smile. "I will think about everything you said, Grandfather."

It wouldn't make a difference, though. Drew couldn't hurt his family. An admirable trait, in any other situation. But in this, it meant allowing the murderer of her parents go on to live a fine life. Her anguish caught around her heart and tightened. The pain was real, physical. She managed to hold back the tears until her grandfather kissed her forehead and had gone to eat Banbury cakes with the children.

Chapter 17

Sweat dripped from Drew's hairline and stung his eyes. At the same time, the dampness his body expelled cooled his shirtless skin. A vague part of his mind registered the coppery taste of blood.

The bruises he'd received over the past two hours from well-timed punches of his many opponents were sore and growing numerous in correlation with his exhaustion. His legs were losing agility. The usual threat of his blows had waned. Even if he'd been aware of these impediments, however, he would not have stopped boxing.

He threw another punch and made a weak effort to gain some measure of gratification from the landing of his padded fist against the side of Lord Chesson's head. He reaped none. In the back of his rattled mind, the strange notion floated about that he might be garnering more satisfaction from the punishing strikes his body was taking.

Drew had long lost count of how many matches he'd fought within the ropes of Gentleman Jackson's Boxing Club. The first few ended fast, his opponents taken down with brutal efficiency. For a while, no one was willing to step into the ring with him. Then a group of three young pups with more arrogance than experience took their turns. They all hit the floor within seconds.

But his tiring body now lolled at the edge of its limit. His mind and heart, however, were too charged with volatile emotions to quit. It left him with an increasing vulnerability to the counter attacks of Lord Chesson, a man close to his equal in age, size, and skill.

Drew ducked his opponent. He threw a solid punch to the side of the man's jaw as he straightened. Chesson wobbled back, wide-eyed and stunned. Not surprising, considering at this point Drew should have been an easy take down.

The faces of the men he'd challenged today, or had been fool enough to challenge him, blended in a lost and pointless tally. Drew had taken on anyone and everyone who was willing to fight him. Several of his opponents outweighed him. At least three possessed a good measure of experience and admirable skills. Drew had yet to lose a single match.

He reeked of sweat. Lodged frustration permeated his nostrils and slithered down his throat as the rancid taste of despair further confused his moves. His mistakes were growing. Instead of his step to the left evading, it put him right in Lord Chesson's path.

A sound blow to Drew's cheekbone caused him to stumble. He managed to find his balance before falling, but it was close. And the turning point in the match was in view.

Lord Chesson's eyes sharpened, like a wild beast who has spotted a wounded animal. His chin dropped a tad at the same time his gaze rolled into acute focus. The men circled each other. While Drew endeavored to rally his dwindling energies, his galvanized opponent hunched and readied for the kill.

From the crowd of men outside the ropes ascended

a round of encouraging shouts and cheers. He ignored them. Most were in support of Chesson anyway. Drew's previous opponents, some holding cloths to a lip or an eye, were enthusiastic in their eagerness to see him fall.

His wits were intact enough for him to see the next punch coming, but his reaction time lagged, and the hard blow to his midsection folded him over. Shouts of encouragement to Lord Chesson's probable victory resounded.

Drew rallied enough to straighten and throw out another punch. It was sloppy and weak, and struck nothing but air. He swung again with his left fist, and once more with his right. Chesson skipped back, hopped to the side, and grinned at the ease with which he ducked Drew's weak punches.

The blow Chesson returned after another one of Drew's missed, pitiful efforts landed hard over Drew's left brow, splitting the skin, and hurling him to the floor.

Chesson made a slow circle around his crumpled form. After raising to his elbows, Drew spat blood and struggled to haul himself up to his hands and knees. Chesson stopped in front of him and lifted his bare foot several inches. Drew readied to be kicked over.

Since none of the matches were pre-arranged, neither Drew nor any of his opponents had a knee man to kneel with one knee up and offer a brief sitting spot between rounds. In fact, there weren't even rounds. The fights had gone on until someone cried off or was carried out. Nor had they arranged for a waterman to provide drink and a damp sponge. Most important, though, neither men had an umpire to handle questionable practices.

Chesson lowered his foot and made another circle.

Then his opponent, a gentleman at his core, hung back, giving proper wait as Drew's sluggish limbs dragged him back to a standing position.

He'd scarce come full upright before Chesson's padded fist knocked him down again. How he managed to get to his feet a second time, Drew couldn't guess. His body swayed. His limbs were trembling with fatigue, blood flowing from the cut above his brow mixed with sweat and ran into his eye, and his brains were scrambled enough to leave him unsure as to what his next action should be.

Drew stood for a second or two before his knees buckled. Once again, he worked to get back on his feet. The accomplishment was more credit to his legs than to the depleted strength of his arms. Though, his legs were also on the verge of rebellion.

With but one functional eye, as the other was stinging and too clouded with sweat and blood to be of any use, Chesson's punch readied before his face. Drew couldn't duck it. Nor could he block it. He couldn't even manage to care he was about to go down again.

But a bare hand slapped a grip over his opponent's wrapped knuckles before it could slam into his face. A man's voice sifted through the murkiness clogging his head, a familiar voice.

"Enough. It's clear to everyone you've won the match. No need to kill the man."

It was Burke, Lord Darington, his friend.

"Come on, Drew," Burke said, latching onto his arm and helping him through the ropes. "You've had enough punishment for one day."

He walked Drew through the jeering crowd, which parted with obvious reluctance. Both men ignored the shouting complaints of men who were angry at having been denied witness to the final fall.

****

An hour later, after a good washing, some fresh clothes, and a chance to gather his wits, Drew sipped brandy from a gold-rimmed snifter in the Darington's front parlor. The momentary stinging aside, the fine brandy did much to soothe his aches and cleanse the taste of blood from his mouth.

Rose, Burke's lovely wife, dabbed another spot of anise-scented salve on the cut over his eye, apologizing when he winced. Burke sat in a wing-back chair across the settee from them.

"There," Rose said on an exasperated huff. "At least it's stopped bleeding. I've no doubt you're going to be sore for a while, but you should heal well."

"I'm glad you at least had sense enough to wear mufflers," Burke said, referring to the padded bandages Drew and his opponents wore over their fists. Some men fought bare-knuckled. Had Drew partaken in the boxing matches so, the damages he suffered would have been far worse.

Rose shook her head and muttered something Drew couldn't understand, but the tone implied he was being scolded. He glanced at Burke. Was the man smiling into his brandy?

"Thank you, Rose," Drew said, bringing his attention back to her. "You're an angel."

Rose tossed the cloth atop the jar of salve, which sat on the mahogany Sheraton table between them and Burke. Next to the jar was a creamware bowl of water and another cloth she'd used to clean his wounds.

"If I live to be one hundred, I swear there are things about men I will *never* understand. Goodness, letting yourself be beaten to a pulp!"

"Rose, dear," Burke said in a mollifying tone. "He didn't intend to be beaten to a pulp, did you Drew."

Cleaned up, he'd regained the vision in his left eye, well, most of it. There were some limits due to a bit of swelling. He directed his eye and a half toward Burke. The man was trying to ease the concerns of his pregnant wife. Both men had a clear understanding that while Drew might not have set a goal of getting mashed, he'd not have exited the ropes on his own decision.

Burke said, "Your skills just weren't as up to snuff as you'd thought, isn't that right, Drew?"

Drew was one of the best boxers Gentleman Jackson's had ever produced. Not that one would guess such a thing by his present appearance. And Burke's wife was in a state over his condition. So, to keep the ireful worry from Rose's good heart, he choked down his pride and went along with the story.

Shooting a wry and weary glare at Burke, Drew said, "Apparently."

Rose gave him a gentle pat on the shoulder. "Perhaps boxing isn't your strong suit. You should try something a bit more docile." Her arched, blonde brows furrowed in concentration for a moment or two, and then she brightened with an idea. "Like archery."

"Yes, Drew," Burke said from his chair, a slight grin tugging up the sides of his face as he swirled brandy in the crystal snifter. "Some men are not built to box."

Rose gave a comforting squeeze to his arm. "It's

nothing to be ashamed of, dear. Who knows? With time and practice, you may well become one of London's finest archers."

Drew indulged her with a grateful smile, as the dear woman had his best interest in mind. "A man can dream."

After an encouraging pat on his hand, Rose stood. She gave her skirts a shake and brushed them down. From his wingback chair across from them, Burke's contented attention paused on the swell of her belly. Their son was just walking, and already she carried their second child. The pang of envy coursing through Drew caused him more suffering than all his physical injuries combined.

"Now if you boys will excuse me," Rose said, gathering up her jar of salve, her cloths, and the bowl of water. "I have some other, much younger children to attend to."

Burke was on his feet in an instant, setting down his glass, taking her burdens and returning them to the table. "I'll have a maid see to these things. In fact, the children are fine in the care of the nannies I've hired. You should go lie down and rest, Rose. You've already done too much today."

Rose swept loving fingers over her husband's jaw. To Drew she said, "He would prefer I lounged in the sun parlor all day stitching samplers and sipping tea with my feet on a padded stool." Returning her attention to her husband, she said, "But you know I'd be bored out of my mind in minutes."

Burke clasped her delicate fingers in his and bent to brush a quick kiss across her knuckles. The smile Rose bestowed upon her husband could outshine a thousand candles. Warmth flooded Drew's heart. It then receded, laying bare tender emotions too raw to abide.

Dove.

"Promise me you'll rest if you get the least bit tired," Burke said.

"You have my word." She patted the small protrusion of her belly twice and said, "I'll be diligent in my care of us, just as I was before."

Rose swept from the room, her joyful glow powerful enough to brush across Drew's battered body. It taunted him with what might have been.

A moment later, Rose poked her head back in.

"Drew, please do consider giving archery a chance. You might find it rather enjoyable."

She'd suffered great trespasses in her life, yet her heart was as big as the world. Her life was full, content, and happy. She exuded joy, now. For Rose, the worst of her times led her to the best. Her story, her example of what might be overcome, allotted him a glimmer of hope.

Drew sent her a solemn nod. "I will devote great consideration to the sport this very week."

With a satisfied nod, Rose once again disappeared. Many seconds passed before Burke caught Drew in the corner of his eye. His expression bore a tiny hint of surprise, as if every part of his being focused on Rose and he'd forgotten his guest. With an unabashed grin, Burke took his seat.

Drew shot an affronted glare to his friend. "You realize I could box you off your feet in less than a full round."

"You could try."

Drew took another swig of Darington's fine

brandy. It caused a bit less of a sting on the cut in his mouth this time. With some rest, he had no doubt he could outbox his friend. They knew each other well enough so Burke couldn't doubt it either. Drew's pugilistic abilities were renowned. His friend was jesting with him. In his present condition, however, Burke's pregnant wife would stand a fair chance of knocking him off his feet.

From some distant room, a child's shriek was followed by a long peal of laughter and the quick, padding footfalls of children running. Another bout of laughter ended with the hard closing of a door.

"How many children did you take in?" Drew asked.

"Six. Three girls, three boys, and a dog named Raisin."

"A dog?"

"The dog belongs to one of the boys, Brennan. He's the one who likes to sing. The child sure has the voice for it."

"Is he the one who once had you wave goodbye to a dog?"

Burke chuckled. "Yes. Same boy, same dog. Anyway, Brennan said he would sooner sleep on the streets than abandon his dog. Have to admire such loyalty." Burke shrugged then. "The furry beast just adds another layer to the chaotic fun. The staff is handling the situation well. It's good practice for them, as Rose and I plan on having a large brood. Besides, my young son is enjoying all the new playmates."

Drew remembered a time not so long ago when Burke's plan of revenge on his abusive father was to never marry, never have a child, and to let the earldom die with him. Burke was last in the line without so much as a distant relative to whom the title could pass. At the time, his anger and history led him to believe it was a line best put down. Drew shook his head at the massive span of his friend's transformation.

"It's the love of a good woman," Burke said at Drew's expression. "It changes your world."

Drew gave an almost imperceptible shake of his head as his heart contracted. "My situation is more complicated."

"Only because it's yours. If you remember correctly, I, along with all of London, once judged Rose guilty of a horrible crime. I believed her the worst sort of human being." A tautness altered his face for a moment, its retreat slow.

"The difference is, Dove is set to commit a murder."

"That turn of events has yet to occur and may never if we can find proper justice for her. Besides, I'm not at all certain she could do it. Rose and I have worked with Lady Barrow on the Foundling Project, and I don't see the capability in her. It's one thing to concoct a fantasy about killing someone who has taken your family, quite another when faced with the ordeal."

"I've had the same thought. The problem is, I worry she believes she's already too mired in crime. To exact revenge, in her eyes, I fear, dispatching a trio of villains would add little more to her sins."

"So far, she's done no permanent damage. The time for her salvation has not passed. Remember, you and I are the only ones who know of her alter-identity. Well, us and her man, Renny."

"Dove has been hurting for so long now. I worry

she lacks clarity of mind on the matter. But your point is valid. In my heart, I do not believe she has the constitution to commit cold-blooded murder. Then again, I would say the same about either of us. But Burke, in truth, what would you do were someone commit an act of such atrocity against your family, murdered the people closest to you?"

Burke's jaw tightened, and his countenance grew hard. Drew also pictured himself in the situation. What if it had been his mother and sister murdered? Rage gripped him at the mere thought. Yes, either one of them would vow to murder someone who would do such a thing, and mean it.

"My point exactly," Drew said. "Dove hasn't yet passed the point of no return. But if I cannot find an alternate solution…"

Burke shook his head. Drew imagined he was trying to shake off the horrific image of suffering such loss.

"I take it you haven't yet spoken to your uncle," Burke said.

"I've been to his house several times, now. Either his butler is lying to me or…or Charles has absconded. Since I was angry and tipped my hand by leaving the bag on his desk in which the brooch was kept, my guess is he's disappeared. Perhaps for good."

"Has your mother an idea where he might be?"

"I don't believe she's aware of his absence, yet. Now that I'm handling the ledgers, I can keep the knowledge from her, for a little while. Speaking of family," Drew said, throwing back the last of his brandy. "I must be going. Mother and Ollie will be sitting down to dinner soon, and I don't want to be late."

This time there was no mistaking Burke's astonishment.

In answer to the unasked question, Drew said, "I've learned a new appreciation for the time I spend with my family."

Something in the vein of approval softened Burke's surprise at Drew's statement. "I see Lady Barrow has already had a positive effect on your life."

Drew answered with a slight tip of his head and a smile marred with sadness. He set down his empty glass. A moment later, he stood to leave.

Burke remained in his chair, his elbow on the brocade cover of the armrest as he gave a thoughtful stroke to his jaw. "Would it make a difference to Dove if your uncle hadn't been the one to pull the trigger?"

Drew stilled, and his mind shifted. This angle had never occurred to him before. And yes, it was indeed possible such a difference could change everything. "I hadn't considered that. I should have."

"There were three men in hoods there that night, am I correct?"

"Yes. Since my uncle had the brooch, I assumed he was the one who'd murdered them. Perhaps it was a rash assumption."

Burke set his glass on the table beside Drew's and stood. "No doubt your uncle was there. And he might have committed one, or both, of the murders, but perhaps not. The difference could put a distinct alteration to her thoughts, and perhaps her actions."

"It might also make Charles more amenable to disclosing the names of the other two men who were there that night."

"Yes, if he can keep his own neck from the hangman's noose by turning on the others."

"Exactly. Even more reason for me to find that blasted man and speak with him." Drew strode halfway to the door before he stopped. He said, more to himself than to Burke, "Or Renny."

"Renny?" Burke said, approaching him. "Her driver, the one who was with them that night?"

"Yes, there and shot one of them, my uncle. Perhaps he can tell me if the man he winged was the same man who pulled the trigger on the Barrows."

"I thought he remembered nothing after he was shot. In the papers, it said he was shot first. He didn't even know the Barrows were dead until later."

"So Dove told me. Maybe if I prod him a bit, some scrap of memory might return, some tidbit he didn't even know he possessed. I don't believe Dove ever pushed him. She would have been too worried for his health."

"Keep in mind, Drew, it might not matter much to Dove if your uncle did not pull the trigger. All those men were in on the deed."

"It might not matter much, but it could matter enough," Drew said. "After dinner, I'll go and speak with Renny. I have to find some resolution before Dove goes too far."

"For all her pain and threats, seeing them all brought before the magistrate could well sate her thirst for revenge. But, Drew, your family would still suffer the scandal."

"I'll traverse that muck when it's laid out before me. I've an idea or two bouncing around my skull. In the meantime, I'll gather all the information I can and present it to Dove, see if I can reason with her. Bye the bye, something has been picking at my mind. I'd like your thoughts."

"Of course," Burke said.

"It's about the fire at the foundling home. Do you remember the chair downstairs, the one burning in the main hall?"

"Yes. Hmm, now that you mention it. It was out of context, as the fire had not yet spread to the first floor."

"It was the only thing in the whole of the downstairs aflame. Even the far more flammable items had not yet caught, the ancient muslin curtains, the rag doll on the floor. Yet the chair was engulfed in fire."

"It's as if... As if someone had set it on fire deliberately, as if they'd been stopped before they could complete the task."

Drew nodded. "Yes. The notion is in my head and I can't get it out. Nor do I think I should."

"When we first ran in, I swore I detected the odor of coal oil. At the time, I was so worried about Rose, I didn't pay it any mind."

"Coal oil. Dear God."

"Why in the name of all that is holy, would someone want to burn down the foundling home? The children are a threat to no one."

Drew's rubbed his temple as if the horrid ideas pounded to get out.

"What is it you're thinking?" Burke asked.

Drew paced back into the room and didn't stop until he stood before the hearth. The hearty fire did nothing to ease the vicious chill biting into him.

He pivoted back toward his friend. "I've had a grim thought eating at me, about how the two crimes might be connected."

"The murders of Dove's parents and the fire at the foundling home?"

"Yes," Drew said. "We know the only thing stolen from Dove's parents that night was the brooch. Her father had coin in his purse, her mother wore other jewels. Nothing but the brooch was taken. The ruby wasn't cut into smaller pieces to make it easier to sell. As we know, the piece wasn't altered or sold at all, as the papers hypothesized."

"It's clear the crime wasn't for monetary gain."

"The brooch was taken, I don't know, as a memento?"

"If the murders weren't part of a robbery gone wrong, perhaps it was personal. However," Burke said, pausing. "If I remember right from what I read in the flurry of articles after the crime, there wasn't a single person who had a negative thing to say about Lord and Lady Barrow. They were fine people and had no enemies."

"Who we know about."

"Who we know about," Burke conceded. "How do you see the murders linked to the fire?"

"What if Dove's parents were murdered on the grounds of bigotry? We know these attitudes exist. I've never known any to surpass gossip and snubs and venture to such an evil extreme, but it's not outside the realm of possibility. What if…" Drew started. He shifted his gaze from one horrid image to another. "What if my uncle and his small band of killers are on a mission to rid the world of what they consider 'undesirables'?"

"Such as those involved in mixed marriages, and

children without proper parentage," Burke said, disgust thick in his tone. "That is beyond evil."

Drew paced to the beveled panes of the bay window. A book of stories lay angled on the red, cushioned seat with an orange pillow propped on one side. He took scarce note of any of it. His mind could not even register the sun drooping in the sky. Speaking aloud the concept that had crept about in his mind's murk, cast it with a sound of believability. Horrid possibilities darkened the small ray of hope he'd had moments before.

"Have you any thoughts on who the other two men were? Friends of your uncle's you may know, perhaps?"

Drew shook his battered head. One hand came to rest on his sore ribs. He forced his attention, faced Burke and said, "I don't know the men with whom he socializes. Frankly, I always thought him a loner. It's rare he attends parties, and he manages to avoid all but the most essential of social events. I will set my course to learn of his associates, I assure you."

The gilt clock upon the mantel caught Drew's eye. "I must be on my way if I'm to dine with my mother and Ollie. We'll discuss this more later."

"Perhaps I'll take a ride down to the site of the fire, see what I can find. Then I'll ask around, discreetly, of course, and see who might have a mind toward such extreme hatred."

"Good idea. And Burke, thank you for tonight."

"I think that makes us even," Burke said.

Drew didn't need an explanation as to what his friend meant. He'd once rescued Burke's drunken semblance of himself from public humiliation. If Burke saw that as a debt to be paid, it was his right as a gentleman.

"And," Burke said, a slight grin on his face. "I look forward to challenging you at a target with bow and arrow."

Drew chuckled. "Ah, yet another sport for me to trounce you with my superior skills."

Returning his good humor, Burke said again, "You can try."

The men walked to the spacious foyer. It was too early for the chandelier to be lit, but the crystal drops adorning it caught enough sunlight from the window over the door to cast glimmers of rainbow color onto the white marble floor. Burke's efficient, silver-haired butler strode in with Drew's coat but a moment after them.

"Thank you, Timmons," Drew said, donning his coat.

Timmons bowed his balding head and said, "My lord," before opening the front door.

"Thank you, Timmons," Burke said. "You may go now." Once the butler had gone, Burke continued. "We could have a Bow Street Runner track down Charles."

"I don't want to alert the authorities just yet. Since I've grown so sure of my uncle's guilt, I've devised a plan to send my mother and sister on a long holiday. I'm hoping to get them gone before this ugliness bears fruit."

"Good thinking. By their return, the gossip will have settled."

"Yes. I'm hoping when the time arrives for Ollie's come out, the *ton* will have their tongues wagging over something far more current."

Burke nodded, and Drew readied to leave.

"Oh, I'm appalled I forgot to ask.," Drew said, spinning back in the doorway. "Have you seen Durham? When I stopped by, his butler told me he was asleep. Though I don't feel certain the man was being honest."

With a pained shake of his head, Burke said, "I tried to see him, too. Derek won't take visitors."

"Do you know what the doctors have said of his recovery?"

"Rose took over a basket of cakes and, though Derek wouldn't see her, she did manage to charm a bit of information from his butler. It's not much more than what we already know. He'll heal, but his disfigurement will be severe, and permanent. At present, I'm more concerned over the state of his mind."

"He'll need his friends to rally."

"Indeed. However, it's going to be difficult if he won't even see anyone. I'll wait a couple of days and try again."

"I'll do the same. Perhaps if I request an audience to give my gratitude, he'll feel obligated to see me. He's still a nobleman. When he's feeling better, I'll extend a dinner invitation. If Derek declines, I'll insist. The man helped save my life. I'll not give up on him."

"Nor shall I. We'll talk soon, Drew."

****

The conveyance stopped in front of Drew's house, ceasing the rattle of carriage wheels on cobblestone and the clomping of hooves. His head was so busy mulling over his conversation with Burke, his next course of action, his uncle Charles, his friend Derek, and of course, Dove, the sudden silence rather surprised Drew.

He hadn't even known he was close to home.

The coachman, ever efficient, opened the door and Drew exited the carriage, his attention directed toward the dinner he was about to share with his family, and hoping he wasn't tardy. He'd found oft times it was difficult to catch up if he popped in too late on one of their conversations. And he loathed being left out of even a small portion of whatever topic they may be discussing.

Cool evening hovered not far off, primed by nature to dim the day's bright light. Crickets already chirped in their ritual amongst the sweet scent of hyacinths, tucked neat in their flower beds in front of the three-story, columned house. The whiteness of the flowers was so clean and vibrant, even when night fell they would still be visible.

The coachman directed the horses to carry their burden around back to the carriage house, leaving silence in the wake of their fading clanks and clops. Drew took note of all these things on his peripheral as the clack of his bootheels beat a brisk pace on the paving stones.

Light peeped through the mid-split of the closed drapes in the front parlor. It was the single candle his sister always insisted the servants left lit for him in the center of the room so he could find his way through the house long after the other residents had retired. Like his mother, Olivia cared for him, always, even when he was too absorbed in his wayward pursuits to pay her much mind.

The resonant pace of Drew's bootsteps quickened along the walkway. By the time he reached the top of the steps, their butler stood to welcome him at the open front door.

"Thank you," Drew said when Hubert took his coat.

The pleased look upon the man's face roused Drew's curiosity, for a moment. Hubert had been with his family for years. While it mattered not a whit if the butler approved or disapproved of his behavior, Drew found an odd degree of liking in Hubert's reaction to his presence.

"Have my mother and sister sat down to dine yet?"

"It's been no more than a minute or two since they entered the dining room, my lord."

Drew took long strides down the corridor, a smile burgeoning at the prospect of this time with his family. After all that had transpired, and everything lying ahead, the respite was needed. And yes, such was how he viewed them now. They weren't obligations from which to flee. They were not nuisances with whom he shared walls. They were his safe harbor, his quirky kindred, his loving home.

He'd never given proper appreciation, or respect, for the healing affect those two had on him. Regrets at the time he'd wasted jabbed at him, but he shooed them away. He'd not let guilt taint this precious time.

At the open doorway to the dining room, Drew stopped with such abruptness, he almost stumbled.

His smile vanished.

Rage boiled anew from his belly up to his brain and threatened to dissolve his control.

Drew's seat at the head of the table was empty, but his place setting awaited him. The footman busy at the buffet had not yet served any of them. His mother and sister beamed at his presence. The dinner guest beside his mother, however, stared at him, expressionless.

"Drew," his mother said. "I'm so glad you're here. Look, your Uncle Charles has decided to join us for dinner."

Chapter 18

Before taking his seat, Drew used his well-practiced gaming face to bestow a pleasant smile on his sister and mother. Showing any measure of welcome to his uncle, however, required falsity beyond his limits. He did his best, though, to keep a civil countenance. He would not upset his mother and sister's delicate sensibilities with the ugliness Charles had wrought upon this family.

Beside Ollie's chair sat the two scruffy little dogs of mixed shades of browns, ears up, brown eyes attentive as they awaited their evening tidbits. It was quite improper. He should have put his foot down long ago. However, since his authoritative foot had been occupied elsewhere, it was a habit too ingrained to change. And frankly, though he would never admit to it, he rather enjoyed their furry little faces.

Raising his head, his mother snagged his attention, staring at his face with a bit of distress in her expression.

"Drew, your eye is swollen and bruised." Tipping her fretted gaze upward, she added, "And whatever happened to your head?"

His fingers gave a brief and cautious tap to the cut over his brow. At the sight of Charles in his home, he'd forgotten the battering he'd taken within the ropes at Gentleman Jackson's. Drew settled into his seat while

239

tamping down the glare meant for his uncle.

"It's nothing, Mother. I took a stumble today whilst working at the new foundling home. I assure you, I am fine."

His mother placed her fingertips on the edge of the table near her plate. "Do try to be more careful, dear. It's a fine cause, but perhaps working with your hands isn't your forte. Might there be something else you could do to lend your support?"

"I'll explore other means of assistance, Mother."

"Oh, I know," Ollie said. "You could be one of those men on the construction site who tells others what to do. You know, the person in charge, the, oh, what is the word I'm searching for?"

"The foreman," their mother told her.

"Yes! Thank you, mother. Drew, you could be the foreman."

It was the second time today a female told him he was engaged in a line of physical activity beyond his abilities. And for the second time, to spare feelings and hasten along the conversation, he acquiesced. It was a good thing his self-esteem enjoyed fine health. Otherwise, a day like this might reduce him to a doubting mass.

"I'll consider changing my status," he said, without mentioning not only did the foreman engage in physical work but possessed knowledge and experience Drew did not. However, he wasn't up to the conversation. Not now. He wanted this dinner to come to a hasty finish so he could get Charles alone as soon as possible.

"What a wonderful idea, Ollie," his mother said.

"Thank you, mother. All right, me now," Ollie said, her mood approaching something close to giddy at the change of topic. "Drew, you'll never guess what happened today."

As tumultuous as his emotions ran at present, the sight of his little sister so excited about something she was near to bouncing in her seat, gifted him with a genuine smile. A mad curl of her red hair, restrained with countless pins, slipped from one loosened on the side of her head. He tucked the curl behind her ear for her. She was too excited to notice.

"What's happened, Ollie?"

She leaned forward, the whole of her beaming. Even her light spray of freckles exuded a lively impression. "Lord Foxboro joined us for tea."

Drew couldn't help but slant a quick glance to the other side of the table. Beside his mother, Charles kept his eyes averted, his attention directed to Ollie. What thoughts ran through his head? Had his uncle honed excuses, or was he ready to confess all? Getting through this meal with even a semblance of normalcy was going to require the best of Drew's skills.

The man's presence caused a deep distraction, and it took a moment for Drew to process his sister's words. He was nodding before what she'd said sank in. Hadn't Derek mentioned at the masquerade something about Foxboro having an eye on his sister?

"Foxboro?" Drew said, his voice flattening as he focused on his sister. She had his full attention now. "Looking for me, I hope."

"You?" Ollie said. "You scarce know the man."

"I know enough of his reputation," Drew muttered, dreading the answer to his next question. "Why was he here, if not to see me?"

Ollie beamed. "He was here to call on me."

"You! He's twice your age."

"Not even close, silly," Ollie said in a flippant manner, his outrage failing to intimidate her. "He's quite refined, and ever so handsome."

Drew folded his arms. "He's a cad. I forbid it."

"Forbid what? He's already been and gone. You can't forbid what's already happened."

"That's not at all what I meant, and you know it."

"Drew," his mother said as a footman spooned stewed tomatoes onto her plate. "It was a cup of tea and some polite conversation. She's excited because he was her first gentleman caller."

"You were here to chaperone, I hope," he said to his mother.

She drew up and raised both arched, golden brows high over the affronted widening of her eyes. "Of course. Do you think me so old and feeble-minded I can't keep to proprieties guide?"

"No, of course not, mother. I didn't mean to imply such." Drew uncrossed his arms and flattened his hands atop his thighs. He shot a brief glance toward his uncle.

Charles sat beside his mother, staring at his plate as if the decorative gold dots around the edge were fascinating. Drew's fists balled under the table. Maintaining a civil conversation with his family was like trying to enjoy an afternoon tea while cannons blasted about his head. But it's what he would have to do, lest he topple their lives by losing control of his temper and spilling his uncle's ugly secrets all over the table settings.

"Lord Foxboro," his mother said, picking up her fork. "Was a perfect gentleman."

Foxboro was the worst sort of cad, and far too

reckless with his coin. He'd not allow such a man to court his sister. His present state of anger, however, was inflamed by far more than a scoundrel sniffing at Ollie's skirts. He could deal with Foxboro in an easy enough fashion. The man who tore apart Dove's life, however, was a catastrophic matter sitting at Drew's dinner table.

Were his mother and sister not here to witness the violence, he'd pound the man to a whimpering lump, and then get every question answered. They were right here, though, and unaware of the evil deeds done by a family member that were about to change their lives.

Drew slanted a meaningful glare at his uncle. Charles must have sensed it, because he raised his head and blinked. His uncle then dropped his head to stare at his plate.

The footman finished serving and resumed his position at the sideboard. Ollie speared a chunk of potato with her fork but used the loaded utensil to add to her dramatic tale, waving it as she spoke in a manner bordering on besotted. Drew let her garner all his attention, lest he forget all else and tear into Charles.

"Mother, did you notice how fine his manners were?"

"I did. He was quite proper. Don't wave your food around, dear."

Ollie stuffed the potato into her mouth and chewed with great relish. For a minute or two, the only sound in the dining room was the light clink of silverware to plate.

"His ears are too big for his head," Drew said, homing in on a physical flaw. He had to steer Ollie clear of that rake before her infatuation evolved into something deeper, and more difficult to dissuade. This he hoped to accomplish without delving into Foxboro's more unsavory characteristics.

"They are not!" Ollie said, bouncing her empty fork in his direction. "His ears are quite proportional. Besides, I find a bit of symmetrical imbalance attractive."

"You see, Olivia, you're making no sense. Are his ears proportional, or are they not? You're letting a bit of attention from a man sway your thoughts."

"And you're letting a man's imperfection sway yours. It matters naught if his ears are a bit too large for his head."

"Ah, so you admit Lord Foxboro is imperfect." He had her now.

Satisfied with his clear, sensible triumph, Drew forced himself to continue with his own meal. Not that he was the least bit hungry. But the sooner they finished dinner, the sooner he could lead Charles away for a private conversation.

"Indeed!" Ollie said. "Isn't it wonderful? I'd hate to be saddled with a husband who is ordinary."

Drew coughed on the bite of potato as it was making its way down his throat. As soon as he swallowed, he said, "Husband! He's not spoken to me of an offer."

Nor should he. Foxboro wasn't near to good enough for his sister. Along with being a known rake, the man had already gambled away much of his family's fortune. Another year or two of his reckless activities in London's gambling hells, and he'd not even be able to support himself, much less a wife. More possible than not, the cad was seeking marriage to a woman who would come with a sizable dowry, like Olivia.

"Well of course he hasn't made an offer of marriage yet, silly," Ollie told him. "First he has to make a formal request to court me."

Drew set his fork down on the white, linen tablecloth as if its precise placement was of the utmost importance. His gaze bore into his sister's. "Is that his plan?"

Ollie mocked him by setting down her fork in the same slow, deliberate manner, and imitating his dire tone with complete and utter disrespect. "I don't know."

"One, you will not speak to me with such insolence. Two—"

"One, I will not be treated as if I am a child."

"You are a child. Two—"

"I'm almost seventeen years old and not far off from having my come out. The reign of what little grip you have on me is near to an end."

Drew's brows knitted together to form his most blistering scowl. "You make it sound as if I've been a harsh lord. As you well know, such is not at all the case. Perhaps it should have been," he muttered, glancing at his mother who was most attentive in her dissection of a tomato slice. *So much for expecting her assistance here.*

Reaping what I've sown.

Shaking off the self-recrimination, Drew intensified his focus on his sister. This change in her, this girl with too much pluck for her own good, must be taken in hand. Her defiant attitude was not to be borne. It boggled his mind, as she used to be such a sweet girl.

"When did you become this impertinent little

brat?"

Ollie raised her voice, right there at the dinner table. Another sign he'd been remiss in overseeing her proper education in etiquette.

"Brat!" Ollie said. Her tone escalated further. "How dare you!"

"How dare I? You're the one behaving as if you've no refinement whatsoever. Yelling at the table like some fishwife. And I'll tell you something else—"

Her glare on him narrowed in its focus. "If you call me another foul name I swear I'll order both these well-trained dogs to devour you! There will be nothing left of you but some scraps of fabric dangling from your boots."

"The only thing those two useless mutts could devour is Cook's fine dinner."

"*Mutts*! I'll have you know these are two of the finest dogs in all of London. Fernley is a most attentive watchdog, and Liston is an expert performer. Watch and see for yourself."

Ollie picked up a length of sliced potato from her plate and faced the dogs. Everyone, even the footman, craned their necks to see what would happen next. "Liston," she said. "Beg."

Both Liston and Fernley gave a slight lift to their heads, black nostrils expanding and contracting as they sniffed toward the treat she held.

"See! Ollie said, self-satisfied in her victory. She broke the slice of potato in two and gave half to each dog.

"What I see are two dogs interested in tidbits from your plate," Drew said. "Neither of them begged."

"They're subtle. You should consider yourself

lucky to have them living under our roof."

Amusement made a fine effort to soften Drew's aggravation with Ollie. He would not allow it. How his reprimand had gotten so far off track as to be distracted by non-performing mutts, he couldn't say. One thing of which he was sure, though, he must instill his authority over his little sister's attitude. It was for her own good. He leaned toward Olivia.

"For now," Drew said, needing to set proper emphasis to this discussion. Namely, Lord Foxboro. "We'll set aside the validity of the training and pedigree of your pets. Your behavior, however—"

"Drew, dear," his mother said, intervening before he could give his sister a full and deserved rebuking on her intolerable conduct.

He faced his mother, his indignation not lessened in the least. She should have had Ollie's behavior under control. And if she wasn't up to the task, then she should have come to him for help. His mother could make no viable excuse for this. He may not have spent a majority of his waking time here, but he *was* in residence.

"Why are you so riled over a visit from Lord Foxboro?" his mother said.

She had the gall to sound puzzled. The woman must have heard the rumors about Foxboro and his reckless gambling habits, among other things. Besides, this discussion was about far more than an unsuitable admirer, and she was too astute to not be aware of such.

His mother then said, "Ollie is merely dipping a toe in the waters. Why, she hasn't even had her first season yet."

"It sounds to me as if she's ready to gather her

dowry and be wed. Besides, you heard the way she spoke to me. And as far as me being riled, it is my responsibility. I'd be remiss in my duties were I to be tolerant of such ill-mannered behavior."

"You've no one to blame but yourself," his mother said to him in a matter-of-fact voice.

He expected his own reprimand, a brief lecture on how he'd been remiss in near to *all* his duties to this family for quite some time. It mattered naught the point was valid. He was still lord of this household and entitled to due respect.

As he constructed a defensive response, his mother surprised him by saying, "You should know her better than to taunt her so. Your high-handedness has inspired your sister to tweak your nose."

Drew blinked. She was speaking as if they were both little more than out of their infancy. "In case it has escaped your notice, we are no longer children, Mother. And high handedness, is it? I *am* master of this house. Or has that fact slipped from both your minds?"

"Brother, dear," Ollie said, in a sweet tone so placating it grated. "While we are thrilled to have you back in the fold, over the years mother and I have become rather..." After twice circling her empty fork in the air, she sent a questing glance across the table.

Their mother responded with, "Son, dear, what Ollie is trying to say is, well, as you've been pre-occupied these past few years with your...activities, the two of us have become rather, autonomous."

"Yes!" Ollie said. "The exact word I needed. Thank you, Mother."

"You're welcome, dear."

"Autonomous," Drew said, letting the word, and its

implications, sink into his brain. "Are you saying you deny my authority?"

"Not deny, dear," his mother said. Her mollifying tone was sincere, which made the annoyance of her statement even worse than Ollie's. "It's more like, well, let's say, we decline the offer."

The appalling blow of her proclamation sent Drew slumping back in his chair. His position in this household should not be in question. His authority wasn't an offer for them to accept or decline. They hadn't the right. It, it just wasn't done. Women didn't detach themselves from their lord's rule. In all his years, he'd never heard of such a thing, not ever.

Well, there was Burke's wife, Rose, and her actions before she was his wife. But her situation was altogether different. Her guardian, her brother-in-law, was a lecherous tyrant. She'd no choice but to find her own way. Such was not the case here.

"Mother, you cannot declare yourselves independent of my rule. As you are aware, that is not the way of things in this world."

While slicing a cucumber round in half, his mother said, as if they were discussing nothing more important than the day's weather, "Well, dear, perhaps now that you have reinstated yourself, we could manage to find some compromise. You know, to maintain your pride. And of course, neither of us would ever gainsay you in public. Isn't that right, Ollie."

Olivia nodded her consent. "Of course, Mother. Not in public."

"Not..." Drew straightened and placed his hands on either side of his plate. This went beyond the pale. His presence these past few years may have been a bit scant, but it did not diminish his position in this household, not in the least. He would put a stop to this nonsense posthaste.

"There is nothing to compromise," Drew said in his sternest voice. "I am lord of this house and my word is the final word."

Ollie and his mother glanced at each other with indiscernible expressions. However, the clout of rebellion clung to their postures. From the corner of his eye, Drew caught sight of his uncle fidgeting with his cravat. That matter, the man's involvement with the murders, was of more importance than this. However, getting his family in proper order was far from insignificant. Drew huffed a sharp sigh. This night was overrun with impediments.

His mother opened her mouth, but Charles, speaking for the first time, cut off words certain to enhance the uprising.

"Perhaps we all need a moment to catch our breaths," his uncle said.

"Splendid idea, Charles," his mother said to her brother. "Why don't the two of you go and enjoy a brandy while Ollie and I take an evening stroll in the gardens. Let tempers settle and we'll all sleep on our thoughts. Tomorrow we can have a calm, reasonable discussion."

Drew had serious doubts as to whether a new day would produce a calm discussion on this matter. He would not have his position of authority reduced to a figurehead. A brandy, however, sounded like just the thing. Besides, he could take care of this family dissension later, as well as Foxboro. He needed to deal with his uncle, tonight.

"Yes, Mother," Drew said. "On that you are correct." He pushed back from the table, sent his sister a short but polite nod, and then led Charles into the study.

Chapter 19

Burke kicked over a chunk of rubble with the toe of his ash-coated boot. All he found was more rubble.

He'd devoted his afternoon to coming down to the burned-out ruins of the foundling home in hopes of finding a clue as to what may have started the fire. So far, all he'd gotten for his time and trouble were soot-stained clothes and a nose full of ash.

The acrid odor of smoke and burnt wood hung strong in its stagnancy, and evoked memories of the crippling fear he'd experienced the day of the fire, the moment he'd learned Rose was inside the burning building. He'd never forget it. If he lived a thousand years, he would not forget.

Rose was safe at home. Dove was safe, too. At least for the time being. But Lady Dove Barrow had a belly full of rage and hurt. He well knew the awful decisions such turmoil could inspire. Hence, his presence in this horrid reminder of what had happened. He could suffocate on the knowledge of how much worse it might have been.

The roof was gone to ashes, as was the second floor. Much of the perimeter stones around the first floor remained in place, blackened, and without doubt, unstable. The top of what was left of the walls was jagged in their nonuniform destruction. They imitated ancient ruins against the late day sun.

Picking his way around the back of the toppled and charred remains, Burke continued his search. What he was looking for, he couldn't say. It was doubtful there was anything to find. Whatever clues or proof had been here, if there'd even been any, was now damaged beyond recognition.

Using his booted foot, he shoved aside debris, broken and blackened stones, scorched wood. All he found was more of the same. Every bit of it reeking of the fire's after-stench. In a few places, thin spirals of smoke still rose, like charred spirits escaping Hell. He had no concerns of the fire flaring up again. There was nothing left to burn.

He rounded the back corner, careful to step over a pile of lumber, burned black, still soggy from the futile attempts to quell the fire. Something on the ground, near the empty gape where the back door had been, caught his eye. He took a few more steps.

It was a brass bucket. Soot covered most of it, but enough streaks of its color showed through to snag his attention. It lay tipped on its side next to a pile of large, blackened stones, that used to be a wall.

He squatted on the ground beside the bucket and set it upright. Thick liquid, dark and pungent, rolled in the bottom, it's slick spillage puddled on the ground where the bucket had lain. Burke lowered his head to the top of the bucket and sniffed. Coal oil.

Marching around the building to the black and listing, wooden stub of what was left of the front door. Burke crossed the stoop, still marred with the red of Derek's blood, and into what was left of the interior.

It took some careful shuffling, but he found the remnants of the chair that had been burning when he

253

and Drew first rushed into the home. He lifted it a bit and ran a finger along the chair leg and then sniffed his hand. Coal oil. The fire *had* been set deliberately.

A string of vile profanities burst from his fury and landed on the devastation around him.

Rage flared from his core as hot and destructive as the fire that had destroyed the foundling home. That someone had wanted this, had done this, was beyond horrific imaginings. It was a miracle all the children and women had made it out alive. And Rose, his precious Rose. If Drew's uncle was indeed involved, Drew would no longer have to worry about Dove's actions. Burke would kill the man himself.

"Oh!" a startled voice said from behind him.

Burke spun around, still wrapped tight in his rage. A woman stood in the open space of the doorway. Hester, one of the women who worked here with the children. She was a thin, mousy woman of her middle years with a warm smile and kind eyes. At present, however, there wasn't a hint of her smile, and even in the dimming light he couldn't miss the nervous clutch of her hands, and how fear pried her brown eyes wide.

Burked schooled his features and managed to control his rage. The last thing he wanted to do was frighten this saint of a woman. She and the other women who worked and lived here had dedicated their lives to caring for orphaned and abandoned children.

"Lord Darington," Hester said, bowing her head a bit.

"Hester, my apologies. I didn't mean to frighten you. I…I wasn't expecting anyone to show up here."

"Yes, well, I suppose I surprised you, too. And this place," she said, sweeping a saddened gaze across the still smoldering ruins of what had been her home. "It was never fancy, but it's downright eerie now. I was hoping something might be salvageable." She made another slow, visual search of the burned out remains of the building where she'd lived and worked for so many years.

"I'm afraid there is nothing here to be saved," Burke told her. "But Rose has organized a charity drive. Deliveries of clothing are already being made. When the new foundling home is finished, it will be furnished with everything needed, and then some. You have my word."

She smiled at him, her fear replaced with warm gratitude. "You and Lady Darington have been so kind."

"Many people are putting forth effort to help."

"Yes, but we know who is behind it all, and we are every one of us ever so grateful."

"Where are you and the other women staying?"

He'd been so consumed with the children, the cause of the fire, be it accident or deliberate, and helping Drew with his situation, he'd not considered the women of the foundling home. Rose would have, though. She would have seen to their needs. Rose was a true angel.

"Like the children, we're scattered about," Hester said. "Thanks to you and your wife, everybody has a place to stay until the new home is finished."

Burke nodded. "Hester, did anything unusual happen the day of the fire?"

"Oh, well," she said on a sigh. "Jeremy had fallen. The children were running through here and the boy stumbled over a rag doll left on the floor. He cut his head on the edge of the table. It wasn't a bad cut, but it bled something fierce. While we were tending to Jeremy, two of the older girls got into a squabble over a dress. Everything was rather chaotic that day." She chuckled a bit. "Well, more than usual."

Her face changed then, distress contorted her features, deepening the creases time and worry had stamped on her face.

"What is it, Hester?"

"Jeremy was hysterical," she said, clutching her hands before her. "Some of the children were blaming each other for his falling. There was some crying, some yelling. The sight of blood had a couple of them upset. The dress the girls were fighting about ripped, and they got even louder. Elsa was working to settle their argument. She had to raise her voice to be heard. Raisin was barking and Brennan couldn't settle him. Rose and Dove were upstairs with some of the other children."

Hester squeezed her eyes shut for a moment before opening them. She continued her story with a trembling voice. "In all the uproar, I'm worried that…you see, I'd just put a kettle on the boil, and I was cleaning when Jeremy started screaming."

Her head twisted, stopping to focus on the blackened hearth at the end of the room that had served the home for heat and cooking. The dented kettle still hung from a rod over the iron coal grate, cold as death, now. Most of the wooden shelves once hung on the wall beside it were burned away. What was left of the home's simple dishes and cooking utensils sat broken and blackened, more parts of the rubble about the floor.

"I dropped the rags I was using to clean, maybe, maybe too close to the fire, and ran to Jeremy, and…then the girls were arguing. Usually I'm so careful, but I just don't remember." Misery was clear in her droop. "This may all be my fault."

Hester slapped a hand over her mouth and made a valiant effort to control her emotions.

"Hester," Burke said on a gentle tone. He needed her head to be clear so he could get some answers. If he told her what he knew right now, it would further clog her mind. "I'm sorry to make you talk about this, but it's important. Did any visitors come here to the foundling home the day of the fire?"

She took a breath, straightened her simple, dark blue skirt, and then, a spark of remembrance showed through her watery eyes. "Yes. With everything that happened, I'd forgotten all about him. It was during all the commotion with the children when a man knocked on the door. He wasn't a visitor, though."

"Who was he?"

"He might have told me his name. I don't remember. He said he was from the city inspection office, here to inspect the building."

Burke had to force a façade of calm. "Had you ever seen him before?"

"No."

"Has anyone ever been here to inspect the building before?"

Hester thought for a moment. "Well, I've been here near to fifteen years. In that time, I don't recall anyone ever coming here to inspect anything, not even once. We've always been left on our own. Without your wife, and her campaigning charity for the children, our situation would have been wracked with hardships. Thinking about it now, it was odd, that man showing up here."

"Hester, did the man carry a bucket?"

"Hmm. Yes, he did. A brass bucket with a cloth over the top. I assumed he carried a few tools with him. I didn't give it much thought."

"Did you see where he went, what he did?"

"He first walked through the rooms down here," she said, a sad glance drifting over the charred remains of the home. Bringing back her attention, Hester said, "The last I saw, he was walking up the stairs. I was too busy with Jeremy and the situation down here to go with him. While Elsa was handling the girl's argument, I carried Jeremy in back where we keep the stores, you know, so I could tend to the cut on his head."

Burke nodded.

"I got him fixed up and calm, and then I heard the children yelling fire. After that, well, we were all in a frenzy trying to get everyone out. I forgot all about the man. Do you think he got out in time? I don't remember seeing him in the crowd. But I was so worried over the children, and Rose and Dove, well, I just don't know." Her hand clutched at her chest as if to keep her breath calm.

"Ease yourself, Hester. Lord Worthington and I searched through every room. Nobody died in this fire."

Ellen, the girl the women had gone back into the building to save, crossed his mind. Perhaps she hadn't fallen and hit her head in a frantic attempt to escape the fire. Maybe she saw something she wasn't supposed to see, and someone tried making sure she wouldn't tell. He'd find out from Rose where the girl was staying and go talk to her.

"Can you tell me what the man looked like?"

"Well," Hester said, rubbing her hands together before clutching them again. "He had blond hair, very light in color and not so thick. His skin was fair. He was thin, maybe four or five inches shorter than you. I didn't pay much attention to the man. As I said, it was a hectic day."

Her description could fit dozens of men he knew. Perhaps Ellen might have something more useful to add. Burke glanced up past the remaining, blackened walls, and into the sky where the sun had lowered beneath what was left of the foundling home. Nightfall was not far off.

"We should go," he said. "It's getting late."

As he walked her back to her hackney carriage, Burke said, "Hester. The fire was not your fault."

"But I'm just not sure about the rags I'd been using to clean, and I saw at least one of the chairs on fire when I ran back in. Maybe there were more burning, probably. It could have started the whole thing. I don't know. All I could think of was getting the children out."

They each skirted a sludgy puddle and met on the other side. "Hester, you're not to blame for the fire." He hated having to tell her the fire was intentional. However, he could not allow her to continue berating herself, worrying over something not her fault. "I believe the man who was here claiming to be an inspector set it deliberately."

Hester stumbled, and Burke caught her arm and steadied her.

"Deliberately? But why? Why would anyone do such a thing? There was no profit to be made. The building was near to useless to anyone but us. And we're not far off from leaving it. We weren't a threat to anyone. I don't understand why anyone would do such a thing."

"I don't know. But I promise you, I'm going to find out."

Chapter 20

"Close the door," Drew spat at his uncle.

By the time the door clicked shut, Drew had stridden across the room to the polished, umber side cabinet and poured a brandy. He did not offer one to Charles. Drink in hand, he rotated with deliberate slowness until he faced his uncle.

Charles stood but a couple feet inside the closed door of the study, more spacious and better appointed than the dim box of a study in his own home. Though his uncle had been in the room many times, as he'd tended the finances for years, his gaze shifted from one item to the next as if seeing it all for the first time.

A square Aubusson carpet centered the glossy wood floor. Several low-backed chairs with embroidered cushions offered comfortable and sufficient seating. An inset of shelves on one wall held the family ledgers, going back many years. The other walls, all papered in pale green, bore the added adornments of several landscapes in oil. The hearty fire in the hearth and several candles about the room gave them plenty of light.

His uncle sent a longing glance toward the crystal decanter upon the cabinet, more than half full of Drew's fine brandy. He said nothing, though.

After downing a hearty swallow, Drew set his glass on the cabinet and glared at his uncle. "Start talking."

Micki Miller

"They weren't supposed to die."

Well, at least he didn't dance around, pretend he didn't know what all this was about. The man got a bit of credit there. It didn't even begin to cover his debt.

"Your story rings false. You expect me to believe you and your compatriots attacked the Barrow's carriage, hooded and armed, to what, frighten them?"

"Yes! Exactly! I can explain everything," Charles said, more stirred than Drew had ever seen him. So much to this man he'd known his whole life yet didn't know in the least.

His uncle appeared to stumble in his thoughts before taking another direction. "By the by, how did you discover the pendent? I told your mother never to open the bag." Charles let loose a snide chortle. "Lest the magic spill out."

Drew endeavored to set aside his uncle's belittling tone directed at his mother, Charles's own sister. It would not be forgotten, though. The cost of his condescension raised the sum of his misdeeds another notch.

"If you did not want the brooch for yourself, why did you steal it?"

Stiffening at the offence, as if stealing was a worse crime than murder, Charles said, "I'm not some common thief. The piece was exquisite. Far too precious to be handed down to their tainted spawn."

Drew's jaw tightened to the point of pain. Keeping a calm façade was more difficult a task than he'd ever had in even his most challenging card games. He did it, though. He had to.

"Once I got it home," Charles continued, oblivious to the roiling pot of danger he stirred. "I realized I

262

couldn't keep it. I painted some nonsense markings on a velvet bag and made up a story for your mother, made sure she gave a severe warning to her chambermaid to never, ever open the bag. It would be safe kept under her pillow."

Charles paused for a moment. "How did it find its way into your hands?"

"Never mind about the pendent for now," Drew said. Now or ever. He would never tell Charles about how the brooch came to be in his possession. "Tell me about that night."

His uncle's lips pursed, and then crept back into his jowls, as if perturbed. "All we had planned to do was frighten them into leaving London."

"Why?" Drew asked. Though his suspicions were already strong, he needed to hear the confession from his uncle's own mouth.

"You never saw her, did you?"

At Drew's stony silence, Charles's composure faltered a tad. He rallied, though. The man had a defense to construct.

"The woman Lord Barrow brought back from the Colonies, she could never assimilate, no matter their efforts to refine her. There are characteristics fine clothing and manners cannot conceal. The dark tone of her skin, the foreign form of her face. She looked as if she'd stepped straight out of some portrait of those savages from over there. It was appalling."

Drew kept his casual stance, going so far as to lean back against the cabinet. Beneath his pretense, though, seethed a rage toxic enough to poison his stratagem. Forcing his tone to remain calm, he said, "Go on."

"At first, they were snubbed, of course. No decent

263

home would have them. I…we, thought they'd weary of their ostracism and leave London, move to some little village on the outskirts, perhaps even out of the country. Anywhere but amongst polite Society."

Charles shook his head and twisted one flat palm against the other in what one might view as a cleansing motion. "Then, there was word floating around some duke found the woman fascinating. There was a rumor he even had them to his house for tea. I don't know if any of it was true, but it made all the difference in how she was viewed. In a bare instant, the woman was accepted. The Barrows' paraded her around to every social event. Most of the *ton* considered it an honor to host her. Can you even imagine such a thing?"

Drew held his tongue but failed to restrain in full his glare of contempt. The power of even that small portion of his fury jostled his uncle's composure. Charles paced to the sash window, left open half a foot or so to let in the fresh breeze. After but a moment, he pivoted from what little there was to see in the night and continued his explanation.

"After rumors of the duke's acceptance and the consequent change in Society's attitude, we knew we had to act. We *had* to. Suppose more of her kind sailed here to make London their home? What would become of the upper classes were we to be inundated with immigrants from this other culture?"

He shot a haughty glance at Drew, as if his point was valid and should close the conversation. At Drew's silence, Charles continued.

"We had meetings, the three of us, to decide the best course of action. We could think of nothing feasible. We circulated about town, to different events, testing the waters and keeping our ears open to assess the general mood. After a time, scarce word of the woman was spoken. However, we were all confident if others like her arrived in our fine country, more would join our cause."

"Were there anymore immigrants from the Colonies?"

"No, thank the good Lord. So we held still. That is, until the situation turned ruinous."

"Ruinous? What do you mean?"

With an expression of utter distaste, Charles said, "They had a child."

Dove.

"Mixing the blood of nobility with the blood of savages. It was an outrage, an affront to civilization."

Drew's fingers squeezed into the polished wood of the cabinet with unseen fierceness. If he didn't cling to the heavy piece of furniture, he might well disembowel his uncle with his bare hands.

"We bided our time," Charles continued. "We assumed they would not want to raise their child where it could never belong. Good God, she was a damned hybrid. It's one thing for the family to damage their own lives by living outside the proprieties of the upper crust. But to subject their offspring to such humiliation. We were certain the tide would turn at any moment, the proper cuts would return, and they would be forced to leave."

"The snubs didn't return, though, and the Barrows didn't leave," Drew said. Without a doubt, the cabinet would forever bear the imprints of his fingers.

"No. Well, a few snubs, but not many and none severe. The child came. The entire family remained in residence without a drop of shame to show for what they'd done. In fact, they thrived. All because of that damned duke's approval, they continued to be received. It was as if it was a natural thing for them to blend in. When thought of at all, the half-breed child was viewed as exotic."

Drew gritted his teeth at the ugly epithet, thrown at the woman he loved. He said nothing, though. He wanted the names of the other two men. Until he had the full story from his uncle, he would toil for restraint. After that…

"We were at a loss as to what we could do about the situation, but in agreement we must do something. The new gossip going around made us decide to wait before we let ourselves be drawn to action."

"What new gossip?"

"It was rumored the duke was going to take up permanent residence at his country estate. His health was waning, and he sought a quieter life. And the duke did leave, eventually. The child was about, oh, eight or nine, by then. We believed in his absence, society would find their good sense and turn on the Barrows. It never happened. There was always new gossip to sway their attention from the matter. The atrocity of the situation had long lost anyone's interest. It was as though those people belonged, as if it were all acceptable. They'd become…rooted here."

Charles paced, continuing to spew his malice, unaware of the fast approach of his reckoning.

"Years passed and the girl grew. Nothing changed. She was granted associations with other children by far too many lords and ladies. The mother was already grown, already claimed by a man. This child they created, however, she would go on, furthering the line and mixing refined English blood with her savage lineage. It was beyond intolerable. Still is, now more than ever, as the half-breed is of marriageable age."

Charles flexed his fingers a couple of times while he stared at nothing. He muttered his next words, but he might as well have shouted them for the power they wielded. "Perhaps it would have been better if their child had been with them that night."

Shaking with rage burgeoned too potent to restrain any longer, Drew lunged at his uncle. He grabbed Charles by his wide lapels while shoving him back against the wall hard enough to rattle the painting beside them and rock it askew.

His uncle stared at him, shock altering his face. The man believed righteousness was on his side and it was clear this reaction baffled him. Then something else emerged from the man's dark depths. An ireful acknowledgement.

"There is a rumor floating about," Charles said. A goading smirk overtook his surprise. "Someone had the gall to say you were courting the young savage. I must assume she is but another of your conquests, convinced your feelings run deeper, correct? Do you care for her? No, of course not. Not you. You've just taken personal offence of my depiction of your paramour. Even you wouldn't sink so low as to pledge yourself to a subhuman. Tell me Drew, as I must admit I am curious. Does her savage blood run her wild beneath the sheets?"

With a barbarous growl, Drew lifted the man by his clothing until his feet scarce touched the floor. His uncle struggled to breathe as the collar of his shirt cut into his throat. The sudden appearance of fear in his glazing eyes showed too late to snap Drew to his senses.

"Your passion for hate makes a fool of your tongue, Uncle. Answer me this. If our courtship is not unfounded gossip, will you kill her to stop us? Would you kill me? Would you slit the throat of your sister's son, your own flesh and blood?"

Charles gasped for air. His face had gone red for lack of it. "I told you," he was scarce able to choke out, panic replacing the arrogance of his hate. "We meant only to frighten them. The murders were not supposed to happen."

"But they did happen. And you've yet to tell me about that night, other than your preposterous proclamation they were not supposed to die."

Charles struggled against his strong hold, yanking at Drew's arms. He failed to gain his release and had to exude pressure from the toe tips of his shoes to keep high enough to garner some relief.

"It's the truth. If you'll let me catch my breath," Charles managed to say on a wheeze. "I'll tell you everything."

With great reluctance, as his fury still burned crimson, Drew unfurled his fingers. Charles slumped against the wall as he tugged at his collar and sucked in air with a course rasp. His eyes watered, and he blinked several times, to clear them, or perhaps to gather himself from the shock.

Massaging his throat, he said, "It can't be true. You're not going to tell me you have feelings for the—" At Drew's lethal expression, Charles scooted along the wall. Drew stalked him, keeping his shadow over the man.

"Continue," Drew ordered.

Charles shook his head as if to lose an impossible thought. With another quick and wary glance at Drew, he sucked in and released a deep breath, and continued his story.

"As I said, we'd planned only to frighten the Barrows in hopes they would leave London and live elsewhere. The girl was coming of age. We had to act before she stepped into the marriage market. Frankly, Drew, I'd think you'd be appalled at the horrid rumor she's started of the two of you. A courtship, for God's sake."

He paused to stare at Drew. Bafflement mixed with the alarm on his scarlet-tinged face. Drew read it clear as print. Charles was struck with the sudden worry the rumor of his courtship with Dove might be true, that his own nephew's feelings for her ran too deep to avert a permanent joining. It was the man's fret of all frets.

Drew hovered over him, no longer schooling his features to hide his rage. Let him see what his deeds had wrought. "Tell me what happened the night of the killings."

Charles paused long to massage his throat before he began his tale in a tone far more docile than before.

"We had a secret meeting place, a shack hidden back in a wooded area. We met there and donned our dark costumes, hoods and all. As we'd learned the Barrows would be attending a dinner at a private residence, we knew where best to intercept their carriage."

Drew used his advantage of height to look down his nose at his uncle. "The short, but lonely stretch of road they had to take to get home. No one would hear them cry for help, three innocents against three armed villains. How very brave of you."

Charles shot him an irritated glance before continuing.

"I pointed my pistol at the driver to keep him in place while the others had the Barrows step out of their carriage. The plan was to threaten them, to make them believe there would be dire consequences, deadly consequences, were they to remain in London. It was only supposed to be a threat. We were certain if we made it believable enough, frightening enough, they would leave London. Before we could even begin our prepared speech, I looked away for but a second, and their driver drew a pistol and shot at me. Everything flew out of bounds from there."

"His ball hit you."

"Yes, well, grazed me," Charles said, his hand giving a brief touch to his long-healed shoulder. "He should have kept his damned weapon pocketed. The escalation was all his fault. And then…then one of the others shot him. The driver fell from his perch and lie still on the ground. We thought he was dead. The woman was screaming. Lord Barrow shoved her behind him. There was another shot."

"From your side, on an unarmed couple."

"Their driver was armed, and he'd been more than willing to kill us."

Bending toward his uncle, Drew said, "What was he supposed to do, stand by and allow you to murder them all?"

"I told you, they weren't supposed to die!"

"But they did die! How were any of them to know

your plan was but a cruel purpose, that you only meant to terrify them?" Before Charles could answer, Drew spat another question into his face. "Who committed the murders? You?"

"No, not me. I told you, it was not our goal. At least it wasn't for two of the three of us. My pistol wasn't even loaded. I thought none of them were. They were supposed to be used for intimidation, nothing more."

"Your two partners had different notions on the matter."

"No, just one of them. I think perhaps he had his own plan from the start."

"Who were they? I want their names."

"Drew, first you have to listen to me. I can better explain our righteous motives—"

Drew had heard enough of his nonsense. There were no excuses for what they'd done. He didn't bother with theatrics, this time. He threw a punch, sending his uncle bouncing against the wall before landing in a hard fall. Drew then hauled the man to his feet and clamped his hands around Charles's throat. He was angry enough to kill his uncle right there in his study, consequences be damned.

Charles clutched at Drew's wrists. He couldn't so much as loosen the determined grip. With the further contraction of Drew's fingers, Charles's face turned red, then deepened to purple.

"Your mother," Charles choked out before his glazed eyes fluttered and his body slackened.

Drew let go of his uncle with a shove and strode away. The thought of his mother or sister finding Charles dead on the floor was the only thing that could have stopped him. With his back to his gasping uncle, Drew said over his shoulder, "You will give me the names of the other two men, or I will kill you."

Drew spun around and stalked to his uncle. Charles, wheezing and stunned, had managed to get into a seated position. Drew squatted before him, the menace in his voice matched his expression and was a clear warning his threat was real.

"Do you hear me, Uncle? I *will* kill you."

With his chest heaving, Charles rolled his eyes toward Drew. "Lord Ephraim. He shan't be any concern to you, though. As of two days ago, he's dead. I already planned on telling you about the other."

At Drew's dubious expression, Charles said, "It's true. The man you seek is Lord Eric Flynn. He's the one who was prepared to kill that night. Like me, Ephraim had not loaded his pistol."

"Who brought the knife? Tell me who used it." His uncle's face retracted in a slight cringe at the mention of the knife. "I read in the papers Lady Barrow had been stabbed to death. *Who brought the knife?*"

"Flynn. It was all Flynn. After he shot their driver, he dropped his pistol and withdrew another one from a pocket, already loaded. He killed Barrow but a mere second or two later. The woman fell to the ground beside her husband, weeping, in hysterics. Flynn withdrew a knife from what appeared to be and endless cache of weapons, and he attacked her. Even after she…"

"What?"

Charles tipped his head down, as if to shame his quieted words into a less vile state. "Even after she was dead, he didn't cease his stabbing until he'd exhausted himself."

Sick anger pounded in Drew's head. He wasn't aware of the violent extreme of the woman's murder. *Did Dove know the further gruesomeness of her mother's death?* Dear God, he hoped not.

"Ephraim and I had no part in that, I tell you. None. It was all Flynn."

"You claim your innocence, Uncle, say your own pistol was not even loaded."

"It's true! I would never go so far. I am not a savage."

"As you claim the woman of foreign blood to be. But look what skin tone committed this heinous act."

Drew's damning words hit the mark. Charles grew stiff with insult, but of course, he had no viable retort.

"Yet, as told in your own story, Uncle, neither you nor Ephraim made any attempt to save those innocent people from Flynn's murderous rampage."

"Everything happened so fast. One moment, Ephraim was about to deliver our speech, then in the blink of an eye, they were all dead. Well, we thought the driver was dead. Flynn's determination ran deeper than either of us could have guessed. After that night, both Ephraim and I ended our association with Flynn, of course. Since there was nothing we could do to change the past, it was pointless to go to the authorities. All we'd accomplish was dooming ourselves, and to what end? Scandal for all of you?"

His expression pleaded to Drew for understanding. Perhaps even due gratitude for his protecting the family from a devastating scandal. Drew only hated him more. Keeping scandal from the family was but a fortunate consequence of his efforts to keep his neck from the hangman's noose. At Drew's unyielding gaze, Charles deflated, but continued with his story.

"Flynn contacted us a few weeks ago, insisted we meet with him. We learned his bloodlust was not sated, but has simmered over these past three years. Ephraim and I met with him, thinking we could calm him, make him understand how fortunate we all were to have escaped prosecution for what we'd already done. Besides, what he wanted us to do this time, what he's already done…"

"What do you mean?" Drew asked, his neck prickling. "What did he do?"

"He's the reason I'm here tonight, Drew. I came to see you with every intention of telling you about Flynn. He's is why I've scarce been at my home. I'm here to ask for your help. You see, things have gone awry."

Chapter 21

From her small, leafy spot concealed in the mass of shrubbery outside the open window to Drew's study, Dove missed nothing.

After she'd seen Charles enter the house, and not long thereafter, Drew, her insides were charged with the knowledge she was nearing the end of her long mission.

She'd crept around the outside of the house to Drew's study, anticipating it would be the room where the men would go to speak after their evening meal. Using both hands, she lifted the bottom half of the sash window so she could hear everything. Then, with patience so thin it stood only out of necessity, she waited.

She recognized both names he had given to Drew. She was familiar with one of their homes, Lord Flynn, as she had made a search of it on one of her expeditions. Flynn had no wife. He lived alone. She'd searched his home anyway, as she would leave no possibility unexplored. The other name no longer mattered. If what Drew's uncle said was true, Ephraim was dead. Flynn, however…

These past three years, she'd thought her mother had died in an instant from a single knife wound, a tragic, but quick death. It's what her grandparents had told her. She should have been suspicious when they forbade her from reading the papers. At the time, however, she'd been too grief-stricken to foster a quarrel.

When she heard Drew's uncle tell of the excessive violence her mother had suffered in the last, grisly moments of her life, Dove had to crush her hand over her mouth to keep the scream from escaping. Her tears flowed, though, rolling over her hand and dropping to the ground, a silent patter of anguish. With significant effort, she managed to hold quiet and still.

After Drew's uncle finished his story and the men made their exit from his study, Dove used her sleeve to wipe her face, and then wove her way out of the shrubbery, catching her simple, deep brown skirt on a twig.

The dark color of her clothing was a deliberate choice. When she'd left home, daylight still lingered enough to prohibit her from smuggling out her Bandit attire. Especially with all the extra people wandering about the house. Yet she'd needed to be as inconspicuous as possible in case a scenario such as this arose.

Dove shook loose her skirts and continued at a brisk pace toward the carriage.

At the edge of the scythed lawn, she paused, listening for approaching carriages. Nothing but a slight and silent breeze wafted through the darkness. It brushed cool against the last traces of dampness upon her face, helping to shroud her grievous fury.

She crossed the street at a long angle, blending in with the night as best she could. Renny awaited her with the carriage, positioned at the border of two large properties with a partial concealment of several fat elm trees. It was a perfect place for cover. Much needed, since they'd parked there before the sun had set in full.

At her approach, Renny emerged from the shadows cast by the elm's blockade of the three-quarter moon.

"Were you seen?" he asked, his head swinging from one direction to the other. "I don't like this at all, you out undisguised, traipsing through yards. And at such an early hour. People are still up and about." Renny scrubbed a hand down his face and shook his head.

She and Renny had been alternating their watches between Drew's house and his uncle's. The man she sought was bound to turn up sooner or later at one of the residences. Tonight, luck played on their team.

"Don't worry," Dove told him. "I wasn't seen. I did learn something, though."

"What's that?" Renny asked as he hurried to open the carriage door.

"We already knew Drew's uncle was there that night, knew he was the man you shot. But now I know he was not the one who killed my parents."

Renny froze in the dark frame of the open door. He twisted his head enough to gaze back.

"One of the men, Lord Ephraim, is dead. I'm not dismissing Drew's uncle. He was there, a part of it, and he will pay. But he's not the one I most want, the one I've been searching for all this time. At long last, I now know for certain the name of the man who murdered my parents."

Renny made a slow rotation to face her. The moon shed enough light for Dove to see his expression, surprise mixed with a good dose of worry. For he was aware of the next step in her plan. It was the step, she was certain, Renny thought would never come.

"Dove," he said.

She hated the bilious dread in his voice. Had she not needed to be out at such an early hour, she would have gone on this mission alone. This was the part to which she'd always planned to exclude Renny. Both homes were close enough she could have walked in a reasonable amount of time. There'd been no choice, though. She couldn't be walking around all alone. She couldn't even ride. It would draw unwanted attention, and stir gossip of her going out unchaperoned.

Even in the broken light of the moon, speckled by countless leaves and branches of the elm trees, Renny's paling complexion was clear. This new swell already reaped a toll from him.

"It's all right, Renny. You don't need to worry. Drew is handling it from here."

"He…You're allowing it?"

She wouldn't, no. This was what she'd waited for. She'd earned the right to exact justice, to execute the overdue sentence, and stand witness to the villain's spilled blood. For three years she had practiced what she would say to him, at what moment she would fire the lead ball into his soulless heart. And every day without fail, she anticipated the conclusiveness of witnessing the life depart from his eyes.

Even if she wanted to, which she didn't, she couldn't make a report to the authorities without revealing she was the Creeping Bandit. One way or another, it was sure to come out. Nor would she endanger Renny's fragile health by telling him her mind had not changed. If it meant she had to lie to him, then that is what she would do.

"Yes, Renny. Drew will speak with the magistrate.

I've tempted fate long enough," Dove told him, unable to look him in the eye. They'd always had such a close and honest relationship. She feared he might read the lie on her face.

Dove ascended the carriage steps and settled herself while Renny stood in the open door. For the better part of a minute, the only sound was the quiet rustling of her arranging and rearranging her skirts. She was quite sure he wanted to believe her, and just as certain of his doubts. Her friend's worry did at last recede into the arms of his wish, but at a sluggish pace.

"We're going home then?" Renny asked several moments after she stilled.

His belief balanced on the precarious edge of her lie. Dove looked him straight in the nose and said, "Yes. After these past days, I think we both deserve to find our beds early tonight."

"Yes, little bird," Renny said with an unmistakable sigh of relief.

It inspired a quiet one from Dove. He believed her tale, believed she had relinquished control of the mission to Drew. The closeness she'd shared with Drew, his knowledge of her secret identity, his assistance, the way he'd put himself at risk, all gave support to her story. Renny stepped back and bent in an elegant bow.

His very proper decorum gave her a smile, as they'd long ago done away with all such formalities, when not in the company of others.

"Home it is," Renny said before closing the door.

The coach rocked as he climbed onto the driver's box and took his seat. Fifteen minutes later, she was home.

"Good night, Dove," Renny said before climbing up again and steering the carriage around back to finish his duties for the night.

"Sleep well, my friend," Dove whispered at his back as he drove away.

She entered her house in time to help tuck the children into their beds. It was a ritual she and her grandfather had taken from the nanny they'd hired because it so pleased them both.

"How is Lady Darington? her grandfather asked as they ascended the stairs behind the four little ones they'd taken in. The children took slow steps, reluctant to call an end to the day, and yet too tired to extend it any longer.

Dove sent a bare shift of a glance his way. She'd told him Rose was ill, and she'd gone to sit with her this evening. This day, the lies poured from her mouth in a fountain of deceit. *Every lie was necessary for the protection of the ones she loved.*

"Feeling better," Dove said. "The babe she carries makes her stomach quite nauseous. But she managed to sip some vegetable broth tonight and eat a bit of bread."

Before he could question her further, the girls popped into their room with assurances she and her grandfather would be back soon to tuck them in. The rest of them continued down the hall and into the boys' room.

They'd assigned the two girls, Marion and Elizabeth, five and nine, to one room, and the two boys, Elmer and Mark, both seven, to another. There were enough rooms in the house for them to each have their own, but they were used to sharing and Dove didn't want any of them to wake up alone in unfamiliar surroundings. They saw to the boys, in no hurry at all to listen to the children's thoughts and ideas, before blowing out the candle, and closing the door.

The girls had already changed into their nightclothes. In a trice, they were tucked snug in their beds, with warm blankets and soft, fluffy pillows. Marion smiled up at Dove when she sat on the edge of her bed. Dove used her fingers to comb away strands of wavy gold hair from the child's sweet little face. A small ache twisted in the center of her chest. It had ricked her in the boys' room, too.

The last couple of nights, for the first time since before her parents were killed, Dove thought about children of her own. What might her world be like? With the end of her long ordeal close in sight, life beyond her goal of finding the killers made a sudden demand for her attention. The heavy ramparts surrounding her obsession shifted with a slow grind, and parted. Just a smidgeon, but it was enough for her to get a glimpse of beguiling possibilities.

Might normalcy lie in her future? It was a lovely thought, but still too far out of hand to settle a belief. If she was caught tonight, a risk truer than ever before, her life would be over. *As would any future she might have with Drew.*

Drew. Her grandfather said he was a good man, and he was right. She'd had covert watch over the scene with his uncle tonight. At some point in his reckless life of indulgences, a man had emerged from his adolescent existence. A good man. A strong man. A man who cared to his core and bore a keen sense of justice.

A man she loved, could love forever.

Her parents. Keep focused. She mustn't fall out of

step now. Not when justice was so close. If she were not killed or arrested this night, then, then she might look forward and explore a fresh path. For now, it would be foolish to allow her mind to wander toward what might never be.

With the children nestled in their beds for the night, Dove kissed her grandfather on the cheek and wished him pleasant dreams. After a quick stop in the library, she sequestered herself in her bedchamber, and she waited.

For a while, she attempted to read the novel she'd chosen to help her pass the slow-moving time. After reading the same page three times, and still not knowing what she'd read, she set the book on her dressing table, and she paced. First to the white lace covered window, then to the closed, paneled door, back again, circle the half-tester bed and the old cedar chest at the foot. Repeat.

At the proper time, she blew out her single candle, lest someone see the light seeping beneath her door and check on her. Enough moonlight shone through the window, and of course, she knew the room well enough to pace it in the dark.

Fifteen minutes later, she raised her hand to her mouth to smother a yawn. The last days had taken such a toll on her emotions as to rob her of needed sleep. Pausing beside her soft bed, she considered lying down for a nap. The consideration passed almost as soon as it arrived. Without a doubt, any attempt to nap would be as futile as her effort to read. So Dove resumed her pacing, and thinking about everything she'd heard from outside the window of Drew's study.

Charles said Ephraim was dead, killed by Flynn.

Lord Eric Flynn, one of the three men who had attacked her parents' carriage. He was the one who had come armed that night, ready with two loaded pistols, and a knife.

Now Flynn had taken the trio's guiding motives in a new direction, a direction more extreme than his cohorts had ever imagined.

Dove was still in shock the man had gone to the foundling home and set it on fire. Flynn was on a mission to rid London of every life he deemed unworthy. It was unfathomable. For even having the thought in his head he should hang. He wouldn't hang, though. The monster wasn't going to live long enough to see a trial. Nor would Drew's uncle.

Odd as it was, Dove managed to set aside those thoughts. After all the waiting, the crying, the sneaking around in people's homes, the ordeal was quite near to the end. By the morrow, it would be over.

Drew's Uncle Charles and Lord Ephraim were clear in their condemnation of Flynn, at his plan to set fire to the foundling home. There was a limit to even their extended boundaries of bigotry. Flynn thought them weak and ineffectual, and had been outraged at what he saw as their treason. Nothing would stop Flynn. *Nothing but death.*

Ephraim was already dead, drowned in his own courtyard fountain. Flynn had smashed the man's head against the concrete side first. With all the blood, it appeared to have been an accident, as if he'd taken an unfortunate stumble into death.

Had it not been for the appearance of two men taking a shortcut through the alley behind the tavern where Flynn confessed this to Drew's uncle, with a knife to his throat, Charles would not have lived long enough to tell the tale to Drew. His death would have appeared to be a robbery of the worst sort.

Tonight, Drew and his uncle were going after Flynn.

They were to meet in front of Drew's house at midnight. They would ride to where Charles thought Flynn might be hiding. She would be close behind them. All this was decided as she stood outside the window to Drew's study, and didn't require further thought. After all, she'd been planning for three years.

It was what else she'd seen and heard this night keeping space in her head, and her heart.

She couldn't stop thinking about Drew's reactions to what his uncle said earlier in the Worthington study. From her spot outside the window, she had a clear view of the eruption of his fury, ignited by his uncle's foul words. Drew stepped up to her defense, to the defense of her parents, who he never even met. His outrage wasn't for show. He didn't know she was there to witness his behavior. Yet Drew was driven to threaten his own uncle with murder for his part in the crimes against her family. And he'd meant it.

No one who saw the rage on Drew's face in that moment could doubt his seriousness. Nor did it escape her what broke his control. His uncle's vicious comments already had him coiled. The remark about how it was a shame she hadn't been with her parents the night they were murdered, sprung Drew into lethal violence.

Could a man react so if his heart was not immersed? And if their love was indeed true, was there a chance it could overcome everything standing between them? The second question shifted in her head until she saw it from every direction. She would have her answer by sunrise. For then, the question would be posed to Drew.

With significant effort, she steeled herself for the probable answer. After she murdered two men before Drew's eyes, one being his own flesh and blood, she wouldn't have to bother querying him about what lay in his heart. More expected than not, he'd be the one to deliver her to the magistrate.

Dove paced her room some more.

In time, the house quieted. At the closing of her grandfather's door, her anxiousness to get going increased to an almost unbearable point. She waited, though. She waited until she knew the servants completed their nightly tasks and were in their rooms, until she was confident the household was asleep.

And then she opened her mother's cedar chest at the foot of her bed. From beneath the array of folded blankets and old clothes she used for cover, she removed her Bandit costume. On this night, she did not carry it in a bundle until she was secluded within a carriage driven by Renny. She changed clothes in her room.

Before leaving, she plunged her arm to the bottom of the chest again, and glided her hand to the back, left corner. There it was. Her fingers wrapped around the beaded sheath and withdrew the piece of her mother's heritage. She tucked the simple trade knife into her coat pocket.

As quiet as she could, Dove took light steps down to the first floor. The darkness didn't matter, as she knew the house well enough to get where she needed to be without the assistance of a candle. She had no trouble finding her way to her grandfather's study.

At his desk, in the bottom drawer, she slipped her hand to the back and tapped around until she felt it. She withdrew her grandfather's pistol. From the same drawer, she removed the box he kept there, and knelt on the floor beside the window. She opened the box containing several pouches.

In the generous shaft of moonlight, she first checked to make sure there was plenty of flint left to give a proper spark and avoid a misfire. She poured in the powder, dropped in the wad, and then, of course, inserted the lead ball. Sliding out the ramrod from beneath the barrel, she used it to tamp it all down. Once she'd primed the flash pad with a bit of fine powder, she closed the frizzen and lay the pistol on the floor. She shut the box and returned it to the drawer.

Dove stood and tucked the pistol in the other pocket of her coat, separate from the knife, tipped up so she wouldn't loosen and lose what she'd packed. She opened the window of the study and slipped out to land on the ground with a soft thud.

In the stables, she saddled her horse as quiet as she could. After leading her gentle mare down to the street, Dove mounted her horse, and disappeared into the darkness.

Chapter 22

"He's not here," Charles said with little more than a hasty glance at the pathetic little structure.

The hut's small size and evident tone of abandonment helped conceal it back in the thick growth of woods. The lack of so much as the flicker of candlelight gave credence to his uncle's conclusion.

With hope and a touch of fervor, Charles said, "Maybe he's done us all a favor and left town."

Drew shot a quick, narrow scowl at his uncle. "When there are still those about London who don't deserve to live?"

Charles shrunk at the sarcastic anger. Or perhaps it was his failure to extract himself from a dangerous situation. Either way, Drew gave not a wisp of concern for the man's wants or fears.

His uncle had been making excuses since they'd met in front of the stables at Charles's home. They'd arranged the midnight rendezvous hours before, following the scene in Drew's study, and some bullyrag persuasion on Drew's part. His uncle's original plan was to have Drew take care of Flynn, whatever he meant by *take care of*. The insinuation was murder. Drew introduced a new plan, and made it clear he would suffer no discord.

While seeing both men dead would put a quick and just end to this retched ordeal, he was not an executioner. It was his intention to haul Flynn to Bow Street and let the proper authorities manage his future. He was prepared in full to turn over his uncle, too. Charles was unaware of this portion of his plan, hence the extra rope hidden in Drew's saddlebag.

Tomorrow, he would make immediate arrangements for an overseas holiday for his mother and sister. A long one.

His uncle's complaints commenced right at the start when Charles refused to ride a horse. Drew had grabbed him by the scruff of his cowardice neck and told him he'd have to forgo his fear of horses and ride tonight.

"Like you did the night of the murders," Drew told him.

"I was younger then," Charles argued.

"It was three years ago. Are you even afraid of horses at all, or was the claim part of your guise?"

"I don't care for horses. I would never ride for pleasure. Sometimes, though, one must adjust. Couldn't you just go yourself? I'm sure to be a hindrance anyway."

Drew didn't spend another word debating. He released Charles, entered the stables, saddled a horse, and led it out. Drew then sat upon his own steed with feigned patience as his uncle made a clumsy mount.

They'd ridden according to his uncle's directions. Two to three quiet miles from town, Charles stopped at a massive, fallen oak off to the left. It lay at an angle, the bottom nearest them, dirt-caked roots dangling over the edge of the road.

"There's a path on the other side of this felled monstrosity," Charles said, nodding at the prone tree.

"It leads to a small cottar's hut back in the woods. The three of us used to meet there."

"Ah, yes, a fine place to convene and plan the cold-blooded murder of people who'd done you no wrong," Drew said while scanning the woods.

His uncle had the gall to sound exasperated. "I've been over this with you already."

"Yes, they weren't supposed to die. You only meant to terrify an innocent man and woman. And their driver, of course, for having the poor sense to be in their employ. Your excuses do naught but further condemn you, Uncle, so keep them to yourself."

Drew guided his horse over the fallen tree. Once on the other side, he twisted back to his uncle. "Let's go."

With reluctant resignation, Charles managed to direct his horse over the tree, and then he followed Drew down the narrow path.

Enough patches of moonlight survived the fall through the leaves to light their way. A frog croaked, so loud in quiet of the woods. Drew was grateful for the cover. He didn't see or hear signs of anyone else in the vicinity, but that meant nothing. Flynn might well be expecting trouble. There were endless smears of darkness where he could hide, to lie in wait for a surprise attack.

Some small critter, rustled into disturbance by their passing, scurried away through the underbrush. From behind him, Charles sucked in a quick breath at the sound. Out of his comfortable, well-ordered, civilized settings, with a killer's ire on his back, his uncle must be terrified. Good. It was but the beginning of his punishment.

They stopped in front of the hut and dismounted.

Even the soft cast of moonlight couldn't endear the old structure's dilapidated condition. The window was but a glassless opening, a gapped tooth in a rotted mouth. Thin log beams lay exposed on part of the low-sloped roof where the thatch had deteriorated. Strands hung limp down from the front left corner in a stringy teardrop.

Perhaps it was the wear of the roof giving the illusion, or the low light of the night, but the hut appeared to be listing a bit to the left.

If the window opening hadn't shown it was dark within, the breaches between the planks of the front door did. Drew tied the horses to a tree. Charles pushed open the door and they entered the hut.

Inside the pitchy confines, Charles used flint and tinder to light a brimstone match, and then a candle. He had no trouble whatsoever finding the candle and tinderbox in the dark. Yes, his uncle knew this place well.

"This is a waste of time," Charles said. He flicked a gesture about the single room. "Flynn's not here."

"Nor was he at his home, and this was the only other place you could think he might go."

Drew took the candle and made a slow perusal of the hovel. Dirt floor. Mud hut walls. A crude, rectangular table upon which sat the tinderbox, and some cloth stacked at the other end. Three chairs of the same rough makings slanted in various positions at the table. A cornhusk mattress without adornments lie on the floor along the back wall. A rough blanket crumpled at one end.

In the corner sat an old stove. Beside it lay a pile of fresh split logs. Drew crossed the room in but three strides, and with due caution, neared his hand to the stove. Warmth radiated from the iron onto his skin.

"He's been here recently," Drew said, eyeing the table.

Folded neat on the edge was not mere cloth, but a set of men's clothing. Drew sifted through them. Fine fabrics, custom cut. He glanced at his uncle.

"Yes," Charles said. "Those are Flynn's. He must have donned his costume."

"He's gone to cause more destruction."

"It's the only reason he would have changed clothes here. It's what we did that night." Charles clutched his hands before him and tapped his knuckles on his chin several times. His fair skin had gone ashen. "Perhaps he's gone after me."

"He wasn't at your home and we didn't pass him on our way here," Drew said. His heart picked up speed at a horrid possibility. The room was too small for a proper pace, but he did anyway.

"If your partner in crime was determined to eliminate the children, he might go back for them, one by one." They were spread over several different homes. By the time they traveled to all of them, it might be too late. He spun on his uncle. "Where would Flynn be? Where would he start?"

"I've no idea." At Drew's glare, Charles said, "Don't you think I would tell you if I knew where he was? I showed up on your doorstep to ask you to help me."

"Think! He must have mentioned something, perhaps someone, one of the children he found more egregious than the others."

"As I said, after what happened with the Barrows',"

Ephraim and I disassociated ourselves from him. At every event, we avoided him as much as possible. Up until recently, there'd been no more than a polite nod between us for almost three years now."

"No secret meetings whatsoever to discuss further plans?"

"No. The man terrified us. We spoke to him for the first time a couple of weeks ago when we met up here. Flynn requested our presence here through a missive, using a code we used to have. Ephraim and I met him out of fear he'd decided to turn himself in to the authorities. We were worried he'd confess, and…"

"And?"

"And he might shape a different slant to what happened the night he killed the Barrows, make it out so he was innocent of the murders, blame us, who knows? I told you, the man is brainsick. For God's sake, he killed Ephraim."

"And two others."

"Yes, of course, and two others."

"And attempted to murder a house full of children."

"When Flynn told us of his plan to burn down the foundling home, we made every effort to convince him it was a bad idea. It's the truth. We did. We based our arguments on the grounds he'd be caught, rather than the cruelty of it. We thought the angle would be a better convincer. Flynn wouldn't be swayed."

"I don't understand. When you refused him, he allowed you to leave this place, the perfect, secluded setting to kill the men who witnessed what he'd done, and knew what he was about to do, only to go to Ephraim's home later and kill him there?"

"Ephraim refused him straight out. Said he'd keep his mouth shut, but made it clear he would not be a party to such a thing as what he had planned."

"And you?"

"Don't look at me like that. As I said to you in truth, I would not have anything to do with burning down the foundling home. But I...I told him I would consider it. You didn't see him, Drew! He's gone bloodthirsty. I thought he would kill both of us that night, right here in this room. However, if he believed he could coax me to go along, I was sure I'd live long enough to get out of here alive and search out some sort of solution."

"And poor Ephraim lacked your deviousness."

"Ephraim didn't have sense enough to feign the possibility of accordance. I think Flynn hoped I might persuade him to change his mind. Flynn paid a visit to Ephraim to see if he'd come around. Snuck up on the man in his own gardens. When Flynn realized Ephraim wouldn't go along, he saw Ephraim as a liability, and killed him. He bragged about all of it to me, told me how he'd made it look like an accident by slamming the man's head against the fountain first."

"Yes, so you've already told me. Were you with Flynn when he burned down the foundling home?"

"I *told* you, I was against him. He led me outside, behind the tavern and told me what he'd done to Ephraim, then proceeded to tell me the time and details of his plan for the foundling home, what my part was to be. He told me it would be best to go at night, when the they would all be asleep."

Drew clenched and unclenched his fists, scarce able to contain his seething rage. "Ah, yes, less chance for anyone to escape being *burned alive*."

Charles winced, but the worry roiling below was all for him, and the simmering pot of trouble he was in.

"But the fire was set during the day," Drew said. "Why would he change his mind and not go at night?"

"I don't know. Perhaps he didn't want to go to that part of town alone at night. I told him I would meet him at sunset. But my lie of cooperation must not have sounded convincing. The way he stared at me, he knew I didn't mean it. Good God, the man nearly slit my throat right there in an alleyway."

Charles covered his throat with his hand, as if Flynn's blade still posed close to his tender flesh. "If it hadn't been for those two men chancing to pass through…"

"Why did you not go to the authorities? You knew what he was about to do. Oh, wait, I know. You would rather see a house full of children burn to death than risk punishment for your own evil deeds."

"I hadn't done anything! Not really. I told you, it was all Flynn. Besides, I thought the threat was over for the home since he knew I wasn't with him, and I knew the details of his plot. When the night passed, and nothing happened, I assumed he'd given up his plan."

"He didn't."

"I know. He rode there the next day. And now he's coming after me. You have to help me, Drew!"

Drew took a determined step toward his self-serving uncle. He would take him to Bow Street now, and work with the Runners to find Flynn. His foot slid a bit. Drew squinted into the dimness around his feet. The heel of his boot lay upon a slip of foolscap. He bent and picked it up, then held it to the candlelight to read the scrawling.

"What is it?" Charles asked.

Drew held in his hand a list. The first item written, the Barrows, had a line drawn through it. The foundling home was second on the list. A line ran through that entry, too. The third item on the list remained unfinished, waiting for completion before it too could also be crossed out.

Drew stared at it, heart racing, head pounding with every accelerated throb until he beat down the terror and threw himself into action.

"What is it?" Charles asked, taking the sheet of foolscap when Drew didn't answer.

Drew shouted as he ran out the door. "Flynn's gone after Dove."

Chapter 23

Dove guided her horse along the edge of the road near the woods, slow and quiet. Moonlight pearled the road and the outer leaves. At times, when the road ahead curved and Drew and his uncle were out of sight, it was as if she was in a world vacant of civilization and human life.

She made sure to keep enough distance between herself and Drew and his uncle, so if they should glance back they wouldn't see her. Keeping to the shadows on the side of the road, dressed in black from the top of her hood to the tip of her half boots, the risk was minimal.

The hoot of an owl sliced through the night. A bat fluttered across the yellow glow of moonlight. Every now and again, some creature burrowed into its hidey-hole when she passed. None of it caught much of her attention.

When Drew and his uncle stopped, she stopped, too, edging her horse to just inside the cover of the woods. The men were talking, but she was too far back to make out what they were saying. After a couple of minutes, they cut into the woods and she lost sight of them. Chewing on her left thumbnail, she waited, giving them time and distance, waiting to see if they'd return with Lord Flynn.

While sitting atop her horse, she slipped her right hand into her pocket to again feel the beaded sheath as she'd done several times tonight. This time, she unhooked the thin strand of twine from the button and folded back the flap. She rested her hand on the wooden handle, taking comfort in the solidity.

The simple knife was more familiar to her than anyone knew, the piece her mother had carried with her when she'd come to England and taught her how to use.

The weight of the pistol in her other pocket was disproportionate to the weight of the knife, tugging her coat to one side. But she was glad for the presence of that weapon, too. Nothing would be left to chance this night.

Enough waiting. Wherever they had gone, she needed to follow. No sooner was the decision made and the reins in her hands, when a horse and rider emerged from the woods at the same place where Drew and his uncle had entered. But the rider was neither of the men she'd been following. The horse turned her way, and in a spread of moonlight loomed a larger version of herself.

The rider was dressed in full black, just as he had been the night of the murders, including a black hood. It was Lord Flynn. The man who had murdered her parents. She was sure of it.

Dove stared at him, hating him from her core; her spirit ardent with a fierceness worthy of the great warriors from her mother's tribe. *Keep your mind. Keep your wits.*

In a quick and silent flow, she dismounted and edged beside a tree.

The man on the horse twisted in his saddle several times, taking glances at what lie at his back. He must have seen Drew and his uncle approaching and hidden until he could make his escape. Now, after three years of hunting, her prey was riding straight into her eager clutches.

He rode slow, keeping quiet until he gained enough distance to get out of earshot, she assumed. Every few seconds he twisted around for another look over his shoulder. As his attention was focused more on what may be behind him than what was in front, Dove had a valuable advantage. Everything was set her way this night.

As her heart pounded with anticipation, she slipped a hand into her pocket to retrieve her grandfather's pistol.

Hidden in the shadows, dressed in her own set of dark clothing, the killer didn't see her until he was near to right upon her. He bent low, ready to gallop away. She stepped out into the moonlit road, feet planted, eyes focused. Her pistol was pointed right at his chest.

"What—"

"Get off your horse, slow," she ordered.

At the sound of her voice, he said, "You...you're a woman."

"My woman's fingers work as well as any man's." To make her point, she cocked the pistol, and relished his sharp intake of breath at the unmistakable sound. "Do as I say. Make one sudden or unapproved move, and it will be your last."

Approved or unapproved mattered not. This fiend's life ends tonight.

He held out his gloved hands, fingers splayed. Then, holding onto the pommel, he used caution to dismount. Good. She did not want his death to come before he knew the person about to dispatch him to hell.

"Take off your hood," she ordered.

Using the same due caution, he did as he was told. Lord Flynn dropped his hood to the ground. Thin wisps of blond hair rose in disarray, catching light from the moon and adding menace to his appearance.

"Who are you," he asked across the ten feet or so separating them. "If you've come to rob me, have done with it and be gone. I've important matters to attend to."

"Matters or murders?"

"…Who the blazes are you?"

Keeping the pistol steady in one hand, she used her other to remove her hood. She let it fall to the road before again gripping the heavy pistol with both hands. The initial shock marking his face was soon replaced with revulsion.

"It's you. Don't tell me you're the Creeping Bandit."

"Yes," she admitted. It was of no consequence if he knew her secret. He wasn't going to live long enough to tell anyone.

He laughed, small at first, and then louder before quieting. He twisted another quick glimpse behind him. No one was there.

When he faced her again, Dove said, "I am the Creeping Bandit, this half-breed savage."

"Proving such to be true, I see."

"This, from a merciless, cold-blooded killer."

"I'm not a killer, I'm a cleanser. Society should kneel before me and give thanks for all my work to keep the upper classes pure."

The cool, silver inlay of the pistol grip pressed into her damp palms. Her finger trembled on the trigger.

"My parents did nothing to you, committed no crimes, no misdeeds."

"They were an abomination! They might as well have been a mix of species with their detestable marriage. What right did they have to live amongst decent people?"

The ripe ache in her chest tightened to the point of pain. Her finger firmed. *Pull the trigger. Why was she waiting?*

Behind Flynn, from the place where Drew and his uncle had entered the woods, a horse and rider bounded and veered to the right. It took no more than a few seconds for him to get to them. Drew reined in behind Lord Flynn, leapt from his horse, and stood to Flynn's left. His uncle arrived a moment later. After an awkward dismount, he stood on the other side of Drew.

"Don't do this, Dove," Drew told her.

"I have to. It's all I've thought about for three years, all I've planned for."

"Why is she dressed like that?" Drew's uncle asked him.

Flynn gave him his answer. "She's the Creeping Bandit, you idiot coward. Look at her. She proves me right. Now do you see why the family had to be eliminated?"

"Your days of eliminating people are over," Drew told Flynn in a tone of finality. "What time you have left in this world will be spent within the walls of Newgate." Shifting his attention away from Flynn, he said, "Dove, give me the pistol."

The heavy flintlock quivered in her hands. *Pull the trigger.*

"Dove." His gentled tone had more effect than had

he shouted. For in that kindness laid his devotion.

Tears filled her eyes. "I was outside your window tonight, listening. What he did to my mother…" She couldn't finish her sentence. The words were choking her, as the image was such a horror. She didn't miss Drew's pained expression. Her suffering was his.

"I'm so sorry you heard that, Dove. With all my heart I wish you'd never known those details. But it doesn't change things."

"You're right. It doesn't. He has to die, Drew!" Her vision blurred. Why couldn't she just pull the trigger and end this?

"The law will take care of him," Drew pleaded. "If you take his life, you'll fall into a darkness from which you may never return."

"I don't care what happens to me."

"Yes, you do. You care because your parents raised you to care."

At the mention of her parents, of their nurturing, her tears overflowed. The warmth of them trailed down her chilled face. Drew took two small steps toward her.

Keeping her eyes on Flynn, she said, "He'll tell them about me. I'll go to prison anyway."

"On top of what he did to your parents, he set out to murder a house full of children. Even if he dares to spew lies, no one will believe him."

"Lies?"

"You have a solid alibi for the nights of several of those break-ins."

For the first time, Dove shifted her gaze from Lord Flynn to Drew.

"You were with me many of those nights Creeping Bandit was breaking into homes, as I was a visitor in your home," Drew said. "With your grandfather there to chaperone, of course. I was also by your side at several social events during which the break-ins occurred. I'll tell the authorities. I'll swear to it. My reputation may not be pristine, but my word is."

For a man to risk his honor so was no small matter. Grandfather would not be a problem. Even if his faulty memory told him different, he would lie for her, too. But Drew... "You would do that for me?"

"How could you doubt my love for you, and how far I would go to protect you? Did I not enter a burning building for you?" He smiled when he said this, speaking in a light manner as if he'd no more than presented to her a fist full of flowers at her door.

She nodded, and more tears slid down her face. "You did. You came for me."

"Haven't I already proven I care for you more than my own life?" Another step and he was beside her. He held out his hand, palm up.

The moonlight illuminated a good portion of his face. A beautiful mix of love and desperation confirmed his words, as did his stance. His hand wasn't more than a couple inches from the pistol. He could grab it from her if he wanted. He didn't, though. The decision was hers.

Dove stared at his palm. In his strong hands might lay her future. Marriage, family, everything her parents would have wanted for her. What would they think of her now, like this, with a pistol poised and readied to kill a man?

These past three years her heart was too broken, her mind too full of hatred and vengeance to stop and wonder what her life's mission might look like from her parents' point of view. This sight would devastate them. When you loved someone, you wanted them to be right with the world.

It was what Drew wanted for her right now. She wanted it, too.

When Dove laid the pistol in Drew's hand, his relief was evident in his exhalation and the slight curve of his body. And then she was in his arms, safe, free. Crying, but weightless.

"You can drop her weapon onto the road now. And step apart."

Both Drew and Dove raised their heads from the cradle of their consolation to see Flynn with his pistol pointed at them.

Flynn laughed when Drew swore a string of curses under his breath. Drew let go of the pistol, its thud in the dirt rang an eerie death knell on the quiet road. He and Dove stepped back from one another and faced Flynn.

"You were so worried about her shooting me and throwing her life away, it never occurred to you to relieve me of my pistol. Ah, stop right there," Flynn said when Drew shifted to the side to position himself between Dove and the pistol aimed their way. "Stand apart. Yes, that's good."

"You can't kill all three of us with one lead ball," Drew said.

"I only have to shoot you. For her," he said, tapping his coat pocket. "I have the same knife I used on her mother."

Dove stiffened as her hatred flared in raging ferocity the likes of which she'd never known. For now, she was on the cusp of a new life, complete with a love match deep in the realm of what her parents had so treasured. The same man who took it all from them, now threatened to take it from her.

"You can't possibly believe you'll get away with this," Drew said.

"I'm very good at getting away with this sort of thing." Flynn then eyed Dove. A grin, slight, but chilling, tugged up his entire face.

"Charles, do something," Drew pleaded to his uncle.

Flynn laughed again. "This mealy-mouthed coward?" he said, tipping his head toward Drew's uncle. "He's up to his ears in trouble. He won't say a word, will you, old boy?"

Drew's uncle yanked a handkerchief from his pocket and wiped his brow, damp enough to glisten in the moonlight even though the night was cool. "Flynn, he's my own flesh and blood, my sister's son."

"We'll blame it on the Bandit," Flynn continued. "Say she attacked the three of us on the road and she'd killed your nephew before we could stop her. She's already dressed for the part. She's half savage. Everyone will believe it, and all the *ton* will be relieved the scourge of London has been felled. We'll be hailed heroes."

Flynn raised his pistol and pointed it at Drew.

"Flynn, for God's sake, he's my nephew. Please. Let's give this some thought."

Lord Flynn leveled a disgruntled mien to Drew's uncle. "Here is something to think about. He knows enough to doom us both to the gallows, and his affection for this half-breed will lead him to do just that. Besides, he's nothing but a wastrel anyway.

You've said so yourself on numerous occasions."

Kneading the handkerchief in his fidgeting hands, Charles answered, "I know, but…"

Brightening with a fresh approach, Flynn added, "As the only surviving male, you'll take over as head of the family. This set of circumstances work to your great benefit, my friend."

"If you'll grant me a moment to make my case for the boy."

Twisting enough to give Drew's uncle his full face of disgust, Flynn said, "He's not a boy. He's a grown man who's done nothing of use with his life. Good God, man, for years I have listened to you complain about him."

As Drew was focused on her, and on Flynn, only Dove saw his uncle flick his wrist behind his back. He was distracting Flynn so they could escape into the dark cover of the woods. But to flee would just delay the inevitable, for she had no doubt Flynn would come after her. If not tonight, then another. Perhaps he would try again to kill the children of the foundling home.

No, this ended tonight. And she knew just how it would end.

Flynn was, for the moment, focused on Drew's uncle. The brief distraction was all Dove needed. Before Flynn drew a breath after his last word, Dove had her mother's knife in her grip. But a second later, it sliced through the air like a skilled bird of prey. The blade struck Flynn where she had aimed, dead center of his chest.

Flynn stumbled back and wavered, eyes bulging, his body already fluxing into death. Whether the twitch of his finger was deliberate, or an involuntary action, no one would ever know. But his pistol exploded.

There was a brief flash of fire, and Drew's uncle slapped his hands over the mid center of his body. In an instant, his white handkerchief turned red, saturated, and useless. Blood ran a streaming river over his fingers. Both men hit the ground at the same time.

Drew first checked Flynn to make sure he was dead. Blood trickled from the corner of his mouth and his shocked eyes stared vacant into the moonlight. His uncle groaned. Drew spun back and knelt beside him.

The ball had struck him low in the chest and blood gushed from the hole. Already, his breath gurgled. The man was either going to die where he lay or experience a far more painful death on the back of a horse if they tried bringing him back to town.

Drew set his uncle's head upon his lap as Dove knelt on the other side of him. After all the waiting she'd done for this moment, she took no pleasure in watching him die. Nor did sympathy make its way into her array of emotions. Intentional or not, this man was part of a plot that ended in the death of her mother and father. At the same time, he was now at the end of his life because he'd endeavored to save theirs.

Having just come so close to death, to seeing the man she loved teeter on the same precipice, all she wanted now was to have this nightmare come to an end.

"Drew," his uncle said, on one of the exhales following his jerking gasps. "Your mother. She's innocent. Don't...don't tell..." His body convulsed, and blood flowed from his chest as he strained for another breath.

"She won't know about any of this. No one will. Flynn is dead. It doesn't matter if he takes the blame for everything. You have my word, I'll handle it."

"You are...a better man than I...gave you credit for." Those were the last words the man spoke. His lips quivered. His bloodied chest heaved, and then it was over.

Chapter 24

The revival of summer never better suited a day.

Drew and Dove sat on the terrace at Dove's home, a Blue Wedgewood tea set and plates on the table bore crumbs and specks of cinnamon. A black and white checkered cloth lay over a basket of Cook's Banbury cakes. Drew reached around his newspaper and into the basket for another cake.

The sky shone a warm blue with a few streaks of wispy clouds, reluctant to travel on the faint, balmy breeze. Dove wore a simple, pink day dress with a high, modest neckline. Across the table from her, Drew was ever handsome in his white lawn shirt and earthen, brushed cotton trousers.

Her grandfather and the children were taking advantage of the sun-soaked day, too, playing lawn bowls. Dove giggled and set her cup on the saucer. Drew raised his head from his newspaper to see what made her laugh.

"I'm nearest the jack!" little Marion yelled, hands waving high above her head as she danced in a circle around the lignum wood balls. Green stains marred the knees of her little white dress. They served to make her even more adorable.

The other children shouted, "Let's play again!" Her grandfather joined in the chant.

With a smile of his own, Drew set the newspaper

on the table. After the children and her grandfather began another round, he tapped the paper with his forefinger and said, "The story is at last simmering down. It won't be long before we can start posting the banns."

Dove directed her attention to the man with whom she would spend the rest of her life. "Are you certain you're ready to be leg-shackled?" she teased.

"Are you? No more wild adventures, no more daring fate."

"After what we've both been through…"

He'd credited her for saving them that night on the road, but it had taken the workings of Drew's sharp mind to figure out what to do next. She had been too stunned by what had transpired to grasp a clear thought. Killing a man was no blithe matter, even knowing the villain deserved his early death. She was more than fortunate to have had Drew there to see to things after the killings.

Two men dead, she in her Bandit attire, if anyone had come along before Drew devised a plan and set it to action, things would have gone in quite another direction.

He'd draped both men over their horses, and she and Drew rode together until they neared the city. He then sent her on her way, instructing her to be at her most stealth, to slip into her house and live as if none of this had happened. Fortune abetted her again and she'd made it home without being seen.

When word spread to her house of the capture and death of the Creeping Bandit, she was to act as surprised as everyone else. More difficult was behaving as if she felt any amount of grief over the death of

Drew's uncle. She reminded herself how in the end, he'd distracted Flynn so they could escape, and his efforts had cost him his life.

Perhaps if she and Drew had fled into the dark cover of the woods, they'd all still be alive. Of course, disastrous endings teemed all along that road.

Drew had taken both bodies to Bow Street. The papers printed and reprinted the story of how Lord Flynn, dressed as the Creeping Bandit, had attacked Drew and his uncle while they were out on an evening ride. How Flynn had shot his uncle before Drew fended off Flynn with a knife.

Before dying, according to Drew's testimony, Flynn confessed to breaking into homes for the thrill. His advancements to more exciting adventures in crime had proven fatal. All this was further supported by Ellen, the girl from the foundling home. She'd given a fine description of Lord Flynn, told how he'd struck her when she saw what he was doing. Hester gave the same description.

London's season had ended with an abundance of gossip and gloomy weather. Though the death of the Creeping Bandit was huge, in time, the endless supply of fresh gossip chipped away at its enormity.

Drew still received pats on the back, both for the loss of his uncle and for his heroics in relieving the town of the infamous Creeping Bandit.

As he'd promised his uncle, Flynn took the blame for everything and no one other than Dove and himself would ever know the truth. Renny was the single exception. The poor man was on the verge of an episode when he'd learned what had happened. What calmed him was Dove's promise the Bandit was forever gone.

Fortunately, the mourning period for Drew's family was near to an end. And as Drew said, the banns could soon be posted.

"After what we've been through...?" Drew prompted when she didn't finish her sentence.

"I told you how I learned to throw a knife from my mother. It was our little secret, a part of her heritage passed on to me. Back then, I just thought it was fun. She believed it was an important skill."

"She was right." Drew nodded. He sent a casual glance toward the game being played on the lawn before returning his attention to Dove. "You have yet to answer my question."

"My mother taught me many things. Most important, I would say, was to take the lessons of the past on my journey forward. I'm sorry for the grief your mother and sister have suffered, but I'm not sorry those three men are dead."

"I couldn't expect you to be. Besides, the way it all turned out, I didn't have to send Mother and Ollie away. I'm grateful for that. I would have missed them. As for Charles, he doomed himself when he chose a path of hatred."

"My point is I can't regret the things I've done any more than I can change them. But I can take what I have and start anew." She slid her hand across the table and clasped it atop his. "I love you, Drew."

"I love you, too, Dove."

"My parents would have loved you. They would have been pleased to see their daughter pledged to a man like you."

"And how does their daughter feel?"

"Like the most fortunate woman in the world."

Drew stood and circled the table. His hands caressed her shoulders. He then bent to place a light kiss on her ear, and another on her neck.

Dove's eyes fluttered. She then craned her neck to gaze at his handsome face before flicking a quick tip of her head toward the lawn. "They're quite occupied. They won't miss us 'til luncheon."

"What is it you have in mind, Lady Barrow? You should know, my virginal reputation is stellar."

Dove did a poor job of muffling her giggle. For her impudence, Drew gave her ear a light tug.

"If you deem to ruin me," he continued. "You will find yourself shackled to me for life."

She stood, dragging her fingers up his thigh as she did. Without a word, she took his hand and led him inside.

A word from the author...

I lived most of my life in the wondrous city of Las Vegas, Nevada. For ten years my husband and I traveled several months of the year in an RV and I was fortunate to see every state in this amazing country. Now I live in beautiful Michigan, where I've learned about layering clothes and that boats don't have brakes.

~

Visit Micki at:
https://www.facebook.com/mickimillerwriter

www.ingramcontent.com/pod-product-compliance
Lightning Source LLC
Chambersburg PA
CBHW050020070726
47506CB00015B/381

* 9 7 8 1 5 0 9 2 2 7 2 9 7 *